Surprise!

Jessica climbed the stairway to Viveca's door, key in hand. However, the door already stood open. Cautiously she edged inside, then came to a stop, her bags sliding from nerveless fingers.

Inside was a stepladder, and standing on it was a man dressed in cut-off jeans and no shirt. He held a paint roller in one hand, and his bare chest was slick with sweat and spattered with paint.

He turned at the sound of Jessica's suitcases hitting the floor, and she was faced with his intense gaze. She swallowed, her cheeks flaming with embarrassment. Viveca had failed to mention that she'd be sharing the apartment!

KRISTIN JAMES,
a former attorney, is married to a family counselor, and they have a young daughter. Her family and her writing keep her busy, but when she does have free time she loves to read. In addition to her contemporary romances, she has written several historicals under another name.

Dear Reader:

There is an electricity between two people in love that makes everything they do magic, larger than life. This is what we bring you in SILHOUETTE INTIMATE MOMENTS.

SILHOUETTE INTIMATE MOMENTS are longer, more sensuous romance novels filled with adventure, suspense, glamor or melodrama. These books have an element no one else has tapped: excitement.

We are proud to present the very best romance has to offer from the very best romance writers. In the coming months look for some of your favorite authors such as Elizabeth Lowell, Nora Roberts, Erin St. Claire and Brooke Hastings.

SILHOUETTE INTIMATE MOMENTS are for the woman who wants more than she has ever had before. These books are for you.

Karen Solem
Editor-in-Chief
Silhouette Books

Worlds Apart

Kristin James

Silhouette Intimate Moments
Published by Silhouette Books New York
America's Publisher of Contemporary Romance

Silhouette Books by Kristin James

Dreams of Evening (IM #1)
The Amber Sky (IM #17)
Morning Star (IM #45)
Secret Fires (IM #69)
Worlds Apart (IM #89)

SILHOUETTE BOOKS
300 E. 42nd St., New York, N.Y. 10017

ISBN: 0-373-07089-6

First Silhouette Books printing April, 1985

10 9 8 7 6 5 4 3 2 1

Worlds Apart

Chapter 1

JESSICA STARTED LAUGHING. IT GREW AND GREW, until suddenly, a few minutes later, hugging her sides, tears streaming down her face, she discovered she couldn't stop. That was when her laughter had turned into tears.

It had been one of those days. Or rather, one of those weeks. Alan Connolly, her partner in their small management consulting firm, had come down with a stomach virus, and she had had to take over his presentation in Memphis yesterday. She had rushed out to the airport when she finished the lecture and found that her plane to Atlanta was thirty minutes late. She had begun to fret. She had an appointment in Charlotte, North Carolina, at four o'clock. It was the biggest prospect she'd ever had, and the thought of being late for it had turned her blood to ice. First impressions were so important, and men were especially quick to judge a woman who was late,

dismissing her as "a typical female." She'd worried all
the way to Atlanta and then had run from her airplane
through the terminal to another wing in order to catch her
next flight, only to discover that that flight was over two
hours late.

She'd bullied the attendant at the gate into finding her
a flight on another airline that arrived in Charlotte only
forty-five minutes later than her originally scheduled
one. That meant she arrived in time for her appointment,
but didn't have time to go to the hotel and freshen up
first.

Then Mark Banacek, the head of the training section
of the personnel department for the North Carolina bank,
the man with whom she had the appointment, had tried
to put the make on her. She wasn't surprised; it had
happened to her before.

Jessica was an attractive woman. Her hair was a bright
reddish gold, the color often labeled as "strawberry
blond," and she wore it pulled tightly back into a French
braid from the crown of her head to her neck. It was a
style only someone with excellent bone structure could
wear, for it completely exposed the face. On Jessica it
was striking. Her face was triangular, with wide cheek-
bones and a determined chin. Her brows were narrow
slashes of light brown above her eyes. The straight line
of her nose led down to a firm, uncompromising mouth.
It would have appeared a hard face except for the
softening impact of bright, intelligent green eyes and a
light sprinkling of freckles across her cheeks and nose,
pale golden flecks that warmed her skin.

At five feet six inches in her stocking feet, she was a
trifle too thin, and there was nothing graceful about her
movements. She appeared all angles and points, changing and re-forming in quick succession, moving in

staccato. But there was an appeal to her angular face and figure, an impression of charged-up energy that was compelling, and her thin figure showed off her stylish clothes well. She was the sort of person one couldn't help but look at a second time, not pretty, but undeniably attractive. Paradoxically, the very restraint of her femininity created by the severe hairdo and conservative, almost masculine suits she wore gave her a certain challenging allure.

More than one man had tried to take up the challenge. For some reason, some men assumed that an independent career woman, especially one who traveled a great deal, was automatically promiscuous. Or maybe they figured that if she wanted to sell them a program, she would be willing to throw in her body as part of the bargain. Whatever the cause, it was something she had learned to deal with. She had to walk a fine line between offending a customer and encouraging him in his mistaken belief.

But it was especially annoying that it should happen on this account, which was so important to her. Fortunately, Mark had already arranged for his boss, Art Simmons, to sit in on their meeting, which made it harder for him to make any advances. Simmons had been very interested in her proposal, and she had taken the two men out to dinner. Finally, after several hours, a heavy meal, two drinks, and countless cigarettes, she had parted from the men. Art Simmons invited her to return the following day, which threw her schedule all out of order, but she quickly agreed. Mark had managed to wangle his way into carrying her supplies out to her car, and she had had to fight off his kisses and embraces.

But the next day she learned she'd won the contract for their educational program, and Simmons had introduced her to another vice-president who wanted a proposal for one of their branch banks that was severely mismanaged. Despite her weariness, she'd returned to Atlanta in high spirits.

As always, because she'd been out of her office for so many days, there was a huge pile of work on her desk waiting for her. She'd sent her secretary down to a nearby delicatessen for a cold sandwich and an extra package of cigarettes, and then Jessica had settled down to work.

The past year their firm had grown tremendously, so much so that she and Alan were considering hiring an assistant or perhaps even taking on a new partner. Both of them were constantly on the run, dashing from city to city to make presentations of their training program or to consult with firms. Whenever Jessica was back in Atlanta, she had mounds of work to do and always wound up staying late at the office or carrying home her papers. Because of her schedule, she rarely got enough sleep or ate properly. In fact, in the last six months she'd lost six pounds. If she didn't watch it, she thought, her stylish suits would be baggy on her.

Tonight she had worked until nine o'clock and was just starting to leave the office when the cleaning woman, Carrie, came in. Jessica knew the woman well, as she was often still in the office when Carrie and her crew arrived to clean. She had stopped to chat with Carrie for a moment, and Carrie had told her a joke in her wry, slightly ribald way. That was when Jessica had started to laugh and been unable to stop.

As Jessica's laughter turned into tears and then sobs, Carrie stared at her in dismay. "Miss Todd!" she exclaimed, coming forward and taking hold of Jessica's arms. "Miss Todd, what's the matter?"

"I—don't—know!" Jessica had gasped out between hiccuping sobs. "I don't know!" Her tears increased.

Without further ado, Carrie put her arm around Jessica and hustled her out the door and into Carrie's antique Buick. She whisked her straight away to the hospital and into the emergency room.

Forty-five minutes later, sitting on a stainless steel table in the emergency room and wrapped in a skimpy hospital gown, Jessica felt acutely embarrassed. Her tears had stopped several minutes ago, leaving her weak and splotchy-skinned and feeling like an utter fool. As soon as they had reached the emergency room, Carrie had called Alan, and his wife, Lynn, had rushed over to the hospital, leaving a still-sick Alan with their two children. The emergency room attendants had whisked Jessica into the room and out of her clothes, and a nurse had bustled in to take her blood pressure, temperature and pulse. Later a florid-faced doctor, overweight and short of breath, had shuffled in and shone a tiny flashlight in her eyes. He had also checked her nose, mouth and ears and listened to her chest with his stethoscope.

"How long have you had this cough?"

Jessica shrugged. "I was sick a couple of months ago, and I haven't been able to get rid of the cough."

"Do you smoke?"

"Yes."

He gave her a stern look and continued to scribble on the clipboard he held in one hand. "All right, Miss Todd, I've scheduled you for some tests. An attendant will take you to the lab. We're going to draw a little blood, do an EKG and an EEG. Then they'll take you to your room."

"Wait." Jessica tensed all over. "You don't mean you're going to make me spend the night here!"

"Yes, of course. We need to make several tests to determine what happened."

"But it's over now. I've stopped crying. Why can't I go home?"

"Miss Todd, it's far better for you to stay here, believe me."

"I was simply tired," Jessica protested. "I shouldn't even have come here. I was on edge today, and tired, and I just . . ."

He fixed her with a stern gaze. "Miss Todd, I want you to stay here tonight. You need to have these tests made."

"But I can't! I have so much work to do! You don't understand. I haven't gone off the deep end. I just started laughing, and I couldn't stop. It wasn't that big a deal. I shouldn't have come here. I—" Jessica stopped, suddenly aware of how hysterically her voice was rising. The doctor regarded her steadily. She clamped her lips together in an attempt to control their trembling.

Lynn, sitting unnoticed in a corner of the cubicle, came forward now. "Jessica, the doctor's right. You need some rest, anyway. And what if this is a symptom of something more? The office can get along without you for a day. Alan's going in tomorrow."

"But there's so much to do, and I have to fly to Greenville Monday. You should see my desk. I can't waste all that time here. I just can't!" To Jessica's dismay, tears began to flow down her cheeks again.

Lynn's jaw dropped and she stared at Jessica in astonishment. "Honey, what's the matter?"

"I don't know!" Jessica wailed. "Oh, Lord, what's

the matter with me?'' Lynn put an arm around her, and Jessica held onto her, crying.

As soon as her sobs quieted, a nurse handed her a few tissues and swung Jessica's feet up onto the gurney. ''We're going to take you for a little ride now, Miss Todd.'' She nodded at Lynn. ''You might as well go home, ma'am. I'll be taking her up to her room as soon as the tests are over.''

''All right. Bye, Jessica. I'll come see you tomorrow. Okay?''

Jessica gave her a weak smile. Her last bout of tears had sealed her fate. Why had she collapsed into sobs? She never acted that way. Never. She was always the rock in the midst of emotional storms, never giving way to panic or tears. No matter how frightened or upset she was, Jessica managed to retain control of her nerves. Lynn's amazed reaction was proof of how bizarre her behavior had been. Why was she falling apart?

A technician took an enormous amount of blood from her, and then she had to endure the placement of cold metal disks all over her body for the EKG. Next came the EEG, and finally they wheeled her to the elevator and up to her room. Jessica lay passively, worn out by her tears. She felt too tired to move, as if she could sleep for years. When they reached her room, she crawled into her bed and closed her eyes. Within moments she was asleep.

A nurse awakened her early the next morning, and Jessica growled in protest. She felt as tired as she had the night before. Bone-weary, she thought. That old expression perfectly described how she felt. She sat up, plumping the pillow behind her, and listlessly faced the huge breakfast a sour-faced attendant brought in on a tray. They certainly must be used to patients with large appetites around here, Jessica thought as she forced herself to eat a third of the tasteless scrambled eggs. Two eggs, bacon, toast, butter and jelly, coffee, orange juice, and a bowl of cereal. What sick person could eat all that? It was far too much for her, and she was perfectly well.

After breakfast a doctor came in, bluff and cheerful. He examined her eyes once again, then left. For the rest of the morning she was taken here and there, tested, poked, and prodded by doctors, nurses, and technicians. If she hadn't felt so listless she would have given them a blistering opinion of their little tortures. But it didn't seem worth the effort. She thought about the work awaiting her at the office and felt like crying again. It seemed as though she were always running and never able to catch up. This whole mess would throw her even farther behind.

About noon they returned her to her room, and she quickly fell asleep. She slept heavily for two hours and was awakened by the arrival of a doctor. She blinked at him, disoriented for a moment, then identified him as the internist who had examined her that morning. "Hello, Jessica. Sorry I woke you up."

"It's okay." She struggled to sit up and clear her foggy brain. "When am I getting out of here?"

"Tomorrow. I want to keep you under observation for another day."

"Why! What's the matter?"

He looked thoughtfully at his hands for a moment. "I want to make sure you get another day of complete rest. Frankly, Jessica, your general health is rather poor."

"But I'm never sick."

"What about that cold a few weeks ago? What about your cough?"

"Oh, everyone gets them. I mean a serious illness."

"Perhaps you haven't had one up till now, but I'm afraid if you don't start correcting your behavior, you will." He held up his hand and began ticking his points off on his fingers. "Your blood pressure is one thirty-eight over ninety-five; that's too high. The blood tests showed too many triglycerides in your blood."

"Too many whats?"

"It means you need to eat less cholesterol and fat. Your diet the past few months must have been terrible. How much weight have you lost?"

Jessica shrugged. "Five or ten pounds this year. Why?"

"You're too thin. And when you eat, you aren't eating the right foods. Frankly, you're underweight and malnourished. On top of that, you're exhausted. It's obvious from your speech and movements. You aren't getting enough rest, you're under too much stress, and you don't eat right." He paused, and for a moment they stared at each other silently. "Your partner, Alan Connolly, came by this morning to see you, but he talked with me instead. I gained some insight into what has caused all this. You've been working under an extreme amount of pressure this past year. You try to do too much. Your behavior is self-destructive. Have you ever heard of type A behavior?"

"I don't know what you're talking about."

"Well, it's a theory a couple of cardiologists came up with. Boiled down, it's the idea that stress and the way one copes with it are as important in preventing or causing high blood pressure and heart disease as diet and exercise. You have too much stress in your life, and you don't deal with it well. You're always trying to do too much. Alan tells me you never turn anything down, just try to somehow squeeze it into your schedule.''

''I am rather busy,'' Jessica admitted. ''But I don't see—''

The doctor sighed and pushed up his glasses to massage the bridge of his nose. ''You're a smart lady, Jessica. You know what I'm talking about. You smoke a great deal. How much?''

''Two and a half packs a day.''

He nodded wearily. ''You smoke way too much; you don't eat right; you push yourself too hard. You worry and hurry and put too many demands on your body. After a while it can't hold up anymore. Then you catch colds and can't shake them off. Your blood pressure goes up. You start crying and can't stop.''

Jessica sighed and brushed her hands over her face. ''Okay, I get the message. What do I do? Are you going to give me some kind of medicine?''

''There is medicine for high blood pressure, yes. But this isn't a problem that medicine is going to cure. You'll have to do it yourself. To begin with, I want you to take a month off from work.''

''What!'' Jessica shot bolt upright. ''You've got to be joking!''

''I'm not. Your partner tells me you haven't taken a vacation in two years.''

''But I can't possibly leave now. And a month! It's crazy. There's no way I could do it.''

''It's not only possible, it's mandatory.'' His thin, ascetic face set in stern lines. He looked, Jessica thought, like some Jonathan Edwards or John Knox, preaching sin, hellfire and damnation. ''You have to slow down, and you need to start by giving your body a chance to rest and regain its health. You need a lot of sleep, a lot of doing nothing, and a lot of exercise. You also need to stop smoking and cut down on your cholesterol intake. That's for starters.''

"Starters! You've just blown away my entire life.''

He smiled thinly. "Hardly that.''

"No work, no cigarettes, no eating anything good,'' Jessica grumbled.

"What I said was rest for a month, no cigarettes, and cut down on cholesterol. It's not exactly the same thing. You need to start taking care of yourself. After you return from your vacation, you have to find a better way of dealing with the stress and tension of your job. Frankly, if it comes down to it, I'd recommend that you find a new career.''

"Easy for you to say. Don't you think this is a bit much?''

"No, I don't. I'm speaking seriously about your life. You can't expect to keep up this kind of abuse of your body and get away with it. Would you like me to take you down the hall and show you a patient who's had a cerebral embolism? He can't move his right arm or leg, and his speech is gibberish.''

Jessica winced. "But I—I've always been healthy.''

"And you could be again. I'm not saying that you're at death's door. But if you don't change your lifestyle, you will be someday. I don't know how soon.''

"But it's impossible. I have so much work to do. There's no way I could get away for a month.''

"It's up to you, of course. I can't make you do anything. I can only tell you what you need to do, and that's to eat right, exercise, stop smoking, adjust your work schedule so that you have less stress in your job, and *take off some time right now to recover*. In my opinion, you're physically and mentally exhausted. Only a nice, long rest is going to bring you back to good condition. I'll have the nurse give you a list of foods that you should avoid, and also some suggested exercises. I want to see you back here in a month for more blood tests and a blood pressure check.''

Jessica nodded feebly. The doctor made a few notations on his clipboard, fixed her with a last admonishing look and left the room. Jessica slid down in bed and stared up at the ceiling, trying to assimiliate what she had just learned. Exhaustion . . . malnourishment . . . high blood pressure . . . Good heavens! How had she wound up in this state? Tears trickled down her cheeks, and she wiped them away clumsily, unable to stop them.

Alan and Lynn came by to visit her that evening. When she haltingly told them what the internist had told her, Alan sighed and shook his head. ''I knew you'd been working too hard lately.''

''I guess I have. I probably better slow down a little.'' She cleared her throat. ''Maybe I should stop smoking.'' The idea sent her reaching in panic for her package of cigarettes on the bedside table.

''I thought he said you were supposed to take off for a month,'' Alan put in.

''That is what he said. But there's no way I can do that.''

''Why not?''

Jessica gaped at him. ''Alan, you know what our work schedule's like.''

''It's not written in stone. We can change it.''

''We can't afford for me to be gone a whole month!''

''Are you saying you think I can't handle the business?''

Jessica grimaced. ''Don't try to divert me with that

guilt tactic. It's impossible to run the office with just one person. Why, we've been talking about taking on another employee.''

"We'll cut out the sales in your area, and I'll take on the courses and consulting you're scheduled to do.''

"I tried that last week while you were out, remember? Look where it got me.''

"We'll cut out all the sales calls, then, for a month. It won't kill us.''

"It'll set us back by at least a month. It might have more serious effects. If we cancel appointments we've already made, why should those companies give us another chance? It makes us sound pretty unrealiable. What are you going to tell them, that your partner's had a nervous breakdown?''

"You're sick and on the point of exhaustion! People will understand if we put them off for a month. So what if we lose a few sales? We'll be a lot better off with you healthy. When you're rested, you'll have a lot more stamina. Take a month off. I promise you, I'll work everything out.''

"I'd go crazy not working for a whole month.'' Jessica chewed at her lower lip. "But maybe I will take off a week or two and hang around the apartment and rest up. I have to admit that I'm awfully tired.''

"You see? But think about a month, okay?''

"Okay.''

Alan brought forth a card from the receptionist and secretary at the office, and Lynn gave her a fat paperback to read. "You'll love it,'' she assured Jessica. "You won't have to make yourself rest once you start this; you won't want to do anything but sit there and finish the book.''

Soon afterward they left with promises that they

would return the next day to take her home. Jessica
waved good-bye and settled back down in her bed. Idly
she flipped through the various TV channels, but nothing
caught her interest, and she turned the TV off. She
glanced over at the empty bed beside hers and wondered
whether they'd move anyone in before she left; at least a
roommate would relieve the boredom. Already she was
bored with sleeping and doing nothing—imagine what
she'd do after a month! Jessica cracked a grin. Even in
the two weeks she'd given herself, she would probably
be climbing the walls.

Frowning, she turned over and closed her eyes.
Almost immediately she was asleep.

When Alan and Lynn returned the following day at
noon, they brought a softly pretty middle-aged woman
with them. Jessica sat up in bed, her eyes widening in
surprise. ''Mother!''

Viveca Howard moved toward the bed, her eyes
glistening with tears. ''Jessica!''

She enfolded her daughter in a warm, sweet-smelling
hug, and Jessica hugged her back with real affection. Her
mother could be vague, irritating and overly emotional at
times, but Jessica loved her dearly. ''Viv, whatever are
you doing here?'' Jessica asked when at last her mother
released her and moved back a step.

Instead of answering, Viveca studied Jessica intently,
her head tilted slightly to one side. Her narrow brown
brows drew together over her pale blue eyes. ''Darling,
you look awful!''

Jessica had to laugh. ''Thanks. That's just what I
needed to hear.''

''Oh, you know what I mean.'' Viveca impatiently
brushed back her wild mane of reddish-blond hair, so

like Jessica's when she wore it down and loose, and adjusted the wide leather arm-band on her wrist. She was dressed in her usual outlandish outfit, Jessica thought, and as always Viv managed to make it look good. Dark brown trousers were topped by a loose, cowl-necked blouse that was a mixture of four different patterns: a swash of plain dark brown; another of plain white separated by a brown on white grid; sleeves of a white grid on dark brown; and through the middle of the loose fold of the neckline, a jungle pattern of white, brown and tan. A matching scarf twisted into a bandeau held back her vivid hair, and an enormously wide brown leather belt cinched in her still-small waist. "You look very tired."

Jessica shrugged. "I guess I am. What are you doing here, anyway?"

"Well, darling, what do you expect? Lynn called me in New Orleans and told me you were in the hospital. Do you think I could just fly off to San Francisco after that?"

"I guess not. Going to San Francisco again, huh?"

"Yes. New Orleans is too hot this time of year. Besides, I was getting itchy feet."

Jessica smiled. Her mother couldn't bear to stay more than a few months in one place. By the time she was eleven, Jessica had seen more states and countries than most people saw in a lifetime. She supposed that was one reason why she disliked her constant traveling on business now; that was the only aspect of her job that she would really like to get rid of.

"When Lynn called me, I decided to fly here first and then go on to San Francisco."

Jessica's eyes narrowed suspiciously. "You aren't planning to take care of me, are you?" A few days together were all it took for the two of them to get on each other's nerves. Their personalities were almost exact opposites. Her mother was an artist who lived a free-and-easy life in New Orleans, supporting herself on her paintings and on the quick personal portraits she painted of tourists at Jackson Square. She was sloppy, vague and happy-go-lucky, whereas Jessica was neat, orderly and practical. When they were together Viveca created havoc with Jessica's schedule, constantly suggesting wild schemes to set out on at the spur of the moment, or rearranging Jessica's furniture so that it looked more artistic, or urging Jessica to stay up until three or four in the morning, drinking gin-and-tonics and discussing Viv's current philosophy of life.

Once she cleaned out Jessica's refrigerator and stocked it with health foods during a back-to-nature mood. The next time she came to visit she brought a huge box of New Orleans pralines and fixed several haute cuisine dishes she had learned in a cooking school. Then there were her bouts with religion. Most of the time she lived a wildly passionate life: drinking, eating, loving, living life to the fullest. At other times she was seized with religious conviction and would eschew all the things she enjoyed—sex, liquor, rich foods—to live a life as ascetic as a nun's. At those times she would concentrate on what she called her "spiritual" paintings and give up her usual more wordly themes. Jessica found both states difficult to live with.

The fact was, as it always had been, that much as she loved her mother, she couldn't stand to be around her very long. And to have her fussing around, bringing Jessica weird concoctions to regain her strength, and telling her all kinds of mind-over-body Oriental exercises that would relieve her weariness—well, it would simply be more than she could take.

Something of what Jessica felt must have showed on her face, for Viveca sighed and shook her head. "No, I'm not going to stay and take care of you. I know it would drive you crazy. Though I'm on a super vitamin and mineral regimen that I'm sure would help you. There's this wonderful mineral—I take it four times a day—and it's amazing how young and full of energy it makes you feel. I'll leave you a bottle, so you can try it. But, no, I'll fly out tomorrow, now that I've seen you and assured myself that you aren't going to fade away by tomorrow."

Jessica took her mother's hand and squeezed it. "Oh, Viv, I feel like such a bear. Here you've flown all this way to see me, and I—"

Viveca made an airy gesture with one hand. "No problem. Don't worry about it. I think you and I simply have conflicting auras or something. Even when you were a child, you were always too sensible and practical to get along well with me." She frowned. "Maybe it's because I was so young when I had you. I've often wondered about that. But, anyway, I know we have a lot more fun together if we don't see each other long. Besides, I'm eager to get to San Francisco. Ben Carlton called me the other day; he's relocated in San Francisco. Do you remember him? Benny, Debby Carlton's son?"

"Oh, yeah. I remember. A tall, skinny kid with big brown eyes. But, Mother, honestly! He's only two years older than I am!"

Viveca turned her palms upward. "I know. Really, Jessica, you have the most bourgeois mind. We're just going to get together and talk over old times. Do you know, Debby's living out on some old farm in New Mexico?"

Jessica cocked an eyebrow in disbelief. Unless Benny

had lost the good looks he'd had as a teenager or Viv was in one of her nun periods, the odds were that their discussion would wind up in bed. Viveca's predilection for young, handsome men was well known. "Honestly, Mother, I think your psyche froze at fifteen, and you're trying to relive the teenage years you missed."

Viveca's eyes filled with tears, and she said in a low voice, "Jessica, sometimes you can be very cruel."

Jessica chewed at her lip. Viv was right. She shouldn't have said something like that to her mother, especially not with Lynn and Alan standing right there. Viveca was the way she was, and nothing would ever change her; there was no point in harassing her about it. Or in embarrassing her in front of people she hardly knew. "I know. I'm sorry." She turned toward Alan. "I've been snappy lately, haven't I?"

"Just your usual foul-tempered self," Alan retorted with easy good humor, and the moment lightened.

Jessica dressed while Alan and Lynn checked her out of the hospital. Then a nurse wheeled her down to the emergency entrance, where Alan's car awaited her and Viveca. Alan and Lynn dropped them off at Jessica's apartment, tactfully leaving mother and daughter alone. Viveca insisted on Jessica's going straight to bed while she bustled around fixing lunch. Jessica was starving, and when Viveca brought in a tray, she sat up eagerly. Her face fell when she saw what was on the tray: a bowl of thin chicken noodle soup and a few saltine crackers. She looked up at her mother with a pained expression. "Viv, I'm not sick. Couldn't you come up with something a little more solid?"

"Frankly, you're lucky to get this, considering the state of your pantry," Viveca retorted. "I found the can of soup hidden away on the top shelf of your dish cabinet, and the crackers were ones I'd gotten at a restaurant the other day and happened to have in my purse.''

''Oh.'' Jessica chuckled. ''Sorry.''

''I thought this would tide you over. I'll run down to the store and get you something better in a minute. But first you eat that, and I'll tell you an idea I had.''

''What?'' Jessica asked warily as she began to spoon the soup into her mouth.

''Don't look so distrustful. I'm not putting anything over on you. But I think I have the answer for you.''

''Answer to what?''

''To what you're going to do for the next month.''

''I'm going to take off a couple of weeks and rest here. If I feel strong enough I might go to the coast and laze around on the beach for a few days.''

''Surely you don't mean to stay in your apartment! Who could get well lying around staring at four sterile walls?''

''The idea is rest, not action or excitement.''

''But resting someplace prettier would be better, don't you think? And the doctor said a month, not two weeks. I talked to him this morning before I came in to see you. I told him my idea, and he thought it was perfectly marvelous.''

Jessica reserved judgment on that. Viveca was quite capable of making people think the most harebrained scheme sounded delightful. She was also capable of thinking people agreed with her simply because they didn't cry out in protest. ''What is your idea?''

''You could spend the month in New Orleans at my apartment.''

''Now, Viv—''

''Don't worry, I wouldn't be there. I told you I was

going to San Francisco, didn't I? I'm sure I'll be there at least a month, probably all summer. My apartment will be sitting vacant the whole time.'' New Orleans was Viveca's home base. She spent most of the year there, and when she left for Puerto Rico or San Francisco, her favorite places to visit, she kept her apartment in the French Quarter. It was difficult to rent space in the Quarter, especially as charming an apartment as Viveca had, and it gave her someplace to store all her works, furniture and other goods that she didn't want to cart around with her.

"Or at least, it'll be vacant for six weeks. I've sublet it to a couple in August—though why anyone would want to go to New Orleans in August is beyond me. Now, where was I?''

"An empty apartment.''

"Oh, yes. It's available, and you have to admit it's far prettier than this place.'' Viveca was right about that. Her taste was impeccable, if somewhat bold, and her apartment in an old reconverted house was lovely. "Think of the atmosphere, the quaintness. Wouldn't it be more restful than this apartment and Atlanta? There's a little grocery only a block away, so you wouldn't have to go far to get whatever you wanted to eat. And there are all those fabulous restaurants. The doctor said you needed to gain weight.''

"Well, I could certainly do that in New Orleans,'' Jessica agreed with a rueful shake of her head.

"Enjoy it! How many people get a chance to eat all they want without feeling guilty? Anyway, you'd have peace and quiet and good food. If you wanted to get out and exercise, there's the whole Quarter to walk around in.

"Well . . . I don't know.''

Viveca smiled a little mockingly. "What's the matter? Afraid the city will seduce you?"

"Don't be silly." Jessica frowned. There *was* something seductive about New Orleans, particularly the French Quarter, something that beckoned one to stay in its indolent, sultry beauty. Viveca had not made New Orleans her home until after Jessica was grown and in college, but Jessica had visited her mother there a few times. Every time she had experienced a certain strange reluctance to leave. There was no other place quite like it.

"Then what's the problem?"

"I—I'm not sure." There really was no objection to it. It was an ideal place to rest. She pictured herself relaxing in the quiet garden, encircled by buildings, lulled by the warmth of the sun and the delicate tinkle of the water fountain in the center of the patio. She could rest, walk, eat, whatever she wanted. And she would be getting away from overly familiar surroundings, too. Most people would jump at the chance to have a month in New Orleans. Jessica knew the only reason she hesitated was because it was her mother's idea. Simply because Viveca had thought of it, she suspected it must be crazy and irresponsible. "Let me think about it."

"Well, promise me that you'll think positively about it."

"I promise."

Two days later Jessica stepped out of the taxi into the narrow street of old, slightly dingy buildings decorated with wrought iron. The building before her was a faded color somewhere between dusky pink and tan. Like all the buildings around it, it had settled with the years, so that one corner was a trifle lower than the opposite one.

The door, too, was slightly askew, but it was made of sturdy wood and beautifully polished. Jessica had visited New Orleans often enough to know that the place was typical of the French Quarter. Strict codes kept the owners of buildings in the Quarter from altering their quaint, aging facades, but inside the owner had free rein. Often a shabby, narrow building hid an interior of dazzling elegance and beauty.

On one side of the house, between it and the wall of the building next door, stood a wrought iron door with an imposing lock, and behind it stretched a narrow, bricked path. The cab driver set her two bags down on the sidewalk in front of the wrought iron gate, as Jessica directed him. She paid him, and he drove away, leaving her facing the uninviting gate. She dug Viveca's key out of her purse and fitted it into the shiny gold lock. It turned smoothly, and the barred door swung out. After setting her suitcases inside and following them into the narrow entry, she turned to relock the gate behind her. Then, picking up her bags, she trudged along the brick walk, emerging into a small enclosed garden. A low marble fountain decorated the center. It was as old as the building, and the chubby cherub eternally pouring out his vase of water had a few pockmarks on his legs and arms, and his nose was entirely missing. But age hadn't managed to dim the beauty of the streaked black marble nor change the soothing noise of the tiny waterfall.

Jessica set down her bags and soaked in the atmosphere of the garden. A stone bench stood near the fountain, and another was tucked away beneath the shade of a small tree. Greenery grew in orderly patterns throughout the garden, carefully tended and contained. Honeysuckle climbed up the wall of the building next door, its sweet fragrance almost overpowering. Slowly

Jessica turned and surveyed the building curving around the courtyard on three sides. She knew that the old house had been turned into six apartments, all opening onto the courtyard. But only Viveca's had a wrought iron staircase curving down into the patio. The other second floor occupants had to walk down inside stairs to a common door.

Jessica smiled. Already she felt more peaceful. She was glad she'd decided to come. It had taken her several hours to decide that despite Viveca's endorsement of the plan, it made a lot of sense. Then she had called Alan and told him what she planned to do, promising to return in a couple of weeks. He had approved the plan and urged her to stay the full month. She had lazed around for another day before she caught a plane to New Orleans.

Jessica took up her suitcases again and climbed the stairway to Viveca's door, key in hand. When she reached it, however, she realized that there was no need for the key. The door stood wide open. Her heart began to beat a little faster. Had Viveca's empty apartment been robbed or vandalized? Cautiously she edged inside. She came to a dead stop, her bags sliding from her nerveless fingers. Inside was a stepladder and standing on it was a man dressed in cut-off jeans and no shirt. He held a paint roller in one hand and was sliding it along the wall. A tray of paint sat on the top of the stepladder. His bare chest, golden tan in color and bisected by a narrow line of light brown hair, was slick with sweat and dotted with splatters of light celery-colored paint. So were his long, well-formed face and light brown hair, now darkened with sweat.

He turned inquisitively at the sound of Jessica's suitcases hitting the floor, and Jessica was faced with an intense, dark brown gaze. His eyes widened slightly, and his eyebrows went up as his arm paused in midstroke. Jessica swallowed, and her cheeks flamed with an emotion somewhere between anger and embarrassment as the full implication of his presence hit her. Viveca had failed to mention that Jessica would be sharing the apartment with her mother's latest boyfriend!

Chapter 2

THAT WAS WHO HE MUST BE, JESSICA THOUGHT. Viveca was notorious for choosing good-looking men years younger than herself. This man was in his early to mid-thirties, and he was definitely good-looking. From his thick, gold-streaked hair to his taut thighs and calves, he was utterly gorgeous. He grinned, and a deep dimple popped into one cheek. His front teeth were slightly uneven and gave his grin a puckish quality that saved his face from a too-perfect handsomeness. "Hello. Can I help you?"

"Uh—this *is* Viveca Howard's apartment, isn't it?" Jessica didn't know where to begin. How could her mother do this to her? Surely even Viveca wasn't so unconventional that she expected Jessica to stay in the apartment with Viveca's current lover there, too!

"Yes, it is, but she's gone for the summer. Were you

interested in one of her paintings? There are some on view at the local galleries.''

''No. I mean, I know Viveca's gone. She, uh, told me I could use her apartment while she was away. I'm her daughter. Jessica.''

''So you're Jessica. I should have guessed.'' His eyes swept over her thin, erect figure in its flawless white shirt and trousers and double-breasted black suit jacket. Something sparkled in his eyes. Jessica suspected it was amusement. She could well imagine her mother's description of her as a conservative, uptight career woman. Unexpectedly, he explained, ''You resemble her quite a bit.''

''Yes, our hair's the same color.''

He shrugged. ''More than that.'' He set the roller down in the paint pan and tugged a cloth out of a back pocket. He frowned down at his hands as he tried to wipe them clean. ''Viv didn't tell me you were coming.''

''I'm sorry.'' That was the understatement of the year. ''Apparently she got the idea when she flew up to see me. You know Viv. She's impulsive.''

''Yeah.'' He frowned and glanced around the apartment. ''I don't know exactly what to do now.''

''Look, it's no problem. I'll check into a hotel and stay a few days. I didn't really need to live here. I mean, originally I planned to stay in Atlanta. I'll fly back. Simple.''

''No. No, wait. Don't do that.'' He stuffed the rag back in his pocket and hopped lithely off the short ladder. ''I didn't mean to be rude. Please stay. I'll work it out. It's just that I waited until Viv wasn't here to do the painting—it's such a pain to live with the fumes and mess.''

Jessica glanced around at the paint-splotched drop cloths covering the furniture and carpet. She had to agree; it was a mess. Not exactly the peaceful jewel of a setting she and Viv had envisioned. "Didn't Viv know you were going to paint the place?"

"No. She's complained about it a couple of times the past few months, so I decided I'd surprise her with it when she came back from San Francisco."

"That was nice of you."

He shrugged. "Part of the job."

Jessica opened her purse and dug for a cigarette to hide her uneasiness. No doubt he was living off Viv as well as with her. Since the death of Jessica's grandfather three years ago, Viv was financially well-to-do. Even though the trust officer was careful not to give her large sums of money, following the will's explicit instructions, the trust Granddad had set up for his daughter gave Viv ample money to live on. She had always been able to make a living doing sidewalk portraiture, but now her "real" paintings were selling well, too. All in all, she enjoyed a more-than-comfortable income, which she spent freely and enjoyed lavishing on her friends and lovers.

Jessica admitted that she cast a jaundiced eye on all Viv's unorthodox relationships with men, but she was certain that she was right in thinking that two or three of the men in Viv's past had merely taken advantage of her open-handed good nature. But she had never heard one refer to the true nature of their relationship so casually or matter-of-factly, as this man just had, speaking of pleasing Viveca as part of his "job." Did he talk that way around her mother, or was it only with other people? Jessica hardly knew whether to despise him or admire his honesty. But she knew it made her nervous. He stood with arms folded, watching her light her cigarette. Her hand trembled on the lighter. Why was he staring at her?

Jessica glanced up to meet his gaze, then her eyes skittered off to the window on the opposite side of the room. She felt clumsy, naive and foolish. Why did she let him affect her? She was used to dealing with men all the time, and she never let any of them get the upper hand. Of course, the men she was used to dealing with were dressed in three-piece suits, not standing around half-naked. Six feet of smooth golden skin and lean muscle were a trifle disconcerting.

"Stuff'll kill you," her companion announced laconically.

"What?"

He nodded toward her hand. "Cigarettes. Have you ever seen a section of a smoker's lung?"

"No. It's not high on my list of priorities," she answered crisply. She was growing increasingly weary of obnoxious statements about smoking.

"Every smoker ought to look at one. It's a great eye-opener."

Jessica's eyes narrowed. She might have known he was a health nut; it went with the beach boy tan and hard musculature. He probably didn't pump iron; his muscles didn't bulge obscenely. But he'd obviously had his share of exercise to acquire that contained strength. He had the look of someone who'd done manual labor, even down to the calloused, stub-nailed fingers, but he didn't seem the type to work that hard. More likely it was a sport that had toned him—racquetball or tennis. Or maybe she'd been right about the surfer look.

Jessica strolled to the open doorway, studiously ignoring his smoking lecture. He followed her, stopping only inches behind her. Jessica stiffened. She could feel his solid presence looming behind her. Almost powerlessly she turned. Up close she could see the thick brown fringe of his lashes outlining eyes that were the rich, dark color of melted chocolate. His scent tingled at her nostrils, mingling with the pungent odor of paint. He was more than handsome. More than sexy. Jessica couldn't quite put a name to the indefinable quality he possessed. It wasn't power, exactly; yet it was intimidating. Nor was it precisely animal attraction; yet it was compelling. It was a sort of quiet confidence, a sureness in himself and everything around him. Jessica sensed that wherever he was, he would seem to belong there. He *would* belong there, simply because he wouldn't doubt it.

"Sorry," he said, smiling slightly. "I didn't mean to nag. Force of habit, I guess. Here, let me carry your bags to the bedroom."

Before she could protest, he had lifted her luggage and whisked it away through the door into the bedroom beyond. Jessica followed him, protesting futilely, "No, wait, don't bother. I'll go to a hotel tonight."

"The smell won't be too bad," he assured her, dumping the cases on the bed. "I'll finish the coat I'm putting on now because I want it to dry at the same rate, but I'll wait until after you're gone to put on the next coats. The windows and door are open to let out the odor, and if you shut the hall and bedroom doors, the smell shouldn't be too bad in here."

Being in the bedroom with him made Jessica nervous. This man touched off unusual, distinctly sensual responses in her. It heightened her awareness of everything even remotely sexual in their environment. She glanced at him and away, unable to meet his eyes. Her gaze flickered to the bed, but she found that even worse, and she fixed her eyes on his chin. "It's not the paint, uh, Mr.—?"

"Oh, I'm sorry. I'm Kyle Morrow."

"Jessica Todd." She extended her hand politely.

He glanced at his own hand and smiled ruefully, shaking his head. "I'm sure you don't want paint all over you." He held out his hands, palm up; they were splotched with paint.

"Oh. Yes, of course." Jessica's hand dropped awkwardly back to her side. She felt a little foolish, as she had ever since she walked in the door. She cleared her throat and reached over to stub out her cigarette in a wide, flat ashtray, something she recognized as a gift from Viveca's last lover, who had worked in ceramics. Even Viveca had admitted that his talents were dubious. But he'd had a gorgeous tush.

Jessica laced her fingers together, wondering how she could say this tactfully. "Mr. Morrow . . ."

"Kyle."

"Kyle. Your painting isn't the problem. I put up with having our whole office redecorated last year and even managed to get my work done."

"Great. Well, then, everything's fine." Again he smiled, his eyes warm and inviting. A quiver of excitement darted down Jessica's spine. His eyes were deep and dark, fathomless. She knew an urge to trace the line of his cheek, to let her finger skim his jaw and feel the rasp of his day's growth of beard against the ridges of her skin.

Jessica stepped back abruptly. This was crazy! The doctor must be right; she really had gotten weak—at least in the head. She would never have imagined that she would feel even a tickle of attraction to one of her mother's lovers. That wasn't the sort of man she liked at all. There was none of the sleekness nor polish that she was accustomed to. He might be handsome, all right, but he was far too elemental for her tastes, and too much a part of her mother's indolent, irresponsible, crazy world. Jessica didn't understand people like him; she had nothing in common with them. Living with her mother, she had known a great many, but she had never understood them.

"I don't think I'm making myself clear."

He watched her, one eyebrow quirked. "About what?"

"About staying here. It's—well, it's out of the question."

"You're right. You're not making yourself clear. The painting's no problem. Your mother invited you. So why is it out of the question?"

"Surely you can see that it would be awkward."

"No, I can't see. Why would it be awkward?"

Jessica wondered if he were teasing her, trying to tax her patience. "When I told Mother I'd come here, I wasn't aware that you would be here. If she'd told me, I would have refused immediately."

He gaped at her. "You hated me on sight?"

"No, of course I didn't hate you on sight. But, well, my standards, my, uh, lifestyle, are rather different from what they are here in the Quarter."

"No doubt," he contributed dryly.

"It would seem odd to me, well, improper, frankly, to stay here while you're here."

"Lady, you sound like you're out of a different century."

Jessica flushed. "I'm sorry if that sounds prim. I told you, my standards are different."

"Are you sure you're Viveca's daughter?" he asked, laughter brimming in his voice.

Jessica's eyes sparked at his evident amusement. "Damn it! I won't apologize. I'm not a puritan, but I would not be comfortable living in the same apartment with my mother's boyfriend!"

At least her words had the effect of rendering him speechless. Eyes wide, Kyle stared at her for a moment, then burst into loud laughter. Jessica set her jaw. She wouldn't let him intimidate her with ridicule. Or, rather, she wouldn't let it show, any more than she'd let it show that his near-nakedness made her nervous. He laughed until tears formed in his eyes, and Jessica whirled irritably and started toward the door.

"No! No, wait." He reached out and curled one hand around her wrist, capturing her lightly. His hands were large and long-fingered, the skin calloused. His touch shook her composure more than anything else he'd done. Jessica stopped and stood rigidly, her head turned away from him; she didn't dare look at his rich, dark eyes. "I'm sorry. It struck me as funny." He struggled to repress another burst of amusement. "Let me get this straight. You think I live in this apartment? That I'm Viveca's 'male friend.' "

"Yes, of course." Jessica turned her head curiously, a certain eager hope rising in her chest. "Aren't you?"

He shook his head.

"Oh. Oh. I thought . . ." She trailed off, a curious elation flooding her stomach. Relief, she told herself, that's all it was. Just relief that an awkward situation had been resolved.

He smiled. "I know what you thought. Why did you assume I was Viv's lover?"

Jessica colored slightly. She felt embarrassed to say

that it was primarily his hard body and handsome face. "Uh, because you were here painting the apartment. You called her Viv. And you seemed, well, her type, I guess."

He raised an eyebrow at that, but made no comment. "I fix up the apartments, that's all—paint, repair, take care of the gardens, that kind of thing."

"I see." He was the apartment building's handyman. It didn't fit him; there was a quality in his eyes that was too vivid, too strong. Jessica suspected he was both intelligent and educated. And something more— capable, perhaps. No doubt he was another dropout from the real world, like many of Viveca's friends. One of the people who could have done something with his life but opted for the easygoing life of New Orleans instead, not working, or working far below his capabilities, pretending to be an artist or simply bumming around. Jessica thought of such types as escapees from reality.

"Do you?" he responded quizzically to her noncommittal statement.

Jessica frowned. "What does that mean?"

"I'm not sure. I wondered what new picture of me you were concocting in your mind. There was a certain amount of disapproval in your tone."

Jessica shrugged. "Why should I care what you do?"

"Why, indeed?" he agreed cheerfully. "So. Are you going to stay now?"

"Yes. Yes, of course. I'm sorry for the mixup."

"It bothered you more than it did me." He swung away. "I'll get back to painting, if it won't bother you."

"No. That's fine. I'll sit on the patio for a while." He smiled without interest and was gone. Jessica could hear the rattle of the stepladder as he climbed it. She glanced around. The idea of sitting in here waiting for him to finish painting didn't appeal to her. She'd feel as if she were hiding. But neither did she wish to return to the living room with him, because then he'd probably talk to her, and she would have to answer, and all the while she'd be sneaking glances at his naked chest and legs and feeling embarrassed for doing so.

Jessica shook her head. Sheer craziness. You'd think she'd never seen half-naked men before, or had had no experience with men. Of course, she hadn't had much romantic experience; she'd never had the time, and men were usually intimidated by her drive and her accomplishments. But neither was she a naive schoolgirl. She'd had plenty of practice dealing with the passes of office wolves like Mark Banacek, and she'd dated enough that being with a man didn't make her jumpy—or at least she had thought so until she met Kyle Morrow.

As soon as she saw him, she'd felt a strange tingling awareness all over her body. As she'd talked with him, her eyes had absorbed things about him and stored them away, things she hadn't even been conscious of at the time, but now remembered. And thinking of them gave her a strange melting sensation in her abdomen. She remembered the curve of light brown hair across his forearms and the glint of gold when the light hit them; the straight cords running down the backs of his legs; the tight muscles of his thighs; his long hands and agile fingers, sensual and strong. She wondered what his hair looked like in the sun.

Jessica sighed and bent over the bed to unclasp her suitcase. The best plan was to change into cooler clothes and go down to the enclosed garden to relax, as she had told Kyle she was going to. She pulled out a casual pair of white shorts with two bright blue stripes down the sides and a sleeveless, scoop-necked shell in a matching blue. She laid them on the bed and walked softly to the door. She eased it shut, wincing when the hinges creaked loudly.

Stupid. Why shouldn't she close the door? Why did she imagine Kyle's knowing look when he heard the noise? And why did it make her pulse run faster to know he would realize that she was changing clothes? She was behaving like a complete idiot. With sharp, annoyed movements, Jessica skinned out of her blazer, blouse and trousers and pulled on the lightweight shorts and top. She stepped into flat thong sandals and debated whether she should take her hair down to ease her scalp. It would curl and bush out all over the place. But what did it matter? No one was there to see her. Quickly she unpinned her hair and unbraided it. It kinked and coiled, and Jessica brushed through it, then pulled it back from her face and fastened it with a wide comb on either side.

Self-consciously she opened the door of the bedroom and walked into the living room. Kyle glanced around at the sound of her steps. Jessica felt almost as if she were modeling the shorts for his approval, and she held herself stiffly, her eyes darting to the open door to avoid Kyle's. He paused in his work, leaning one hand against the top of the ladder, and watched her cross the room. Jessica went out the door and down the stairs, resisting the impulse to look back at Kyle.

She strolled over to the stone bench in the shade of the trees and settled on it as comfortably as she could. The faint breeze, the distant, intermittent sounds of cars beyond the buildings and the moist heat were soothing, almost hypnotic. But the bench had no back, and no matter which way she twisted or squirmed, she couldn't relax on it. Finally she gave up and stretched out on her back, feet up on the bench and knees bent. It was a hard surface to lie on, but at least she could close her eyes and let her muscles go limp. She threw one arm across her eyes and before she knew it, she was asleep.

She was awakened by the clank of the steps on the metal stairs, and she shot up, startled and disoriented, and almost fell off the narrow bench. Her hands flew out to grip the edges of the stone slab, and she swung her feet down onto the sidewalk. Blinking, she rolled her shoulders and watched Kyle Morrow maneuver the narrow, twisting staircase with his hands full of a paint can, tray, roller and other painting paraphernalia. He set the things down outside a small door and turned back to the stairs. Spotting Jessica watching him across the garden, he grinned and lifted his hand in a casual wave. Even this far away from him, Jessica felt the lazy appeal of his uneven smile.

She rose and crossed the garden to him, faintly surprised to find herself doing it. "Wait." He turned obligingly, the remnants of a smile still curving his lips. "I wanted to tell you that you could finish painting the living room if you wanted to. It won't bother me. Really."

"It stinks."

"I hardly noticed it. And like you said, I can keep the doors closed at night."

"What about the daytime?"

She shrugged. "Oh, I'll be gone soon. I'll probably sightsee, shop, that sort of thing. Besides, I'm supposed to be resting, so I'll be in bed a lot of the time."

"You've been sick?"

"Sort of."

"I thought you looked awfully thin."

"Thanks a lot."

"Sorry. I didn't mean it as a slam. You look good, even though you're thin." Chocolate-brown eyes caressed her briefly. "Well, if you're sure you're game for it, I'll finish the living room, at least. We'll save the bedroom for later."

There was something suspiciously suggestive about his last statement, but when Jessica glanced at him sharply, she saw nothing but blandness in his face. It was silly to think that what he'd said had any ulterior meaning. He wasn't the kind of man to be interested in her; no doubt he liked the big-bosomed, earth-mother type, as indolent and unambitious as he was. Jessica looked away. "Yes, well, that's fine, then."

He leaned against the railing and regarded her steadily, making no effort to close the conversation or leave. Jessica groped in her back pocket for her cigarettes, then remembered that she hadn't brought them down. "It's too bad Viv isn't here to show you around the Quarter," he said. "Have you been here before?"

"A couple of times. Very brief visits. Once I was here at a convention." To have something to do with her hands, she reached out and began to run her thumbnail around the knob atop one of the iron posts of the staircase. "I've, uh, seen a little of the Quarter. We went out to eat at Antoine's, saw the Cathedral, that sort of thing."

He reached out and touched her hand, stopping the repetitive circling of her thumb. Startled, Jessica looked up at him. His hand was warm and enfolding. Jessica swallowed when he began to speak. "You shouldn't spend your first evening in New Orleans alone. Why don't I take you out to dinner? We'll have a real Cajun meal. Then we could hit a jazz place or two."

Jessica froze. She didn't know what to say. In fact, she felt as if her very lungs had stopped moving. Why had he asked her out? And why did she feel a sudden, soaring desire to go? It was crazy. She didn't even know him. They were vastly different, worlds apart. They'd have nothing to talk about; she'd be bored; he'd regret it. "No, please, there's no need for you to do that. I'm perfectly all right by myself. The flight was rather tiring. I'll run down to the grocery and get something to eat, then go to bed early."

"All right, no jazz. I'll bring you home early. But let's have dinner." He held up a hand to ward off her next defense. "I know, there's no need. But I want to. I'd like to be with you."

Jessica glanced at him, a little unsure but overwhelmingly aware that she wanted to go out with him. "Yes, all right," she said breathlessly. "I'd like to. Thank you."

Reluctantly his hand left hers. "I have to run home and clean up first." He glanced down ruefully at his ragged shorts and paint-dotted body. "It may take a while. I'll be back . . . say, seven?"

Jessica nodded. "I'll be ready."

"Good. See you then." He winked and moved away, walking backward for a few steps before he swung around. Jessica watched him unlock the small door in the building and stow the paint cans in the tiny storage cabinet. He turned and gave her a final wave. Jessica was embarrassed at being caught watching him. She scurried up the steps and into her apartment without looking back. When she reached the bedroom, however, she couldn't help going to the window and staring out at the street below. Kyle was ambling up the block, his stride confident and unhurried. Jessica bit her lip and watched as he turned the corner and disappeared. She sighed and faced the room again. What had she let herself in for?

Chapter 3

JESSICA HADN'T REALLY EXPECTED KYLE TO SHOW UP IN shorts and no shirt again, but she was surprised when she opened the door to his knock and found him dressed casually, but sharply, in tan slacks and a tan pullover shirt with three diagonal blue stripes running across it. She had expected something like faded jeans and a T-shirt. His thick hair was shaggy, but she had to admit it looked good on him. He no longer looked quite so much the elemental male animal. Jessica smiled. "Hi. Come in. I'll get my purse."

She stepped into the bedroom and grabbed her purse, then checked her image one last time in the mirror. She was pleased with her choice of dress, especially now that she had seen Kyle. She had wavered between wearing this and something far more casual. The dress was a pale green and plain except for a border of white around the sleeves and collar and down the front on the left side.

Huge white buttons lined the border all the way to the hem of the dress. It was longer than the dresses she usually wore, but halfway down the thigh, the buttons were left undone, showing a slim expanse of leg. Very neat and precise, but subtly alluring, too.

When she returned to the living room, she found Kyle lounging against the back of one of the covered chairs. His eyes settled on her warmly, taking in every inch of her partially exposed leg. She hadn't really worn the dress for that reason—or had she?—but she couldn't deny the exhilaration she felt inside when Kyle gazed at her with admiration. *Now* let him tell her she was too thin!

They walked down the stair single file. Kyle opened the heavy gate for her to pass through, then swung it shut and joined her, his hand slipping easily around hers. Jessica hoped her fingers didn't tremble so much that he could feel it. "Where are we going?" she asked to distract herself from the unnerving combination of rough and smooth that was his palm.

"K. Paul's. He was once head chef at one of the famous restaurants here; this is his own place. It's unique."

They walked a couple of blocks and turned onto Chartres. Across the street from an imposing government building a line stretched out a doorway and down the sidewalk. Kyle led Jessica to the back of the line. "It must be popular," Jessica commented.

"Definitely. If you'd rather go someplace without a line, though . . . ?"

Jessica shrugged. "I'm okay. I live with lines; they're a constant in my life."

His dimple popped in. "What do you do that involves so much line-standing?"

"Bank, for one thing. Mostly, I fly. I stand in lines at the ticket counter, at the gate counter, at the security check, at the baggage claim, to get on the plane, to get off the plane. You name it. I've been in line for it."

"You fly on business?"

"Certainly not for pleasure. I'm a partner in a small firm. I cover the southeast seaboard—Virginia through Florida. I'm always going somewhere or other to consult or sell or teach a course." Jessica wished she hadn't brought up the subject of her business; she had found in the past that it usually had a bad effect on the men she'd dated. Her success and the energy that had gotten her there were intimidating to the male ego. Quickly she cast around for a new subject. "What about you? I mean, do you work on that one building, or are there others?"

"I have three buildings in the Quarter: Viv's, the one where I live, and one over on Conti. They usually keep me busy."

"You enjoy it?"

"Sure. It gives me plenty of time to do the things I enjoy. And I like getting down and digging in the garden or wrestling with ancient pipes. It's a challenge and very . . . basic, I guess." He flashed an amused glance at her. "Not your thing, I take it?"

"I'm not big on physical labor, no. My idea of exercise is walking through an airport."

"They say there's no better therapy than sweat."

"Then let's hope I don't need any therapy." Jessica flashed him a smile, sunny and open. Kyle shifted and leaned against the wall, several inches closer to her. She could see her reflection in the dark mirror of his gaze. Thin lines radiated from the corners of his eyes, and there were deep slashes beside his mouth. She considered his mouth, wondering what his kiss would feel like.

A shiver raced along her spine, turning her body a curious mixture of freezing cold and heat. Jessica turned her head aside. "Are you a native of New Orleans?"

He chuckled. "Is there such a person? No, I'm a Yankee, born and bred. I lived in Philadelphia the first ten years of my life, and the rest of it in California."

"Oh, really? Where in California?"

"San Diego. My father fell in love with it when he was in the navy, and when he got a chance to transfer to San Diego, he jumped at it. Naturally, I loved it, too. It was all swimming pools and the beach to me. Mom hated it; she couldn't stand living year round without snow."

"That would suit me to a T."

"Me, too. But not Mom. When my father died a few years ago, she moved back to Philadelphia immediately." He grunted. "When she got back there, she found that she didn't know anyone there anymore. All her friends had moved or found new friends. So she began to pine for the coast."

"How sad. What did she do?"

"Stayed in Philly. What else? I think even Mom began to realize that she probably wouldn't be happy anywhere. There are some people whose chief pleasure in life is finding fault with what they have. Pris Morrow is one of them." He frowned faintly, then shrugged off the topic. "And where are you from?"

"Atlanta."

"I mean originally."

"You name it, I've lived there," Jessica answered brightly. It was her stock answer to such inquiries. She'd hated her early nomadic life, but if she joked about it, it didn't fill her with such bitterness. "I was born in Virginia. How well do you know Viv?"

"Well enough to know she got pregnant when she was fifteen, if that's what you're wondering."

"I'm sure." Jessica's mouth drew up wryly. "I don't know why I hesitate to reveal her secrets. She'll tell a total stranger her life history."

"Maybe they're your secrets, not Viv's."

Jessica's eyes widened and she gazed at him for a moment in surprise. "Perhaps you're right. I never thought of it like that." Automatically she followed the line forward, lost in her thoughts. "I guess Viv isn't embarrassed by it. Sometimes I am."

"Why?"

"Makes me different, I suppose. I always hated that at school. We moved all the time, and I went to a different school practically every year. I dreaded it. Each school was a horrible test for me. I was always the odd one, the different one, new and unknown and untrusted."

He nodded. "I remember how I felt when we moved to California."

"You know Viv. She loves to travel. The first three years of my life we stayed in Virginia where both sets of grandparents live. Viv married the guy who'd gotten her pregnant; their families thought it was better than scandal." Jessica grimaced. "They were ruled by what the world thought of them, especially Dad's parents. Anyway, we stayed put until he and Viv divorced. Then she packed up her bags and me and took off. She was eighteen at the time, with no skills except an ability to draw, and absolutely no idea where she was going or what she would do. I don't remember anything from those first three years and little about the next two or three. I recall a house where we lived in a couple of rooms on the second floor; I really liked that place. But I don't know what city it was. Then Viv got married the second time when I was five. After that we lived in Florida for three years. That's when she had Dan and Ronny.''

''What happened after three years?''

''Another divorce and another journey. But this time Viv had done more than get her high school diploma at nights. She'd taken art classes at a local college. We moved to San Francisco, and she took more classes at an art institute. That's when she began doing portraits. You know, the kind of thing she does now, quick pastel drawings of whatever passerby will stop and pay her. It wasn't exactly lucrative, and she was always having to break down and call her father for money to get us out of trouble.'' Jessica shook her head. ''This conversation is getting too deep.''

''Too deep for what?''

''For polite conversation. Let's talk about something else.''

''You can't leave me hanging in the middle of the story.''

''There's not much to tell. It was more of the same the rest of my life until I went to college. We lived in . . . let's see, San Francisco; Austin, Texas; New York City; Puerto Rico; Jamaica; Mexico City; Acapulco; Oregon—that was on Viv's back-to-nature phase—Los Angeles; Tucson; Taos, New Mexico. Mmm, let me see, am I leaving anyplace out? Oh, yes, Asheville, North Carolina and Gatlinburg, Tennessee.''

''You're well-traveled.''

''That's one way to put it.''

''I gather you didn't enjoy it?''

Jessica sighed. ''No. People say they envy my having

been so many places. But I didn't enjoy it. I'd have given anything if we had settled down in one place. I wanted to live in the same house for years and years, like other kids. To have two parents.'' She smiled ruefully. ''To have even one *normal* parent. To go to the same school year after year and not be a stranger. I wanted to belong somewhere, I guess, but I was always a fish out of water.''

Jessica turned to him. ''I can't believe I'm telling you all this.'' Usually she was close-mouthed about her childhood. She had little desire to remember the pain and fears of her youth, or to feed others' curiosity about it. Yet here she was spilling it all out to a total stranger. ''You must be very easy to talk to.''

His answering smile was bittersweet. ''That's not exactly what people used to say. Maybe you're easy to listen to.'' He chuckled. ''Why are you giving me that suspicious look?''

''Flattery,'' she said succinctly, and took a cigarette out of her purse. He watched her light it, and for a moment she was afraid he was about to launch into another sermon on the evils of smoking. But he said nothing, merely studied her silently as she blew the smoke out of her mouth in a long, straight puff. She dropped the cigarette package and lighter back in her purse, her movements quick, capable and impatient.

''It's not flattery if it's true, is it?''

''That's right,'' she retorted pointedly.

''Do you always have a comeback?''

''It's one of my major faults—or skills, depending on how you look at it. Does it bother you?''

''No. You needn't get aggressive about it. You can be a very prickly person, Jessica Todd.''

"You mean you don't think I'm soft and cuddly?" she asked, deepening her southern accent and looking up at him through fluttering lashes.

"Mmhmm, soft and cuddly like a baby leopard."

"I'm surprised you risked going out to dinner with me tonight, then. Aren't you afraid I might turn you into the main course?"

His grin was lazy and wicked. Deep brown eyes bored into her, alight with amusement and sensual invitation. "I'll take my chances."

"Daring, aren't you?" Jessica commented, her eyes dancing. She was enjoying their wordplay. There was something intensely exciting about the sexual undertones of their comments, yet the public spot gave her safety, as well.

She stood with her back against the wall of the restaurant, leaning back and propping one heel up against the wall. Kyle had been standing sideways to her, bracing himself by leaning one arm against the wall beside her head. Now he turned toward her and brought the other arm up, effectively trapping her. He stared down at her, his hard body so near that she could feel its heat, his mouth hovering above hers, wide and firm. Jessica's heart began to pound. She could feel his desire like a physical touch. She wet her lips nervously, and his gaze followed her movement. A muscle beside his mouth twitched, and he leaned a little closer. "I think I could handle a man-eater right now," he murmured.

Jessica wondered if he were going to kiss her right there, with all the other restaurant patrons looking on. She wasn't sure whether she would be angry or not. His breath drifted across her lips, and a quick fire curled in her abdomen. His face moved toward her, and for one breathless moment she thought he would kiss her. But he shifted slightly to one side and whispered in her ear, his hot breath sending shivers through her, ''I wish we were back in your apartment. This place is a little public for what I'd like to do right now.''

Jessica's knees melted, and she had to lean heavily against the supporting wall. She would have liked to toss back a fast, sexy retort, but her ready tongue seemed to have deserted her. She could only swallow convulsively and hope that her face wasn't as flushed as it felt. Kyle drew back, but not before nipping her earlobe lightly. He leaned against the wall on his forearms, his body a hairsbreadth away from her all the way up and down. Jessica knew that with any other man she had dated, she would be livid with anger and embarrassment at this public display. But tonight she didn't care.

The exit door opened outward beside her, and Jessica jumped, startled. Two couples emerged from the restaurant, and the line moved forward. With a sigh Kyle levered himself up and off the wall and took her hand to follow the line into the restaurant. Inside, Jessica folded her arms across her chest and glanced around. She felt rudely popped back into the real world, and she struggled to reestablish her usual persona. ''You were right when you said it was unique,'' she commented dryly.

Certainly, in this city of elegant restaurants, it was different. The narrow room stretched back to a waist-high counter, behind which the kitchen was in plain view. The floor was made of bare wood planks, unpolished, and the tables and chairs were wooden and ordinary. Waitresses scurried back and forth with huge round trays of dishes. The hostess came forward and escorted the couples in front of them to their tables. She returned after a few minutes and stopped before Kyle and Jessica. She wore black slacks and a black T-shirt, much worn, emblazoned with the legend "French Quarter" across the front. A yellow pencil rested in her hair just above her ear. "Two of you?" she asked laconically.

"Yes."

"I have room upstairs." She started off at a brisk pace, and they hurried after her across the room and up a narrow flight of wooden stairs. At the top was another room much like the one below. She seated Jessica and Kyle at a table and left. Minutes later a waitress whizzed by their table and handed them single sheets of paper which contained the menu.

Jessica read the menu with some astonishment. There was none of the delectable French cuisine she had encountered in other New Orleans restaurants. She raised her head. "What in the world is blackened Louisiana redfish? And barbequed shrimp?"

Kyle chuckled. "It's very good. Either one. This is Cajun food, not French. You know, jumbalaya, gumbo. . . The redfish is fried in a very hot cast iron skillet, and it comes out black on the surface. But it's really delicious. And the shrimp don't taste like western barbeque. They're unpeeled, boiled shrimp with Louisiana spices on them. They're my favorite."

Jessica returned to the menu. Though the place had none of the almost antiseptic elegance of Antoine's, nor the plush richness of some of the other well-known New Orleans restaurants, its prices were certainly in the same class. A slight frown line formed between her eyes. How could the maintenance man for a few apartments afford to eat here? Jessica felt a twinge of guilt. She couldn't let him pay for her meal. "Well, I guess I'll follow your lead."

"Barbequed shrimp?"

"Uh-huh." She glanced up in surprise as the waitress seated a young man at their table.

"Hello, I'm Stan Furness," he greeted them with a friendly grin.

Kyle shook his hand and introduced himself and Jessica. Jessica managed a smile. Kyle turned to her and explained, "They often seat other people at your table. They're always crowded."

"I see."

Stan grinned. "It takes a while to get used to it, but the food's worth it."

It was indeed. When the waitress brought their plates, Jessica saw that they were piled high with the biggest shrimp she had ever seen in her life. She stared in amazement. "These must be five or six inches long," she gasped.

"Yeah," Kyle agreed without surprise. "I've gotten some that big out of Lake Pontchartrain."

"You're joking."

"No. Go ahead, dig in. There's no way to do it without getting your hands messy."

Jessica began peeling the shrimp, carefully cleaning one after another until she had accumulated as many as she thought she could eat. Then she wiped her hands off on a napkin and dipped them into the little bowl of lemon water the waitress had thoughtfully provided for her. Kyle regarded her with amusement. His fingers were stained with the orangy color of the spices. He peeled one shrimp, then ate it, plowing steadily through his plate. "Methodical, aren't you?" he teased, indicating her neat stack of cleaned shrimp and the pile of discarded shells.

Jessica lifted her shoulders. "I just like to get all the mess over and done with at one time so I can eat without this gunk on my hands."

"I'm sure our methods must reveal something significant about our personalities." He popped half a shrimp in his mouth and chewed, smiling beatifically.

"Yeah." Jessica grinned. "Yours means you're a slob."

"Thanks a lot." His eyes twinkled and he winked. "I won't tell you what yours means."

"Why not? What do you mean?"

"Thought that would get you."

Jessica grimaced at him and started eating her shrimp. Her eyebrows lifted, and her eyes lit up. "Mmmm. These are delicious!"

He laughed. "Told you."

The meal was fantastic despite its messiness, and their unexpected companion proved to be witty and ready to talk. Jessica let Stan and Kyle carry the conversation. It was pleasant to be with people for whom she didn't have to make an effort. She could follow the conversation lazily instead of having to keep her mind razor sharp. There was no need to prove herself intelligent, capable, determined, not given to feminine weaknesses, or anything else. It was a nice change from all her usual business meetings, dinners and cocktail get-togethers. She hadn't noticed until now how wearing they were.

Jessica couldn't finish her shrimp and was far too stuffed to have a dessert. Kyle glanced at her plate and shook his head in mock despair. "Now, how are you going to gain weight eating like that?"

"I ate a lot!" Jessica protested. "You just worry about how you're going to keep from getting fat, eating like you do."

"Ah, but I get a star for belonging to the clean plate club."

Jessica was amazed to see that when the waitress came to take away their plates, she did indeed plant a shiny blue star on Kyle's cheek. He grinned at Jessica, and she couldn't help but smile back. Kyle's good humor was infectious. In fact, everything about him was. That was why he was dangerous. She had the feeling that she could come to like him far more than would be healthy for the state of her emotions. Kyle Morrow was one of those people who were irresistible but didn't last. Charming, then gone . . . like Viveca. She'd learned that the best thing to do with people like that was to stay away from them.

That was why there wouldn't be any repetition of this evening, she told herself firmly. There was pain waiting at the end of any relationship with a man like Kyle. The waitress brought their bill, and Kyle reached into his hip pocket for his wallet. Jessica leaned forward, putting a hand on his arm. "You must let me pay for my dinner."

"I must?" he repeated. "And why must I?"

"I insist. I want to."

He frowned. "But I invited you out."

"What does that matter? I—I'd feel better if I paid for my share."

"Why?" He regarded her steadily. "So it wouldn't feel like a real date? Don't worry. I'll let you off the hook—I don't expect a sexual payoff."

Jessica flushed. "That wasn't what I meant."

He shook his head and tossed a credit card onto the

plastic tray with the bill. "Don't be absurd. When I ask you to dinner, I pay."

"You're being chauvinistic."

"You're being unreasonable."

Jessica, very aware of Stan's interested silence, subsided. She'd done her best. If Kyle insisted on throwing away his money, who was she to stop him? Still, she felt faintly in the wrong, just as she did whenever Viveca bought her something or paid for their meal or entertainment, as if squandering the money were somehow her responsibility. Shaking off the feeling, she rose when the waitress brought the tray back to Kyle. He signed his name in an illegible scrawl, carelessly stuffed the card back into his wallet and followed Jessica across the floor and down the stairs to the exit.

They strolled past what was apparently a permanent line in front of the restaurant and continued down Chartres. Once again Kyle took her hand. Jessica tightened inside, but made no effort to withdraw her fingers from his. She wouldn't let it go any further than this, she thought. There'd be none of that dangerous interplay there had been standing outside K. Paul's; she would make sure of that. Kyle was far too sexy, and for some reason her resistance was down. She couldn't afford to play with fire just because it was exciting while it burned. . . . But surely a little hand-holding wouldn't hurt.

Their steps were lazy and slow. Kyle turned up a side street before they reached the Cathedral and continued on Royal to St. Ann. "This is where most of the antique shops are," he commented as they strolled along. "In the Quarter, that is. If you like antiques, Magazine Street is the real center."

Jessica shook her head. "I'm not all that interested in them."

"Book shops? Perfume shops?"

Jessica shook her head.

"What *are* you interested in, then? Or do I have to keep on guessing?"

"Resting," she replied. "Just lying around reading, sunning, that sort of thing. Sitting in the garden. Sleeping."

"You are an active sort."

Jessica sighed. "Usually I'm going ninety miles an hour."

"What happened?"

"I had a crash."

"Figuratively or literally?"

"Figuratively. One evening I started laughing, and then it turned into tears. I couldn't stop crying, so they took me to the hospital. I had hysterics."

"Somehow you don't seem the type."

"I'm not. That's what worried me. I can't remember ever crying in public, even at a sad movie. But I sobbed." She shrugged, embarrassed even at the memory. "The doctor said I'd been working too hard and needed a rest cure. So here I am."

"Did you have high blood pressure?"

"Yeah. How'd you know?"

He shrugged. "Goes with a lot of pressure. What else did he find?"

"He said I was exhausted and too thin and a lot of other stuff."

"Such as that you ought to quit smoking."

"You got it. Quit smoking, gain weight, rest, exercise." She sighed. "Not much of a vacation, if you ask me."

He chuckled. "There are a lot of people who'd give almost anything to have a doctor tell them to rest and gain weight."

"I suppose. Unfortunately, I'm not one of them."

"Of course not." He let go of her hand and instead curled his arm around her shoulders. "I can see that you're a tough case."

"What does that mean?"

"Just that I'm glad I'm not your doctor. It's risky enough going to dinner with you." Jessica lifted a questioning face to him. "First you seduce me on the sidewalk in front of the restaurant—" At Jessica's indrawn gasp of indignation, his lips twitched, but he held up his hand to silence her and went on. "Then you insult my masculinity by trying to pay for your meal. And when we get to your apartment, you'll no doubt reject my pass."

"At least you've got the last part right." Jessica wasn't at all sure that she'd be able to reject him if he turned on the raw sexual power he'd shown earlier in the evening, but she wasn't about to admit it to him.

"Unfortunately, I'm very perceptive," he admitted with a mock sigh. They turned the corner and continued on a darker, quieter side street. Abruptly Kyle stopped, pulling Jessica with him against the wall of the aging building beside them. She looked up at him, startled, and was surprised to see that his face, despite his comic tone, was harsh and lined. "Damn," he muttered, and then one hand cupped her neck, his fingertips and thumb holding her head still, and he lowered his mouth to hers.

His lips were smooth and firm as they moved against hers, demanding entrance. Instinctively her lips parted to admit him, and his tongue slid over the sharp edges of her teeth and into the depths of her mouth. His breath came out in a ragged shudder as he pressed her body into his, thrusting his lean strength against the soft contours of her flesh. Kyle ground his mouth against hers almost fiercely, at odds with the gentle caress of his fingers on the nape of her neck. Jessica's hands came up to his chest and rested there tentatively, fingers curling into his shirt.

His hands slid into her hair and moved upward, kneading the sensitive skin of her scalp. Jessica felt as if she could ooze right through his fingers and lie in a puddle at his feet. She'd never tasted a kiss as tempting, as sweet, as hungry. The hard texture of his muscles against her body aroused a primitive feminine urge within her, a surging force that wanted to conquer his strength with her own submission. A soft heat pooled between her thighs, and she yearned to stroke her body against his like a cat until the hot ache was eased.

He filled her mouth. He filled her mind and senses. It was a warm evening, but Jessica shivered. She thought that in a moment she might start moaning and twisting against him like a mindless animal, and all he had done was kiss her! Jessica twisted her head away, breaking the seal of their lips, and dragged in huge gulps of air. Kyle leaned his forehead against her hair. She could feel the faint quiver of his muscles. "Oh, Lord, honey, you turn me inside out. I didn't mean to do that. Not just yet, anyway." He paused and sighed, forcing himself to loosen his hold. "Damn! Skinny redheads are dangerous."

Jessica stepped back, tugging and smoothing her dress, carefully avoiding his eyes. *"You're* calling me dangerous? Who's been mauling who here?"

"I confess. I was the mauler." His voice was less

tight now, almost normal, with its usual coloring of wry amusement.

Nervously Jessica licked her lips. She tasted him on them, and her stomach melted all over again. "I—we better go home." Yes, she was sure that was right. She had already determined that she wasn't going to fall under his spell, hadn't she? But the words were difficult to choke out. She wanted to throw herself back in his arms and ask him to kiss her again. Had that been only one kiss? It seemed like a lifetime.

Kyle closed his eyes and released his breath slowly. "Yes. All right."

He started walking again, this time not touching her at any point. Jessica stayed beside him, still unable to lift her head and look at him directly. She'd never felt so naive, frustrated and utterly unlike herself. They reached the black iron gate of Viveca's building. Kyle unlocked it with one of his keys and stepped back to let her pass. He walked at her heels through the narrow passageway and up the steps. With numbed fingers Jessica drew Viv's key from her purse and fitted it into the lock. She turned, forcing herself to face his eyes.

The dark brown eyes were black in the night, but there was no mistaking the brilliant flare of passion in them. His agreement to return to the apartment hadn't been made out of disinterest. She'd wondered why he hadn't protested when she'd suggested it. It had seemed too passive for him. She wished . . . she wished he had said, "No, damn it," and kissed her until she hadn't the wit or strength to deny him. "Kyle . . ." Her voice was soft, faintly wistful.

"What?" He framed her face with his hands, his thumbs outlining her lips. She tasted the salt of his skin.

Jessica shook her head slightly. "I don't know. Nothing."

"You're all wrong for me," he said softly. "I don't know why I'm so crazy. I have the feeling you're going to shake up my world something fierce." He bent and kissed her, hard and quickly. "I'll see you tomorrow morning."

"What?"

He nodded toward the open apartment. "To paint."

"Oh. Well, good night. Thank you for dinner. I— enjoyed it."

His grin was devilish. "Me, too. Especially the dessert."

"What des—" She stopped suddenly, realizing what he meant, and flushed.

"Good night, Jess." He turned and ran lightly down the stairs. She didn't know how he kept from breaking his neck in the dim light. He stopped at the bottom and turned his face up toward her. His skin and hair were pale in the moonlight. "Hey, if we're going to keep on kissing, you'll have to stop smoking."

Chapter 4

IT TOOK JESSICA A LONG TIME TO GET TO SLEEP THAT night. Kyle's parting words had left her speechless, an unusual state for her. Once the surprise wore off she had stormed into her apartment, slamming the door behind her. Then she had paced about, slamming one doubled-up fist into her open palm, muttering imprecations on Kyle Morrow's head, and thinking up all the marvelous, witty retorts she should have made. It had taken her two hours and ten cigarettes to calm down enough to get into bed, and even then she had tossed and turned long after she should have gone to sleep.

As a result she slept far later the next morning than she normally did, not awakening until after ten o'clock. Yawning and rubbing her face, she sat up and swung her legs over the side of her bed. Then she heard it: a small thud in the living room, followed by a rustling sound.

Jessica froze, her eyes turning to the closed door from her bedroom into the hall. There were more sounds of movement, and then a cheerful whistling began. Jessica's brows shot up. A whistling intruder? It seemed unlikely.

Then she remembered. Kyle was supposed to come in today to put another coat of paint on the living room walls. She wouldn't put it past him to have used his pass-key and barged in even though she was still asleep in the bedroom. She frowned, thinking that he had entirely too much nerve. He'd been downright insulting last night, telling her that she'd have to stop smoking if she wanted any more of his kisses. As if his kisses were some kind of prize! As if *he* hadn't kissed her with a great deal of enjoyment despite her smoke-tainted mouth! As if they were going to have some sort of relationship! Jessica tried to work up a suitable anger over his lack of taste and character, but she found her mouth traitorously curling up into a grin. It had been such a blatantly ridiculous statement after the long, passionate scene they'd just played on the sidewalk that it was funny. Some people simply had so much gall that it was impossible not to be amused.

Jessica pulled her feet up on the bed, wrapped her arms around her drawn-up legs and leaned her chin thoughtfully on her knees. Their kiss had been unlike any she'd ever experienced. She wondered if it had had the same powerful effect on Kyle. She grimaced. Probably not. He was no doubt used to sparking fire every time he kissed a woman. But it had been a first for her, an unexpected, overwhelming sweep of desire that had shocked her with its intensity. Feelings had never been her forte; she'd left that to her mother. She had always been the sober, practical one, the one who witnessed, analyzed and *then* acted, not the one who absorbed and exuded emotions. Whenever a problem came up, she set her brain to it, not her heart. She wouldn't have called herself unsympathetic or unfeeling, but certainly she wasn't given to dramatic emotions.

But last night had been sheer epic romance. She had felt hungry, swept away, swooning with pleasure—all those grandiose, unimaginable feelings. It wasn't what one expected from a woman who always thought before she spoke or acted. It was, in fact, downright impulsive. It had also been utterly delightful. Jessica sighed. That was the problem. She had enjoyed it; she wanted to experience it again. She wanted to throw caution to the winds and for once—selfishly, illogically—do precisely what pleased her.

She gnawed at her lower lip. It was an idea that was as frightening as it was intriguing. She couldn't remember acting on impulse before; she wasn't sure how it was done. And what if . . . what if it didn't turn out all right? What if she waltzed into the living room clad only in her short nightie and Kyle coolly rejected her? What if she flung herself into his arms and they enjoyed night after night of pleasure until she left? What would she do at the end of her stay? How could she bear to leave? She had never worried before about what would happen to her if a relationship ended; she had always been confident that it would affect her very little. But she had the distinct feeling that this relationship could completely alter the course of her life. Would the fling be worth it if she had to return to Atlanta broken-hearted, miserable and sniveling?

She didn't know what would happen, and Jessica wasn't accustomed to entering anything without knowing all the possibilities. No, it was worse than that: She knew some of the possibilities, and they were all bad. She and Kyle were not suited for each other. An affair between them couldn't keep from ending badly. There couldn't be any happy-ever-after for a career woman from Atlanta in love with a happy-go-lucky New Orleans bum. In the end she'd lose. They were incompatible. They had nothing in common except a fiercely elemental sexual attraction. Kyle Morrow was like her mother; he represented a lifestyle that she had long ago rejected. She felt sure that they would disagree on almost everything. When the time came for her to leave New Orleans, they would have to part. Realistically, there was no other way.

Kyle had aroused a strong primitive urge in her last night. She admitted that. But was satisfying it worth the trouble? Would it make up for the future pain? Jessica knew she wouldn't embark on any professional project that had such miserable odds. It was being emotional. Irresponsible. Unthinking. Impulsive. All the things she despised. Surely she couldn't allow herself to act like that.

With weary resignation she swung her legs off the bed and stood up. She wouldn't run out and throw herself into Kyle's arms. Instead she would do her best to keep the relationship between them cool and distant. She would have nothing more to do with him than she would anyone else who happened to be painting her living room. She would ignore him and eventually he'd go away. If he became too much of a bother she'd simply pack her bags and return to Atlanta to live out her weeks off. She refused to get into a dead-end relationship with any man.

It probably wouldn't be that difficult, she told herself. Even Kyle had expressed doubts about it last night after he'd kissed her. He realized they were wrong for each other. After he'd thought it over, he might be as reluctant as she was to continue their brief relationship. The thought did little to raise her spirits.

Jessica showered, a slow process due to poor water pressure. Finally, clean and rinsed, she stepped out of the tub and rubbed herself dry with a ragged, stained towel. Jessica glanced at it and smiled. No doubt Viv had once grabbed it to clean up an artistic spill with no regard to how it would ruin the bath towel. It was typical of the things she did.

Jessica toweled her hair and ran a large-toothed comb through it to remove the tangles. She decided to leave it hanging loose to dry. After all, this was her vacation; it didn't matter if her hair hung loose and frizzy. She dressed in a tank top, shorts and sandals, and decided against makeup. There was no point in trying to look pretty for Kyle Morrow when she had no intention of pursuing a relationship with him. At the last minute she smoothed on lipstick, thinking she couldn't let herself go out looking quite so ghostly. She went to the closed door and hesitated, her fingers interlacing and untwining rapidly. She dreaded facing Kyle's eyes.

This was ridiculous. Jessica squared her shoulders. She refused to let herself be intimidated. After all, she could hardly hide in the bedroom for days while Kyle finished painting. She opened the door and walked through the short hall into the living room. Kyle was working along the baseboards, again dressed in shorts, though this time he wore a shirt, unbuttoned down the front and with the sleeves ripped off. He glanced up and smiled, then continued with his work. "Hello, Sleeping Beauty. I was beginning to wonder if you were in there."

"My purpose here is to rest," Jessica reminded him primly and started toward the kitchen. She must not fall in with his bantering as she had yesterday. That was what had set their relationship down the wrong pathway. She opened the refrigerator and found it bare of everything except a few condiments and a wilted bunch of celery. Jessica closed the door and searched through the cabinets. Here she netted a box of cereal, but without milk it wasn't much use. She peered inside the box. It was probably too old, anyway. In this warm, moist climate, food didn't remain unspoiled long.

Jessica tossed the box into the trash can and dug through the drawers until she found a piece of scratch paper and the stub of a pencil. She plopped down at the table and began a grocery list. As she sat there she heard the soft pad of footsteps across the living room floor. Kyle stopped behind her and leaned over to read what she was writing. Jessica glanced up in irritation. "Do you always read over people's shoulders?"

"When I'm curious."

"It's rather rude."

He shrugged and continued reading her list. "You're going to buy a bunch of frozen dinners?"

Jessica lifted her chin. "I didn't come here to spend my time cooking. Besides, these aren't just ordinary dinners. They're gourmet frozen food."

"Do you know how much sodium and additives are in stuff like that? They're high in calories and low in nutrition."

"I'm supposed to gain weight."

"You're also supposed to regain your health. What you need to buy are some good, fresh vegetables and fruits and lean meats. You're sitting here in a seaport, and you haven't got a single kind of fish or shellfish written down."

"Fish smell when you cook them."

One of his long, paint-marred fingers jabbed at another word on her list. "Coffee. Diet soft drinks."

"Do you mind?" Jessica snapped. "Just because you're a health food nut—"

"I'm not. But a person who has high blood pressure and smokes needs to be more selective about her foods. Have you ever heard of drinking water? Decaffeinated coffee?"

"You're getting on my nerves. When I want your advice about what I eat, I'll ask for it."

He shook his head sadly, crossing his arms over his chest. "You obviously need help, lady. Believe me, this is not a healthy diet."

"How do you know?"

"If you'd ever read anything on the subject, you'd know it, too. Didn't your doctor give you a list of foods you should eat?"

"Yes," Jessica admitted grudgingly.

"Where is it?"

With a sigh Jessica retrieved her purse from the kitchen counter and pulled out a crumpled piece of paper. Kyle took it from her fingers and spread it out before her on the table. "Look: decaffeinated coffee, tea and soft drinks. I'll tell you something you've probably never realized. You're a caffeine junkie."

Jessica rolled her eyes. "Give me a break."

"I promise, stay off the caffeine for a couple of weeks and you won't be jumpy like before. The combination of caffeine and nicotine is even worse. If you don't do anything else, cut out the caffeine."

"All right! I'll buy decaffeinated coffee!" Jessica growled through clenched teeth. "Now, will you leave me alone?"

"It's obvious to me that you need help. Come on, I'll help you shop. We'll get healthy, *tasty* stuff." He grabbed her by the arm and lifted her from the chair.

"Kyle! I don't need help. I'm a grown woman, and I'm perfectly capable of shopping by myself."

He took both her hands and stared down earnestly into her eyes. "Do you not have any intention of following your doctor's advice?"

Jessica frowned, hesitating. She didn't want to. She'd like to throw away that list and forget all about the physician's warnings. Jessica thought about the consequences. She must not be stupid. She'd always prided herself on thinking things through and following the most logical course. It didn't make sense to defy the doctor, to pretend that if she ignored her problem, it would go away. She sighed. "I know I ought to. It just seems so grim."

"Stop trying to avoid it. Come on, I'll help you, and after a few days you'll find out it's not so grim, after all."

She hadn't intended this, she thought as she slung her purse over her shoulder and followed Kyle out the door and down the stairs. She hadn't meant to do anything like it. She had planned to be cool, reserved and aloof; she had been going to avoid Kyle like the plague. Yet here she was, walking to the grocery store with him. She was going to let him badger her into buying healthy foods she despised. She would spend thirty minutes or so in close contact with him—and then no doubt when they got home and she fixed breakfast, he would horn in on that, too! Kyle was maddening, frustrating. Why did she have so much trouble building up her anger against him?

Kyle whisked her down the street and around the corner to the small, ancient grocery. A green wood-framed door sheltered the wood and glass doors behind. Jessica stepped over the marble doorframe and into the past. She'd always heard of corner groceries, but she'd rarely seen one. The stores of her childhood were wide-aisled, speedy supermarkets, vast open expanses of food and other products. This store was small and cramped, with aisles so narrow it was almost impossible to navigate a cart down them. Food was jammed into every available space, and in the back a butcher presided over the small meat counter. The floor was of faded, cracked linoleum. A few gumball machines lurked by the exit, but there wasn't sight or sound of a video game machine.

Jessica barely had time to take in the store's quaintness before Kyle set off cheerfully down the aisles, stocking her shopping basket with ripe, succulent plums, peaches that smelled like peaches, fat, glistening green grapes, firm vegetables, and a variety of meat and fish that made Jessica gape. "But I don't cook!" she wailed when he bought a pound of raw, unpeeled shrimp. "Kyle, you don't understand. I don't enjoy cooking, and I don't know how to. There's no point in buying anything that takes any effort to fix."

"Shrimp are no problem. You just boil them. And you just cut up this chicken, remove the skin and broil it. Simple as can be." He peered at a fish through the glass window of the butcher's counter.

"Kyle, don't get that. It's staring at us. I'm not going to eat anything that looks at me."

"After I cook it, you won't recognize it. Trust me."

Sure. She trusted him to weasel his way into eating dinner and spending the evening with her. Obviously she had been wrong in thinking that Kyle had the same sorts of doubts she did, or at least, that he wouldn't pursue her if he did. He seemed bent on pushing his way into her life—and changing it, too! She resented it, yet she did almost nothing to stop it. Jessica was beginning to wonder if something major had snapped in her brain the night she had broken down. This kind of behavior wasn't like her at all.

They carried home three full bags of groceries, all disgustingly healthful in Jessica's opinion. But when they reached the apartment Jessica's fears of Kyle's joining her for breakfast proved unfounded. He merely set the bags on the counter and returned to his task in the living room. Jessica occupied herself with unpacking and putting away the groceries, then drip-brewing a potful of decaffeinated coffee. While the coffee brewed, she poured a bowlful of wheat cereal and sprinkled it with sliced bananas. With the merest dusting of sugar, it tasted delicious, even with low-fat milk instead of whole milk. It was unfair, Jessica thought, that she should be expected to cut down on fats and cholesterol at the same time she was supposed to gain weight. Low-fat milk, plain cereals, little cheese, no butter, no fried foods— she might as well be on a diet. However, she had to admit that the cereal tasted good; she'd worked up an appetite walking to the store and back. And she could tell little difference in the taste of her "fake" coffee.

She offered Kyle a cup, but he shook his head. "Nope. It's getting too hot for it. Tell you what. Tomorrow morning I'll take you over to the Café du Monde, and we'll have some real Louisiana coffee. How does that sound?"

"Heavenly," she admitted. Inwardly she sighed. She wasn't sticking to her plan at all. Lacing her hands together, she fought the temptation to stay there talking to Kyle while he worked. "I think I'll go down to the garden again. It's very restful."

Kyle watched Jessica walk out the open door and start down the steps. He enjoyed the play of her lean buttocks and the long, inviting expanse of her slender legs. She was a little too thin, but Kyle had no complaints about her figure. Everything about her form and face had touched a deep chord of desire in him as soon as he met her. The hunger hadn't diminished with the passage of time or Jessica's continued presence. If anything, it had grown with every moment he spent around her. Her laughter, the delicate arch of her eyebrows over expressive eyes, the clear-cut line of brow and cheek and jaw . . . even the rapid, almost jerky gestures she made, were all subtly alluring. There was little feminine softness to her, but the things she used to hide her femininty—the mannish suits, the tightly repressed hair —only served to emphasize her underlying womanliness and challenged a man to bring it forth.

Kyle thought of the slide of Jessica's skirt over her legs last night as they walked to the restaurant. He remembered the cool touch of her lips and flesh, and the rapid way they caught fire when he kissed her. His lids lowered, heavy and sensual, as he recalled the scene. He'd like to hold her right now . . . feel her small, uptilted breasts pressed into his chest, the tips hard and seeking. He wanted to kiss her and feel the velvet glide of her tongue beneath his. Jessica . . . Jessie . . .

He closed his eyes and shook his head. She was all wrong for him. He'd known it from the moment he saw her. She could disrupt his whole life, disturb the tranquillity he'd fought so long and hard to find. There were qualities about her—the hint of energy and ambition boiling within, the cool shield to ward off intimacy, the rapid movements, the clever, slightly cynical talk—that told him she was a mover and a shaker. Exactly what he had left behind him long ago. He didn't need to fall for a woman who embodied that futile, harried life.

Definitely the wrong woman to want so badly. You couldn't hold a woman like that, not for long. She'd be here for a few weeks, and then she'd be gone, back to her world. Back to the place where he no longer fit, didn't want to fit. And he'd be left standing here, gaping like an idiot with his knees kicked out from under him. Kyle shrugged and began the slow, steady path of his paint roller. Well, if there was one thing he'd learned in life, it was that you hardly ever did anything because it was the safe or sane thing to do. He knew he'd go on chasing her, wanting her on every level, until he had her . . . or until she went away.

Jessica spent the rest of the day dodging Kyle. She took the paperback Alan's wife had loaned her down to the garden and read away what was left of the morning. But the stone bench soon grew hard, and by lunchtime she was more than ready to return to her apartment. She made a tossed green salad and tuna salad for herself, then reasoned that it would seem rude and selfish not to invite Kyle to join her. "Would you like a little lunch?" she called into the living room.

She heard Kyle jump off his ladder. "I thought you'd never ask! Sure. What you got?"

"Not much," she admitted. "Tuna and a salad."

"Sounds great." He cleaned up at the sink, washing

halfway up his arms and splashing water on his face. He toweled off his face and hands while Jessica watched him, unable to jerk her eyes away. It had gotten warm enough that he had again discarded his shirt, revealing a large expanse of tanned, smooth skin. There was little hair on his chest, Jessica thought, following the narrow light-brown line which tapered into nothingness on his stomach. She fought the urge to reach out and trace its path with her forefinger. She had never liked hairy men; Kyle's smooth, firmly muscled flesh was far more appealing, golden brown and beckoning her touch. Jessica swallowed and turned away, sitting down quickly in her chair. She was letting her thoughts get away from her again.

Kyle proceeded to make two thick sandwiches from the supply of tuna salad and devour them completely. "Hard work, painting," he explained briefly. Jessica supposed he must be right. Certainly his flat stomach showed no signs of his eating any more than he burned off. There she went again. She turned her attention firmly back to her plate.

After lunch he helped her clean the dishes and dry them. It made Jessica uncomfortable to have him stand beside her, totally unconcerned about his seminudity, so close that she could smell the faint spicy scent of his aftershave. Her elbow brushed against his as she handed him a dish to dry, and she jumped as if an electric jolt had passed through her. He was dangerous, Jessica thought. Downright dangerous.

After lunch Jessica took her book and retired to her room to rest. She read for a little while, but when her lids began to grow heavy, she gave in to the feeling and climbed into bed. She napped for almost two hours and awoke almost refreshed. At least the bruised, draggy feeling wasn't there; she felt as if she had slept instead of run around the block a few times. Linking her hands behind her head, Jessica stared at the ceiling. It was a luxury she hadn't been able to afford in a long time.

Jessica thought about the fact that there was absolutely nothing she had to do except scrounge up something to eat. It seemed like unbelievable freedom. Some quirk in her mind couldn't quite accept it. What did one do when one had nothing to do? Were there people who lived like this, eating, reading, sleeping, untouched by pressure or hurry? Jessica couldn't imagine it. Even for a brief vacation, it seemed bizarre. Yet she was doing it, and so far she hadn't been the least bit bored.

When she finally pulled herself out of bed she curled up in a comfortable chair in the bedroom to avoid Kyle and continued reading her book. Lynn had been right; it was easy to lose oneself in it. She was surprised some time later to glance up from a page and find that almost three hours had passed. She cocked her head, listening, but could hear no sound from the living room. Had Kyle left? Jessica stood up and limped to the door, her muscles stiff from sitting too long. She leaned her head against the door. Nothing. She eased the door open a crack and strained her ears. There was only dead quiet.

Jessica opened the door and went into the living room. Kyle's ladder was there, but the paint, roller and Kyle himself were gone. "Kyle?" Jessica strolled through the room and into the small dining area and kitchen. He wasn't there. She leaned over the table and lifted a corner of the sheer curtain. She couldn't spot him in the garden below, either. He must have gone home.

She let the curtain drop and shrugged. It was time for him to quit work. Of course, he had said in the grocery store that he would cook the fish for her, but that didn't necessarily mean he would stay and fix it tonight. She ought to be glad; she hadn't wanted him pushing himself into her life. After all, she'd stayed in the bedroom all afternoon just to avoid him, hadn't she? Maybe he'd finally gotten the hint that she didn't want him around. There was no reason for the disappointment swelling in her chest. She would have a nice supper all by herself. She'd fix a frozen dinner and sit down at the table with her book. Then this evening maybe she'd look at TV or read some more.

It sounded incredibly dull. Jessica sighed and reminded herself that it was supposed to be dull; she was taking a rest. She opened the freezer door to choose which frozen dinner she would cook that night and settled on the lasagna. She set the foil dish on the counter and turned on the oven. She was trying to work up interest in cutting lettuce and tomatoes for a salad when there was a knock on the door. Kyle!

Jessica whirled and ran for the door, all the while berating herself for her idiocy. It couldn't be Kyle. Why would he have left and then returned? It was probably a salesman or a friend of Viveca's who didn't know she had left town. There was no point in getting her hopes up. And why was she even thinking of it in such terms? She didn't want Kyle here tonight.

She opened the door. It *was* Kyle. Jessica broke into a sunny grin, realizing only after she'd smiled that she shouldn't have appeared so happy to see him. "I thought you'd gone. I mean, I didn't expect you back."

"When I finished work I went home to clean up and change. I didn't relish the idea of cooking your dinner still covered with sweat and paint."

His hair was damp from the shower, and there was no shadow on his jaw. He must have shaved, as well. He was dressed in khaki shorts, much cleaner and neater than the cutoffs he wore to paint in, and a blue and tan plaid short-sleeved shirt. Despite the typically muggy New Orleans heat he looked fresh and crisp—and utterly appealing.

"Can I come in?"

"What? Oh, I'm sorry." Jessica stepped aside to let him enter and watched him cross to the kitchen. Why did he have to be so darned attractive? Why did he have to have shaggy hair that made her fingers itch to slide through it? Or long, tanned legs, sparsely covered with curling golden hairs? Or incredibly compelling chocolate-brown eyes, or long, sensitive fingers, or an engaging, puckish grin, or . . . The list went on and on. It seemed unfair that he should be so desirable physically and have such a winning personality and yet be so removed in thoughts and values from the kind of man Jessica could love.

Love! Why in the world was she even thinking of the word in connection with Kyle Morrow! If she was interested in Kyle, or he in her, it certainly wasn't in a long-term, deep way. At best Kyle could be nothing more than a brief, uninhibited fling. No doubt he felt the same way; most of the men Viveca knew weren't interested in things like commitment or the future. No, there could never be anything between them except a no-strings-attached vacation romance. Since Jessica had no interest in or time for such romances, that meant there would be nothing at all. It was plain and simple.

Jessica closed the door and followed him into the kitchen, reminding herself to keep everything on a purely friendly plane. He set down a paper sack on the counter. "What's in the bag?"

"I brought some spices I didn't figure you'd have in

stock. You haven't forgotten, have you, that I'm broiling red snapper tonight?''

"I wasn't sure you meant tonight. You know, you really don't have to.''

Kyle shrugged. "I don't mind.'' He glanced at her, his mouth turning up in a grin. "Trying to get rid of me?''

"Of course not. I just didn't want you to feel obligated or anything.'' Jessica turned away irritably. This was ridiculous. Why was she saying things like that? Men like Kyle didn't operate out of a sense of obligation. Had she been fishing for a compliment, hoping to hear Kyle say that he was cooking it because he wanted an excuse to be with her? She must be worse off than she thought.

"I don't. Where are the pans?'' He began a noisy search through the cabinets.

"Beside the stove. Can I help you with anything?''

"Can you make a salad?''

"Of course. I'm not totally incompetent.''

He grinned. "Don't get bristly. You told me you didn't know how to cook.''

"And didn't want to learn,'' Jessica added.

"Why do I get the feeling that your goal in life isn't to marry, settle down, and have three children?''

"I'm already settled,'' Jessica retorted. "And I have nothing against marriage or children. Why should being married and having kids mean cooking and scrubbing floors?''

His eyes danced as he looked at her. "Simply living usually means cooking and scrubbing floors.''

"I'm beginning to wonder what we're talking about.''

"Nothing in particular. Just making conversation. Don't you ever talk without any purpose?''

"Of course I do.'' Jessica paused and considered his

question. "Well, actually, I guess I don't very often. Usually I'm discussing business."

"It sounds like your business occupies all your time. Was it the reason for your collapse?"

"I didn't have a collapse. You make it sound like I had a nervous breakdown."

"No, I was thinking more of your physical problems —exhaustion, high blood pressure, all that."

"I don't know. I guess it must be the reason for the tiredness. It's why I've lost weight. I never have time to eat, or I'm too tired to fix something. I don't know why I have the high blood pressure."

"You mean you don't want to admit the reason."

Jessica glared. "Are you always this obnoxious to people, or is it just me?"

He grinned. "I am known for being a little blunt. It's a great release to realize that one no longer has to be political or ingratiating."

"Ingratiating? You? I can't imagine it."

"You're right. Even when I was supposed to be political, I wasn't. I never could stomach boot-licking."

"You can be polite without groveling, you know."

"Have I been rude to you?"

"Yes. You practically accused me of lying."

"I did?"

"You said I didn't want to admit the reason for my high blood pressure."

"Do you?"

"Why should I deny it?"

"Because you don't want to stop smoking and rushing and pushing. Who wants to give up their lifestyle? I certainly don't."

Jessica sighed. "Well, you're right. I don't."

As they talked Kyle had taken the fish out of the

refrigerator and prepared it for broiling. Now he popped it into the hot oven and turned to her. "Ah, but would you rather die?"

Jessica grimaced. "I though you understood."

"I do." He moved over and helped her tear up lettuce. Jessica stepped a little farther down the counter to continue her work.

"It's a difficult thing," he continued. "But you have to make a choice. The problem is, dying's so permanent. I think it's better to give the other option a try. If it's worse than death, you can always go back to your old lifestyle."

"Are you planning to lecture me all evening?"

He held up his hands in the manner of one claiming innocence. "End of sermon. I promise." He neatly quartered a couple of tomatoes and added them to the bowl of lettuce. "There. You want cucumber and carrots?"

"I guess." Jessica shrugged.

"How about a vegetable?" he asked, turning to inspect the contents of the refrigerator. "Didn't we get some fresh broccoli today?"

"Are we going to be that healthy? It's in the crisper drawer."

He emerged from the refrigerator with a bunch of broccoli, a bag of carrots and a shiny green cucumber. He set the other things down beside Jessica and carried the broccoli to the sink. "I'll steam the broccoli."

"Steaming, yet," Jessica muttered under her breath. "Do you ever eat anything that's nice and canned, full of salt and all those additives? Something that tastes good?"

"This will taste good. As soon as your palate becomes accustomed to it."

"Oh, that's real reassuring."

He chuckled and reached out to take her hand. "Come on. Let's sit down and talk while the food's cooking."

Jessica put the paring knife on the cutting board beside the remaining carrots and followed him. He led her into the living room and jerked a drop cloth off the love seat to make a place for them to sit. Jessica warily lowered her body onto the small sofa, sticking close to the arm of the seat. Being this near Kyle made her uncomfortable. Worse than uncomfortable. It made her heart jerk wildly in her chest, her throat tighten and turn dry, and her breath become decidedly uneven. Kyle flashed her an amused look, as if he knew exactly what she was doing and why, but he made no comment about where she sat.

"What is it you do for a living that ties you up in knots?" Kyle asked casually.

"What? Oh. It doesn't tie me up in knots." The only thing that did that was Kyle's presence. "I like my work. I just need to clone myself to get it all done."

"Okay. What is it that keeps you so busy? Or is it a secret?"

Jessica chuckled. "No, of course not. I'm a management consultant. My partner and I have a small firm, and we do private consulting for businesses all over the South. Also, we have a theory of goal-directed management which we teach in a two-day seminar to various businesses."

"You and your partner are the whole show?"

"Yes. That's one reason why it's so hectic. We thought about hiring a salesman for the various programs we offer, but it wouldn't be as effective as Alan's and my doing it. We know the course inside out and exactly what we can and can't do as consultants. So we do all the selling, as well. We may have to hire someone to teach the course for us. That would ease the workload a lot. There would be some things he might not be able to answer as well as we could, but if we give him enough training, he should be able to carry it off. Of course, then we have the problem of the time it would take to interview people for the job and train the person we hired.''

Kyle seemed genuinely interested in her work, and soon Jessica found herself telling him the details of her job, including her harried trips and irritating romantic encounters with prospective clients. He laughed at her description of Mark Banacek's persistent courting and shook his head. ''You have more problems than I ever did.''

Jessica glanced at him curiously. ''You mean you used to—'' She stopped abruptly, realizing that what she had been about to say wouldn't have been very polite.

''Used to work for a living?'' Kyle finished her question for her, his eyes sparkling with barely restrained amusement. ''Yes, I was once one of the laboring masses.'' He touched her nose with a light fingertip. ''I haven't always been a bum.''

Jessica blushed. ''I didn't say that.''

He grinned. ''You didn't have to. Don't worry. I don't concern myself a great deal with other's opinions, so I rarely get my feelings hurt.''

''That's obvious.''

He tilted his head a little to one side, regarding her quizzically. ''I've found that honesty is usually the best, easiest and least complicated policy. Those little white lies to avoid hurting others' feelings or make you look like a nice guy just end up getting everyone into a worse mess.''

''So you always say what you think?''

He shrugged. "I don't say *all* I think sometimes."

"That's probably fortunate."

His eyes sought and found hers, then dropped to her lips. "For instance, I didn't tell you that I've been aching to kiss you the whole day."

Jessica's breath quickened, and she looked down at her hands, at loss for a response. Kyle tilted up her chin. His eyes were warm and dark. Jessica noticed that though his eyelashes were pale in color, they were absurdly long and thick. How could one man be so desperately appealing? And why did it have to be *this* man?

His hand slid down her throat, coming to rest on her collarbone. He leaned toward her, his eyelids dropping to hide the sudden flame in his eyes. His lips brushed hers lightly, almost hesitantly, and touched them again. Then his arms went around her and arched her body against his, and his mouth moved onto hers. He wanted her. Jessica could feel desire in the heat of his skin, the way his mouth moved against hers, the almost undetectable tremor in his arms.

She didn't resist. She didn't want to. All logic and reason fled at his touch. Jessica pressed herself into his hard body, and her lips opened beneath his.

Chapter 5

ONE HAND HELD HER LOCKED AGAINST HIM WHILE THE other explored her back and moved around to the front to cup her breast through the soft material of her blouse. His thumb roused her nipple, circling the bud until it was hard and thrusting. He went to the other breast, stroking, squeezing. His breath was ragged. He broke the kiss to turn his head and kiss her again from a different angle. Jessica felt the pressure of his teeth behind his lips, the fervent seeking of his tongue. His tongue filled her mouth, reminding her vividly of his ultimate ability to possess her. An aching, moist heat started low in her abdomen. She wanted him there. Wanted to feel him filling her, taking her . . . Jessica clamped her legs together to ease the ache. It didn't help.

Kyle shifted, pulling her onto his lap so that she sat astride his legs, facing him. Even with their clothes between them, the contact was so intimate that Jessica shivered with its force. She moved on his lap, luxuriating in the wild heat and pleasurable torment her movements caused. Kyle sucked in his breath sharply and dug his hands into her thighs, pressing her down against him.

He kissed her face, her ears, her neck, his mouth hot and hungry on her skin. His fingertips crept inside her denim shorts to the soft, vulnerable flesh of her buttocks. One finger traced the lacy trim of her panties. Jessica was breathless and flushed with warmth. She had never felt so soaring, so wild, so out of control. She ran her hands over his shoulders and back. She wanted to touch him everywhere, to sink her fingers into his flesh. She thrust her fingers into his hair and massaged his scalp, enjoying the soft slide of his hair between her fingers.

Kyle buried his face between her breasts, rubbing his cheek against the soft orbs. He pulled back and shoved the soft T-shirt above her breasts. Her nipples were dark and pointed beneath the lacy screen of her brassiere. Slowly, almost reverently, he traced them through the lace, then reached to unfasten her bra and expose her breasts completely to his gaze.

A harsh, shrill buzz erupted from the kitchen, and Jessica jumped, rudely shaken from her haze of fantasy. A muffled oath exploded from Kyle, and he slammed a fist into the cushion of the couch. "The timer! I set the damned timer for the fish!"

Jessica scrambled off his lap and tugged down her shirt, blushing with acute embarrassment. Kyle sprang to his feet and ran into the kitchen. Jessica heard the click of the timer being cut off, then the oven door slamming open and shut. She pulled her knees up to her chest and wrapped her arms around them, struggling to control the trembling of her body. How could she have let herself get into a situation like this? She lost all

self-control around Kyle. It was humiliating how easily
he made her forget all her resolves, all the insurmounta-
ble differences between them, all the reasons why he was
bad for her. She'd always been able to keep men and
romance in their place before. Why did she go haywire
around Kyle?

"I'm sorry." Kyle returned to the living room,
seething with frustration. He'd cursed himself thoroughly as he jerked the food out of the oven. Why had he set
the timer? He wouldn't have cared if the fish had burned
to a crisp, as long as he had Jessica in his arms. But now
the moment of intimacy and passion was shattered.
Jessica was sealed off to him, her body bound up in a
defensive knot. "Supper's ready."

"What? Oh. Yes, thank you." Jessica rose and
walked past him to the small dining table, keeping her
eyes carefully averted.

She set the table while he dished up the food. There
was silence between them as they sat down and began to
eat. After a few bites of the broccoli and fish, Jessica
looked up at Kyle, amazed. "This is very good."

He chuckled. "Don't sound so surprised; it isn't
polite. Did you think I couldn't cook?"

"No, I just didn't think broiled fish could taste this
good."

"Ah. Wait till you taste my broiled chicken."

The first fragile moments eased into something more
ordinary and comfortable. Gradually Jessica relaxed as
Kyle maintained a friendly distance. He chatted casually
with her, making jokes, not referring to the moment of
passion on the couch. When the meal was finished
Jessica tightened again, thinking that now he would
make his move on her. But he didn't. Instead he flopped
down on the floor before the love seat, leaving her the

whole thing to sit on, and continued his light conversation. Jessica was pleased that he was making it easy for her, yet she was curiously piqued, too. Had he enjoyed their kisses so little that he was happy to retreat from their intimacy? Maybe he was afraid that she would press the issue! That was a humiliating thought.

After a few minutes Kyle rose and stretched. "I better go home now. I plan to get up early tomorrow to finish this room." He grinned. "No doubt you'll be glad of that."

Jessica shrugged. She'd never admit that she felt a pang of loss at the thought that after tomorrow he would no longer be in the apartment. "It hasn't been bad." She trailed him to the door. "Thank you for the supper. It was delicious."

"I'm glad you enjoyed it. Maybe you'll let me do it again sometime."

"Of course." That was stupid. It wasn't at all what she ought to say.

"Good." He opened the door and paused in the doorway, one hand on the knob. Suddenly, surprising her, he leaned forward and took her chin between his thumb and forefinger. He kissed her slowly and thoroughly, as though savoring every moment, every sensation. Jessica's knees began to buckle, and she grabbed his shirt to steady herself. He took it as an invitation— and why shouldn't he, Jessica thought bitterly—and his hand moved down her throat and around to capture the nape of her neck. His other hand left the doorknob and came around her waist, pulling her tightly against him.

A sigh of pure enjoyment escaped his lips, and he rubbed his body against hers, as though settling in. Jessica felt open and exposed, horribly vulnerable to him. It was a frightening feeling, but the shivery pleasure of his mouth on hers was too great to pull away. She didn't want to stop him—not just yet. Later she would do it. Later . . . like a million years from now.

It was Kyle who ended the kiss. His hands dropped away, and he jerked back, shoving a hand through his hair. "Lady, you ought to bottle that and sell it."

"What?"

"Whatever it is you do to me. I have a hell of a time keeping my hands off you."

A thrill went through Jessica at his words. He wasn't immune to her, as she had begun to think. He'd been trying to hold back from her and hadn't been able to. She swallowed, incapable of saying anything. Kyle took one of her hands in his, raising it and studying the back. He ran his forefinger down the lines of the slender bones and turned her hand over so that the palm lay up. He kissed her palm, then slid her hand up to curve around his cheek. His eyes closed and he twisted a little to kiss the thin skin of her inner wrist. There was something vulnerable in the thin skin of his closed eyelids, in the yearning way his face fitted into her palm. The contrast between the vulnerability of his expression and the latent masculine power of his arms was sensual and exciting. It made Jessica want him all the more.

If she told him that she wanted him to stay, he would, she knew. Did she really want that? Could she handle it? She wavered, torn by reason, desire and fear. Her indecision turned out to be decision enough. When she made no response Kyle kissed her hand again and returned it gently to her side. He looked at her and managed a shaky smile. "It's too fast for you, isn't it?" he asked.

Jessica nodded. "I'm not—" Her voice trembled. She stopped and cleared her throat. "Casual affairs aren't my style."

"Nor mine." His voice was soft, his dark eyes intense.

Jessica's eyebrow cocked in disbelief. "I would have thought they were."

"Why?"

She stepped back, folding her arms across her chest, flustered. "I just assumed. I mean, the people that Viveca hangs around with seem so loose and carefree about sex."

"I see. The bohemian lifestyle?"

"You're making me sound stuffy, and that's not what I meant. Well, not exactly." She retreated again before his steady gaze. "Oh, all right. Yes, that's what I think. I'm sorry if I seem rigid and uptight to you, but that's the way I am."

"Take it or leave it, huh?"

"Well . . . yes, if you want to put it that way. I won't—I can't sleep with just anybody simply because everyone else seems to do it."

"Don't be so defensive. I told you I don't believe in bed-hopping, either. But you're a very prejudiced woman, Jessica. Being an artist doesn't make one promiscuous. Nor does living in the French Quarter. Nor living a life without a rigid schedule and demands. You lump a huge number of people together in a handy slot and identify them as 'people like your mother.' You don't see them as individuals, or make any attempt to know them. Hell, I don't think you know your mother."

"Spare me the lecture, please." Jessica turned away.

He grabbed her wrist and turned her back to face him. "It's not 'casual sex' that's bothering you, is it? You know as well as I do that it's not casual; there's too much fire between us whenever I touch you. It's something else that keeps you from responding as you want to. Something about me that's unacceptable to you. I'm not an artist, if that's what's bothering you. I can't sing, write, paint, or dance. I'm as uncreative as you could ask for.''

A tiny smile escaped Jessica at his earnest disavowal of skills. "It's not being artistic that bothers me. I imagine there are lots of artists who do something with their lives and their abilities. It's the people who don't do anything, artistic or not, who bother me. And that's what so many people here in the Quarter seem to be. They use art as an excuse to be bums.''

"So it's my job or, rather, lack of one that you don't like.''

"I don't understand people like you. You're obviously bright; you have charm; you're good-looking. There must be any number of things you could do. So why are you wasting your time being a handyman for an apartment building?''

His face set into an unreadable mask. "Maybe I don't consider it a waste. There's more to life than having a six-figure salary or a Mercedes in your garage.''

"Oh! You make me so mad! It isn't materialism I'm talking about. It's personal commitment to something. *Anything!* It's ambition and drive and wanting to be something better, do something better. Striving to achieve isn't the same as greed. It's not collecting expensive objects. I'm talking about a personal quality, a strength.''

"Strength? You call chasing after money a strength? It's more like an illness. It's as addictive as alcohol, or smoking, and equally harmful.''

"It *is* a strength!" Jessica blazed, thoroughly furious with him now. "It's an indication of character. What strength does it take to be a bum?"

"Is that how you think of me?"

"Isn't that what you are? You don't contribute. You're wasting your abilities. You're content with far less than you could be. You let life slide by without taking part in it."

"You can take part in life without getting into the rat race," Kyle answered in clipped tones. "You probably won't be able to understand this, but how much money you make or how much power you achieve is not the only measure of success. Nor is working with your hands something to be ashamed of. What does it matter if I could make more money doing something else? This makes me happy; the life I live is fulfilling. I don't want the mad pace. I don't want the fear and the drivenness, the terror that I won't do enough, won't accomplish more, that someone else will get ahead of me. That's not the quality of life I want. I want time to think, time to enjoy things, time to actually live my life. There are lots of advantages to my lifestyle, though you probably wouldn't recognize them. I don't have ulcers or high blood pressure, and I don't expect to have a heart attack, or a stroke. I don't smoke. Nor do I suffer from malnutrition or exhaustion, like you do. That's the wonderful reward *you* get for running after money and success: You're killing yourself."

Jessica would have liked to have sailed into him, swinging with both fists. He made her angrier than anyone she'd ever known, even her mother. How dare he condemn her for the way she lived and the things she believed in! He was the one who was wasting his life, who was feckless and irresponsible. "It's people like me who keep the world running!'' she barked back. "If everyone thought like you and Viveca and your friends, nothing would get done. Everything would fall apart. Oh, sure, it was fine for Viveca to pursue her art on the sidewalk, making barely enough to scrape by, because I was there to make sure my brothers were fed and clothed and went to school on time. Because I kept the apartment clean and the refrigerator stocked. And it was easy for her to move from place to place because I did the packing and unpacking. Viv couldn't handle that much organization.''

"How did we get onto Viv? I thought we were talking about my being a bum.''

"It's the same issue.''

"It's not the same. I'm not Viv!''

"If everyone thought like you did, we'd be back with the apes. Nobody would have achieved anything! There would be no progress.''

"I have nothing against progress or achievement. They're great. But running yourself into the ground trying to make money isn't necessarily progress. What are you achieving? Success is a meaningful life; it's something inside. But you're so busy chasing your tail you don't have time to look inside you. You don't even know yourself.''

"Please, spare me the pop philosophy.''

"It's the truth. I don't think you know who you are or what you want. Your whole life is a reaction against your mother. Everything you do is based on a determination not to be like her. That doesn't give you any kind of life of your own, just an absence of hers.''

Jessica glared at him. "I think I've had enough of this. Why don't you just go away and leave my life to me!''

"Gladly!'' His dark gaze was as fierce as hers. He

swung around and strode out the door, slamming it shut behind him. Jessica clenched her fists, staring at the blank door, swept with waves of rage. He was impossible. Impossible! Thank heavens he'd gone. He wouldn't come back after that scene. He was out of her life now. And she was very, very grateful for that. Jessica whirled and stomped into the bedroom, venting her anger by crashing the door shut behind her. She stalked to the bed, flung herself across it and burst into tears.

Jessica woke up late the next morning and made her way groggily into the bathroom, where she peered into the mirror. Her eyelids were puffy and red-rimmed. How disgusting! She'd turned into a weepy female the past couple of weeks, crying over tiredness, anger and half a dozen other emotions. Maybe Kyle was right. She was beginning to think that she didn't know herself at all.

Jessica turned on the shower and stripped to step under it. She let the hot water beat on her head and face and run in rivulets down her body. It was soothing, and she loitered there, not eager to get out and face the day. What time was it? Would Kyle be in the living room painting? Or had he stayed away, still seething with anger? She hoped he would be off nursing his wounded feelings; she didn't feel up to facing him today. In fact, she didn't feel up to much of anything.

The water began to run cool, so she finished her shower quickly. She was more awake now, less foggy from sleep and tears. When she left the bathroom she walked quietly to the door into the hall and leaned one ear against it. For a long moment she heard nothing but silence, but then there came the chink of metal touching metal and another, heavier noise. Jessica straightened and walked away from the door. Kyle must be in there.

She dressed in shorts and a casual pullover top and thrust her feet into flat sandals, all the while wondering what she should do. It was her apartment, after all; she shouldn't have to hide in the bedroom until he chose to go away. Knowing she was in the right, she should waltz out and face Kyle calmly. But her stomach clenched with nervousness at the thought. They had parted on anything but friendly terms. If they met again this morning, it would be awkward at best. And if Kyle pinned her with a glare or coolly looked straight through her, it would be too much. She simply wasn't used to such emotional outbursts—or, at least, she wasn't used to being a participant in one. She'd witnessed them in her mother often enough.

She *had* been right last night, although it had been rude to admit she thought Kyle was a bum. But that didn't keep her from feeling that she had made a fool of herself. What did it matter what Kyle chose to do with his life? And why try to convince him that her lifestyle was good? He would believe what he chose to. And so would she. That was the way people were. She'd found out long ago that it was an exercise in futility to argue with anyone about personal philosophies. But last night she hadn't followed her usual sensible course. She'd been argumentative and emotional, letting her anger sweep her away. Jessica hated to think how silly she must have appeared, flushed and earnest and brimming over with anger. It wasn't an image of herself she liked. She always strove to remain cool and calm. That was the way to influence people. Subtlety did the trick where direct confrontation never could.

Jessica didn't want to face Kyle, knowing he would remember her as she had been last night. Besides, what could she say? That she was sorry? That she hadn't meant it? She'd said exactly what she thought. Even if she could apologize and smooth everything over, it was no use. She couldn't deny that she wanted Kyle, but it would never work between them. She didn't want a summer fling, which was all it could be. They were too different for anything permanent. It was best to let the rift happen now. Then she could enjoy the rest of her vacation.

The best way to avoid an awkward situation and any possibility of reconciliation was simply to not go into the living room while Kyle was there. It wouldn't be very difficult. She had stayed in her bedroom all yesterday afternoon reading a book. She could do that again. Kyle wasn't likely to spend the whole day here. He'd said he hadn't much left to do.

Jessica picked up her book and stretched out on the bed to read. Her stomach growled, and she wished she had something to eat in the bedroom. Well, she'd have to tough it out. She'd done without breakfast lots of times. As she read she kept her ears open for the sounds of Kyle's leaving the apartment, which made it difficult to keep up with her story. She had to read several pages twice to figure out their meaning. Finally, around noon, when she thought she was going to have to give in and get something to eat, Jessica heard a flurry of noises in the living room. Jessica tensed, then rose from the bed and tiptoed to the door.

She heard steps on the metal of the landing outside, and the door closed. There was silence. He was gone. She waited a few moments to make sure he wasn't going to pop back in. Then, with a sigh of relief, she twisted the doorknob and stepped out into her apartment.

There was no sign of Kyle. But the apartment walls glistened with a fresh coat of paint. The ladder was gone, and so were the paint buckets and the canvas cloths covering the furniture. With the shapeless cloths removed the living room took on a new and pleasant personality. Whoever had renovated the apartments had done the job well. On the courtyard side the original windows had been removed and new plate glass windows set in, letting in an unobstructed flow of light and a view of the enclosed patio below. At the opposite end, the street side, the French windows had been left undraped to allow as much light to enter as possible.

Viveca had decorated the apartment with her usual taste and flair. The furniture was light in color and design, and left a great deal of open space. A few vivid paintings leaned against the larger couch. Jessica guessed they were meant to go back on the freshly painted walls once the walls were dry. She went closer. Two were signed with her mother's distinctive "V. Howard" signature. The other was done by an artist whose name she didn't recognize. It was a hauntingly beautiful portrait of an Indian woman done in dusty pastels. Jessica studied the paintings for a moment. Her mother's work improved all the time.

Jessica turned away and walked to the courtyard windows. She pressed her face against the glass to peer in every direction. There wasn't a sign of Kyle. He'd left the complex already. She turned and walked into the kitchen, where she pulled out some cheese and crackers. But her appetite was playing tricks on her again, and by the time she sat down to eat, she no longer felt hungry.

She nibbled a little at what she had prepared, then set the plate in the sink and began to prowl around the apartment, looking at the books on the low bookcase stretching across half one wall of the living room. Most of them were metaphysical things or art books in which she had little interest. She began another novel that she had brought with her, but she had trouble getting into it again.

Jessica dropped the book onto the floor with a sigh. She was bored. She had known this would happen as soon as the doctor suggested the vacation. She couldn't stand to be cooped up with nothing to do day after day. It wouldn't take even two weeks for her to start climbing the walls. Jessica stood up and slipped back on the sandals which she had kicked off earlier. She picked up her purse and sunglasses and left the apartment. Perhaps exploring the French Quarter would ease her boredom.

She walked up and down several of the quaint, narrow streets, peering into the windows of bakeries, antique stores, restaurants, T-shirt shops, clock shops, hotel lobbies and dusty little bookstores. It was a pleasant way to spend the afternoon, but nothing caught her eye enough for her to enter a shop, and she soon grew tired of her occupation. She returned to the apartment and tried to nap as she had the day before, but sleep also eluded her. Finally she gave up the attempt to sleep and forced herself to sit down and read.

The evening was equally unexciting, and she whiled away as much as she could of it preparing her dinner and eating it. It was the most elaborate dish she had ever cooked, but since she had plenty of time and nothing to do, she decided she might as well give it a try. It turned out remarkably well, and she thought triumphantly that she'd have to fix that for Kyle next time he came over—then let him joke about her lack of cooking prowess! Suddenly she felt deflated. Kyle wouldn't be coming over again to eat with her.

She sighed and put the dishes in the sink to rinse them off. It would have happened sooner or later, anyway. She and Kyle were destined to disagree. They were too different not to. Jessica grimaced. Wouldn't you know that the first man who had ever inflamed her senses would be someone perfectly unsuitable?

She finished the new novel shortly before lunch the next day. She tossed it aside and yawned as she rose. All that reading had made her sleepy. She glanced outside, and the beauty of the little garden lured her. She slipped out and down the hot metal staircase to the cool shade. She sat down on the stone bench, pulling her legs up and resting her chin on her knees. A scrape in the far corner of the garden startled her, and she turned. She barely kept a gasp from escaping her lips. Kyle knelt beside the wall of the apartment building, pulling weeds from among the flower border. He was turned away from her, obviously intent on his job. He was shirtless, and his skin gleamed in the sun, tanned and beaded with perspiration. Moist black earth clung to his hands. The hair at the nape of his neck was wet and dark from his sweat.

Jessica watched, hardly breathing, as Kyle jerked out another weed and tossed it into the paper sack beside him. The muscles of his lean arms bunched as he pulled, and Jessica could see the paths of more muscles across his back and shoulders. Her heart beat faster, and her breath turned shallow and quick. She imagined running her fingertips down his sweat-slick back, exploring the thrust and curve of the smooth flesh. She could almost smell the hot male scent of his body, elemental and exciting, mingling with the fresh odor of the damp earth. She had thought him the essential, primitive man the other day. He was even more so now, working beneath the sun, tending the earth.

She swallowed, trying to still her sudden trembling. It was terribly hot out here. She ought to go inside. Perhaps if she went in she could fix Kyle a long, frosty glass of ice water and bring it to him. She pictured him looking up at her, then rising to take the glass from her hand, his fingers sliding around the cold wet surface to touch hers. His heat would be sizzling.

"Thanks, darlin'," he would say, leaning down to touch her lips with his. She could almost taste the salt of his flesh.

Jessica bit her lower lip. What was she doing! Sitting out here dreaming up approaches to Kyle, imagining his kiss, his touch. She squeezed her legs together tightly as if that would drive out the molten ache between her thighs.

Kyle didn't want her. He'd ignored her. He must have heard her come out of her apartment and down the staircase, yet he hadn't said a word. He wanted nothing to do with her; that was plain. She must not embarrass herself by intruding on him. Yet how could she escape the situation? How long could they go on ignoring each other in a space as small as this patio? She could close her eyes and pretend to be asleep, but if he spent a long time out here weeding, she could be trapped for ages. If she slipped back up the stairs, he might turn around and they would come face-to-face. But surely if he heard her leaving, he wouldn't turn around and force a meeting; he'd be very happy she was going.

Taking a deep breath, Jessica rose and walked as softly and rapidly as possible across the slightly uneven sidewalk. Every step brought her closer to Kyle. She kept her eyes resolutely turned away from him, feeling that her very gaze might cause him to look around. She was nearly to the stairs when suddenly he pivoted, rising to his feet. He grinned engagingly and said, "Come on, Jessie, do you intend to avoid me forever?"

Chapter 6

WHEN KYLE HAD LEFT JESSICA'S APARTMENT TWO nights before, he had marched, head down, to his own place, propelled by anger. A woman like that was impossible! She was too blind to see what she was doing to herself, and too stubborn even to try. Jessica Todd was absolutely maddening, and he was well rid of her. She'd never learn. Never! It was useless to argue with her. Futile. That scene with her had been the best thing that could have happened to him. Now there was no possibility of his getting involved with a woman so at odds with herself and his life. It would save him a lot of heartache in the future.

When he'd reached home he'd been too keyed up to sleep and had spent the better part of an hour pacing the floor and reliving his argument with Jessica. Finally he wound down and went to bed, setting his alarm for six o'clock the next morning. He wanted to get started on

Viv's apartment early in the hopes that he might avoid seeing Jessica. The sooner he got finished there, the better. He viciously punched his pillow into shape and lay down, closing his eyes. He tried to will himself to sleep, but it took another hour before at last his brain turned off and let him rest.

He had been groggy the next morning when he got up, and he had already worked on Viv's walls for an hour before he really woke up. When he did, he wished he hadn't. He felt unbearably depressed. Why had he let the argument get so out of hand? If he hadn't been so wired up with frustrated desire, it never would have happened. He had seen then that all that aching, unspent passion had been boiling inside him, seeking an outlet. Anger had been the easiest method of release. Any other time he would have let her remarks slide by or turned them aside with a joke. That night he had practically jumped at the opportunity to vent some anger.

Now he regretted it bitterly. He had known what Jessica was like from the very beginning. He couldn't plead ignorance. And really, it was none of his business what Jessica believed, or what she wanted to do with her life. He'd given up telling others what to do a long time ago. But with Jessica he had been as sermonizing as a preacher. A rather bizarre role for him to adopt, he thought ruefully.

Why couldn't he have left well enough alone? He wanted her; she wanted him. Somehow it would have worked out, if he'd given her a little time and space. But he'd been pushy, demanding. And he'd ruined it all. He had stalled with the painting as much as he could, hoping Jessica would emerge from the bedroom and they could talk. However, he'd finally realized that she must be waiting for him to leave before she came out, and he'd given up, packing up his materials and leaving the apartment.

It was for the best, he'd told himself. That girl had heartbreak written all over her. If they hadn't fought, he would have become more and more involved with her; she was one he could fall in love with. But before long she would return to Atlanta and the life she loved, a life he could have no part in. He would be left high and dry, nursing the wounds on his heart. But such reasoning hadn't stopped him from wishing and regretting. After all, what was life if you avoided all love and desire for fear you would get hurt? Who was he to say it couldn't work out? Stranger things had happened. Whatever the odds, he was willing to risk it.

So, after a day of struggling with his thoughts and emotions, Kyle had decided to face Jessica and try to mend the split that had been made in their new, fragile relationship. He was afraid that if he walked up and knocked on her door she might refuse to answer, so he took a weed fork and trowel and went to weed the borders, though he had done it only three days earlier. When Jessica came out of her apartment he kept still, not wanting to scare her off. But she had seen him. She must have, for she had suddenly started back down the sidewalk to the stairs, almost running. He couldn't let her go, so he sprang to his feet and faced her, asking her why she was trying to escape him.

Jessica came to a dead halt and stared at Kyle. He went on cheerfully, "Running from me will ruin your whole vacation, you know. I'm around a lot."

Jessica flushed. "I—uh, well, you didn't seem eager to see me. You must have heard me come down the stairs a while ago, but you didn't speak."

"I thought I'd give you some time to adjust to my

presence. Besides, I wanted to see what you'd do when you realized I was here. I found out—you ran for cover. Why do I scare you so much?"

"You don't scare me!" Jessica retorted, stung by the amusement in his voice. "I saw no reason in forcing a situation that could only be embarrassing for both of us."

"Oh, I see. That's why you hid in your room yesterday morning?"

"I didn't hide!"

He quirked an eyebrow. "No? I'd be interested in hearing what you'd call it."

"I got up late, and then I showered and dressed."

"Um-hum. I heard the water running about two hours before I left."

"Oh, all right!" Jessica burst out. "Yes, I stayed in my room to avoid you. If I'd come out, it would have been an awkward situation for us both. Since I'll be gone in a couple of weeks, it seemed easier to let the moment pass."

"Don't you ever make up after a fight?"

"Of course—that is, well, frankly, I almost never fight."

"With anyone? And here I thought you were a hard-bitten career woman."

"You don't sell much consulting work by fighting with your clients."

"Then in your private life?"

"I haven't had much time for that."

"I guess that's true. So you never cut loose like you did the other night and let somebody have it?"

"No, of course not."

"I'm glad I was around so you could let off steam. Did it make you feel better?"

"Not at all. I'd made a perfect idiot of myself. All I felt was regret and embarrassment."

"Embarrassment. Why? I don't understand. You expressed your beliefs, didn't you? Do you think your philosophy is wrong or foolish?"

"No! You're a very maddening person, did you know that?"

He grinned. "To you, apparently. Others think I'm rather placid."

"Placid! Don't make me laugh."

"You didn't answer my question. If you believed what you said, why does it embarrass you?"

"It was the way I said it. I hate firing up like that. I say things I don't mean to say, and I regret it. I feel like a dope for getting emotional about it."

"What's wrong with being emotional? Especially about something you believe in strongly. Jessie, I've got news for you. That's the way most people are. They get excited when they're defending their viewpoints. They get angry and shoot off at the mouth. But they don't toss out their whole relationship with a person because they had a fight. They face the person again and mend the relationship."

"If there's something there to mend." Jessica sighed and moved away to lean against the railing of the staircase. "Our disagreement was pretty basic. It wasn't just arguing over politics or something. We're completely opposed to each other's entire life!"

He shrugged. "Maybe I don't approve of the way you live your life; obviously you don't approve of the way I live mine. But I still like you. Just you, in and of yourself. Don't you enjoy being with me despite all my feckless ways?"

"Yes."

"Isn't that a good basis for a relationship?"

"I suppose."

"You know, Jess, deep down, I think we're a lot alike."

"Alike? You and me?"

"Yes. It's something more basic, more elemental than what we think up here." He tapped his temple. "More important than what we do for a living."

"But our personalities are different."

"Not as different as you think. Ten years ago I probably would have been on your side of the argument. I once believed in being a super-charged go-getter like you."

"Before you 'dropped out'?"

"If you want to put it that way, yeah. There are similarities between us that you don't see. I know you. We respond to each other. Don't you feel it?"

Jessica backed away farther, starting up the curving steps. "That's called physical attraction, Kyle. It doesn't mean anything."

"Oh, it means a lot." He grinned. "Besides, it's more than that. You know it, but you're scared to admit it."

"I told you, I'm not scared of you!"

"Then why are you edging away from me?"

Jessica rolled her eyes and stopped, her hands gripping the top of the railing.

"You know what I think?"

"I'm sure you're going to tell me."

"I think you're frightened because of the way you respond to me. You don't like the fact that your brain can't rule your emotions or your body when it comes to me. You're afraid of yourself, of all your vast, uncharted regions that nobody's touched before. You don't know

what will happen. You aren't sure you'll be able to keep
yourself from doing something your head doesn't like.
Isn't that true?''

Jessica bit her underlip. Kyle was right. She wasn't
fighting to stay away from him because he was different
from her, but because when she was around him she felt
so little like herself. She had never felt such a strong
attraction to any man, never been warmed to her toes
just at the sight of him, never hungered for a man's
kisses or yearned to touch his body as she did with Kyle.
It scared her. She could fall in love with him; her body
and heart could run away with her where he was
concerned. And then she really would be in an impossible situation.

"Maybe I'm afraid of becoming too involved with
you," she admitted slowly. "There's no way it could
work out."

"Take a chance, Jessie."

She glanced over at him doubtfully. He made no move
toward her, but his eyes locked with hers, warm and
deep and compelling. "Please," he added softly.

"All right." Her voice was so low that if he hadn't
been listening intently he wouldn't have heard her.

He grinned. "Then why don't you sit down and talk to
me while I finish with these weeds?"

Jessica sat on the low brick wall running along the
back of the narrow flowerbed, and they began to talk
desultorily as he cleaned out the weeds. The restless
feeling which had plagued her for the past day or so
vanished. She felt lazy, content and faintly, pleasantly
expectant. As long as they avoided the subject of their
respective jobs, their conversation was enjoyable. They
talked about their college days, professors they had had,

pranks they had played, friends they had made and lost. Their talk trailed off onto books and movies and finally wound up in a hotly contested debate over whether a certain story had been a better movie or novel. The argument had ended in a draw, with both sides laughing.

It occurred to Jessica that she felt wonderfully free with Kyle, able to talk about anything and even to argue. She tried to think of someone else with whom she had this easy camaraderie, this instant, indefinable sense of closeness and understanding, but she couldn't. It was fun to be with Kyle; there was no pressure, no image to maintain. And he made her laugh. All afternoon she was aware of a buoyant happiness inside her that spilled over in laughter and smiles and the bright sparkle of her eyes. She flirted casually and enjoyed the look of appreciation in his eyes. She watched the movement of his arms, the trickle of sweat through the sparse hair on his chest, the grasp of his supple hands around a plant and the quick upward tug that released it from the earth. Deep inside her stirred a warm, visceral pleasure at seeing him this way, and it mingled with an ever-rising anticipation. It was a relaxed sensuality, without the throbbing physical demand she had felt earlier in his arms. Being with him seemed so effortless, so right.

Within two hours Kyle had weeded the small garden and watered the plants. He rinsed off his hands and arms under the spray of the garden hose, then lifted it to let the water run over his hot head and face. Jessica laughed as he spluttered, then shook off the shiny droplets of water like a dog shaking his coat. "I was going to invite you up to the apartment for a drink, but now that you're wet all over, I don't know if I dare let you in," she joked.

He pushed back his wet hair and grinned at her. Beads

of water dotted his face and clung to his eyelashes, matting them together in starry points. Jessica couldn't keep from smiling back.

They went upstairs to Viveca's apartment, where Kyle drank two enormous glasses of water while Jessica fixed tall, ice-cool drinks. They sat down in the newly painted living room to sip their drinks. Jessica slanted the wooden louvered shutters to block the fiercest rays of the sun, throwing the room into a darkened coolness. The waxed hardwood floor gleamed with the patina of age and quality, its expanse softened further by the square Oriental rug in the center, woven in a cream-and-blue pattern. Kyle dug his bare toes into the luxurious softness of the rug and sighed. "Ahhh." He took a sip of the drink, so cold it closed his throat, and rolled his head to relieve the stiffness of his neck. "Delicious." He took another drink and stretched out on the sofa. "You'll make me feel like a planter—drink at hand, fan going, a lovely woman to converse with."

"Are those the qualifications for being a planter?"

"No, the rewards."

"I see." Jessica kicked off her sandals and propped her heels on the low glass coffee table. Kyle reached out a hand, damp from the condensation on his glass, and curled it around her foot. With his thumb he began to rub the pads on the sole of her foot below her toes. Jessica's toes curled in pleasure, and her muscles tightened all up her leg. His fingers could work wonders, she thought, and caught her lower lip between her teeth as his hand moved, massaging the sensitive instep and the tendons along the top of her foot.

"Even your feet turn me on," Kyle murmured, his voice low and thick. He encircled her narrow ankle, and his thumb traced the outcrop of bone there. Jessica shifted unconsciously, her feet moving a little apart. His hand went to the other foot, massaging and stroking it, reaching up to caress her ankle. His arm could stretch no farther, and it made his touch more erotic somehow, knowing that for the moment, at least, his lovemaking could be expressed only there, and only with the touch of his fingers.

He released her feet and rose to cross the narrow space between them. He sank onto his knees before her, his eyes holding hers the whole time. Jessica's breath rasped in her throat, uneven and shallow, and her lips parted slightly. Her pulse throbbed heavily in her ears, and her tongue crept out to wet her lips. She knew what was about to happen, and she was both frightened and unbelievably excited. "Kyle." His name was little more than a whisper on her lips.

He smiled in answer, his mouth widening sensuously. His eyelids were heavy, the lines around his eyes deeply scored. Desire roughened his handsome features and enlarged his pupils until his eyes were almost black. He twisted so that his torso was sideways to Jessica. With infinite care he placed his hands on her legs. They were light on her skin, trembling slightly and fiery hot. Their mere touch sent a scorching bolt of desire through Jessica, and it burst and flamed in her abdomen. Kyle's hands drifted lightly down her calves and then back up, his fingertips exploring every inch of her skin. His touch was slow, almost hesitant, and the very contrast of that with the passionate heat of his skin fueled the fire within Jessica.

His hands slipped upward past her knees to the soft, tremulous flesh of her inner thighs. Jessica stirred and gripped the cloth of the couch with her hands. Kyle bent his head and placed a kiss light as butterfly's wings just above one knee. Jessica stifled a gasp. His breath tickled the sensitive flesh of her thigh, and his tongue flickered out to draw a sinuous line up her leg. He repeated the pattern on the opposite thigh, and Jessica tightened all over. Kyle straightened and looked into Jessica's eyes, revealing without shame the unmistakable marks of passion on his face. Jessica turned to liquid, and any remaining prickles of doubt or logic fled her mind.

As he held her gaze with his, Kyle's hands slid inexorably up her legs, coming to rest at their juncture. He cupped the fleshy mound of her femininity, his palm pressing hard against her. He bent to kiss her thighs again as his hand continued its caresses. Jessica drew a shaky breath and her eyelids fluttered closed. She felt raw and yearning inside, and she was aware of nothing but her need and hunger. Jessica moved her hands restlessly over his arms and shoulders, caressing the curve of muscle, the rigid lines of tendons, the hard planes of bones.

Kyle's hands moved upward, sliding over her abdomen and waist and up to her breasts, searing her through her clothes. He buried his face in her belly, and his hands molded her soft breasts. Her nipples hardened against his palms, thrusting shamelessly through the material. Kyle nuzzled her stomach and murmured something she couldn't understand. He straightened, his face flushed and eyes sparkling, and slipped his hands beneath her thin top to caress her breasts. Still there was the lacy impediment of her bra, and he unsnapped it impatiently.

Jessica leaned away slightly and grasped the hem of her shirt, then whisked it off over her head. She shrugged out of the unfastened brassiere and tossed it aside with the blouse. Kyle's eyes drank in the sight of her breasts, bared for his pleasure. Almost reverently he reached out a finger and traced the curve of each high, taut breast. "You're beautiful," he breathed, his gaze never leaving her body. He touched one turgid nipple, then bent to take it in his mouth. His mouth was warm and seeking on her skin, learning her taste without urgency. Jessica shivered; the sensations he was arousing in her were so delightful it was almost frightening. She moaned and slid her hands into his thick hair.

He wrapped his arms around her waist and trailed kisses across her chest, then closed his lips over her other nipple. Jessica clenched her hands into fists as the tension mounted within her. His tongue and lips played with the nipple, sucking and teasing until Jessica writhed, half-sobbing with the intensity of her passion. Kyle unfastened her shorts and whipped them down her legs, leaving her clad in only a lacy scrap of underwear. He spread one large hand across her abdomen, his thumb teasing downward to the moist heat between her legs. Jessica gasped, arching her hips. Kyle drew a shaky breath.

He rose, pulling her up with him. Jessica stood, not sure what he wanted, but eager to follow wherever he led. Kyle scooped her up into his arms and carried her like a baby out of the room and into the bedroom. His movement surprised Jessica, but when she realized what he was doing, she smiled and curled her arms around his neck. She had never been carried like this before, and there was a sort of excitement to it, a strange and delightful sense of being cherished and desired. He laid her gently on the four-poster bed and stepped back to strip off his shorts and underwear with trembling fingers. Then he leaned over the bed and very slowly drew down the flimsy wisp of her panties, his fingertips lightly caressing her legs all the way down.

Jessica placed her hands on his chest and explored the broad plane of bone padded by muscles. She caressed his flat masculine nipples and followed the narrow line of hair down his chest to the shallow indentation of his navel. Kyle moved onto the bed and covered her, supporting his weight on his elbows, and bent his head to feast on her soft breasts. Jessica's hands moved frantically all over him, touching every part of him that she could reach. She dug her fingers into his back as she moaned out a wordless plea.

Then he slipped inside her, moving his long, corded legs between hers and thrusting deep into her waiting femininity. Jessica gripped the sheets, murmuring his name over and over like an incantation. They merged in a deep, instinctive rhythm, every movement a satisfaction of their aching need and yet a renewal of it. Jessica wound her arms and legs about him, and he cried out, beginning the final, frenzied dance. She sobbed incoherently, swept by an almost desperate yearning toward completion, and then the ball of heat burst in her abdomen, flooding her in waves of pleasure. Jessica called out his name sharply, and Kyle groaned, thrown to his own shattering peak. They clung to each other, lost in a moment where nothing existed except each other and the supreme joy binding them together.

Jessica felt Kyle's body relax against her, and after a while he rolled from on top of her and cradled her against his side. Jessica snuggled her head into his shoulder, adrift in a deep peace. No thoughts intruded on her mind; she was aware only of contentment and pleasure and Kyle's warm flesh beneath hers. Absently Kyle brushed her hair back with his hand and turned his head slightly to kiss her forehead. Jessica smiled and stretched her arm across his chest as if to encompass him. Slowly she drifted into sleep.

"Wake up, lazybones," Kyle's low voice teased her awake.

Jessica opened her eyes and blinked at him groggily. Then she remembered what had happened, and a brilliant smile flashed across her face. He chuckled, and she frowned playfully, poking his arm with her forefinger. "Oh, hush. You needn't sound so smug."

"Why not?"

"It isn't polite."

Kyle pulled back the sheet and planted a quick kiss on one nipple. "You're worried about polite behavior now?"

"Oh!" Jessica had to laugh, even as she put both hands on his bare chest and pushed him away.

He rose, grinning. "I'll have you know that while you've been snoozing, *I* have been slaving away over a hot stove."

"Mmmm! Supper? That sounds marvelous. I'm starving." Jessica shoved aside the sheet and stood up. Kyle's eyes moved lazily down her body, and Jessica blushed slightly at his frank appreciation of her nakedness. But she didn't rush to cover up her nudity; rather, she found there was a heady excitement in feeling Kyle's admiring gaze on her.

Finally he said, "I could easily be distracted from eating." He glanced up devilishly. "Supper, that is."

"Now, now."

He reached out and ran a finger down her side. "But I guess I better feed you. I can count your ribs."

"Too skinny for your taste, huh?" Jessica moved

away in mock indignation and grabbed her robe from the closet. "Well, if I'm offensive to you, I'll cover myself up."

"Don't you dare!" He crossed the room to grab the modest robe and jerk it from her hands. Jessica laughed up at him. He pulled her up in his arms and gave her a very thorough, very unhurried kiss. When he released her, Jessica's face was flushed and her eyes sparkling. "Haven't you ever eaten supper in the nude?" he asked.

Jessica shook her head. "No. I've never even thought of it."

He touched his finger lightly to her nose. "You, my dear, suffer from a limited imagination. Sit down on the bed. I'll be back in a second."

He left the room, then reappeared a moment later bearing a large basket tray. He set the tray down on the bed with a flourish and draped a dish towel over his forearm in the manner of an elegant waiter. Jessica burst into giggles at the ludicrous sight of him completely nude except for the towel across his arm, bowing gravely and sweeping his free arm toward the tray in a grand gesture. Kyle raised one eyebrow sternly, and Jessica put her hand over her mouth to stifle her giggles, pulling her face into a look of prim composure.

"Madame," he intoned, and Jessica fought back another bout of laughter. He picked up a paper plate from the tray and set it on the bed before her. A thick tuna fish sandwich sat in the middle of the small plate, with a pickle spear and a handful of cheese puffs beside it. "The specialty of the house: Le Poisson Tuna à la Morrow." He grabbed a bottle of white wine from the tray and extended it toward her with all the flourish of a sommelier. "May I suggest a light white wine? Delicate but assertive."

Jessica struggled to keep her mouth straight. "Ah, yes, it looks like an excellent year."

"Our best vintage—1983," he assured her gravely, then untwisted the cap to pour a healthy amount into a squat glass decorated with a cartoon character.

"As fine as your crystal," Jessica commented dryly.

"Tsk, tsk." He picked up a plastic bowl filled with grapes and strawberries and plopped it down beside her plate on the bed. "Voilà! Dessert."

"It looks delicious."

"I thought so." Kyle tossed aside the towel and flopped down on the bed across from her, taking his own plate from the tray and pouring himself half a glass of wine. He took a large bite from the tuna sandwich and chewed thoughtfully, then kissed his fingertips. *"Magnifique!"*

Jessica mumbled her agreement, her mouth full. It was an excellent sandwich, and she surprised herself by polishing off the whole thing and even eating a bunch of grapes. They laughed and talked as they ate, feeding each other bites of their food and pausing now and then for a leisurely kiss, until Kyle insisted on eating a strawberry off the tip of her breast, and all thought of food was forgotten. Food and drink and tray were shoved aside hastily, and they made love with slow, gentle care, exploring the wonder of each other's bodies and finally coming together in a white-hot melding all the fiercer because of its delay.

Afterward they lay and talked softly in the age-old pattern of lovers. Kyle spoke of her skin and hair and eyes, punctuating his remarks with kisses and caresses. They discussed their likes and dislikes, their fears and joys. Nothing was too trivial, if it concerned each other. Jessica was consumed with a desire to know all about

Kyle, from his childhood on, and she was frustrated by his lack of interest in talking about his past. He kept turning the conversation back to the present, or to Jessica herself. If she had been less sated and content she would have gotten irritated at his reluctance. As it was, she dismissed the subject with an annoyed sigh and went on into the even more interesting topic of his former girlfriends.

"Have you ever been married?"

"Yeah, once."

"Divorced?"

"Yes. Several years ago."

"What was she like?"

"She was attractive, rather stylish. Her hair and makeup and clothes were always just right."

"Oh," Jessica groaned comically. "That kind of person. I hate her already."

Kyle smiled. "She wasn't bad. She was suited for a particular world. When we got married she was exactly what I wanted. I think I liked what she represented as much as the girl herself."

"How terrible!"

He shrugged. "Unfortunately it's the truth. I loved Beth and had as much interest in her as I was capable of having in anyone at the time. And she used me as much as I used her."

"It doesn't sound like a very pleasant relationship."

He chuckled. "Actually it went along quite smoothly until the end. We each had what we wanted, and we didn't get in each other's way. But then I couldn't give her what she wanted anymore, so she split."

"I can't see you being involved in anything that cold."

"Afterwards, neither could I. At the time it made

sense. That's the terrible thing about mistakes: At the time they seem the right thing to do.''

"What did she look like?''

''She was tall and slender—I guess I've always had a thing for skinny women.'' He winced theatrically at her glare. ''Dark brown hair, hazel eyes. Her nose was a trifle too narrow and her mouth a little too thin, but she was clever at putting on makeup to hide the defects. She always had a faint air of self-satisfaction.''

''Do you ever hear from her?''

''No. She's remarried, thank God, so I'm no longer under the gun for alimony.''

''Did you have divorce lawyers and summons-servers chasing you all over the country?''

''It wasn't quite that bad. What about you?''

''Me? No, no husband. I've never even been serious about anybody, really.'' Jessica bit back the rest of her words: until now.

''Too involved in your career?''

''I guess. I meet a lot of men, but it's always temporary. I'm there, and then I'm gone. There's not much possibility of anything but one-night stands, and I'm not interested in that.''

''So you spend most of your life alone.''

''Yes.''

''Do you prefer being alone?''

''I never really thought about it before.'' Jessica tilted her head to one side. ''No, I don't prefer it. I'm just used to it.''

''Don't you get lonely?''

Jessica shrugged. ''Of course. But I have plenty of work to occupy myself. Except now.''

''I'll give you a guarantee that you won't get lonely here. How's that?''

Jessica flashed him a smile. It was foolish to get involved with him, but she was too happy to pay any attention to the voice of reason right now. Surely, she thought, anyone who'd followed logic as consistently as she had all these years deserved to break out of the pattern once. For the few weeks she was with Kyle, she was going to throw caution and reason to the winds. She would allow herself to enjoy what came along without worrying about the consequences. She'd have the rest of her life for that.

Chapter 7

JESSICA SPENT THE NIGHT IN HER MOTHER'S ANTIQUE bed snuggled against Kyle's warm side. She'd never slept through the night with a man before, cuddled and warm in his arms. Nor had she awakened next to a man in the morning and gazed at his sleeping form, sprawled in sleep, jaw prickly with stubble. She did that morning, and she felt instantly awake and alert and ready to take on the world. She propped herself up on her elbow and gazed at Kyle for a few minutes, smiling, then slipped quietly out of bed and into the bathroom for a shower. When she finished the shower and pulled back the curtain she jumped at the sight of Kyle standing before her sink, squinting at his image in the foggy mirror.

"Oh! I'm sorry. You startled me. I didn't realize you were in here."

He grinned and swished a disposable razor under the

running tap water. "You were making so much noise splashing around in there, you wouldn't have heard a tank drive in."

Jessica wrapped a towel around her and stepped out. Kyle reached out and grabbed her wrist, pulling her to him for a kiss. Jessica melted against him, her mouth clinging to his. "Mmmm," Kyle commented when at last they parted. "I could always finish shaving later . . ."

"Oh, no, you don't. I have plans for this morning. Oh! You got soap all over me."

He chuckled and returned to his shaving. "What plans?"

"We are going to the Café du Monde for coffee and beignets. Viv raves about them so much that I'm determined to try them."

"That's a sure way to regain the weight you lost. All right. I'm game for that. It's one of my favorite spots, too."

Jessica dried her hair and dressed in companionable closeness with Kyle, bumping into him now and then as they moved about the small bathroom. He took a shower and sang loudly off-key, then redressed in the crumpled shorts he had worn the day before. He eyed them doubtfully. "Tell you what. Why don't I run home and change, then come back and pick you up. Okay?"

"Sure. You might even put on a shirt."

"What? And not give all the girls around Jackson Square a thrill?"

Jessica rolled her eyes, and he landed a playful kiss on her bare shoulder. By the time Kyle returned, Jessica was dressed in shorts, sandals and a stretchy tube top. She felt wonderfully free as they left the apartment's courtyard and started up the street. It was nice not to be encumbered by a skirt, blouse, jacket, slip, hose, high heels and her briefcase. It made her feel like a schoolgirl on holiday, her uniform stuffed into a closet back home.

They walked toward the Cathedral and Jackson Square. There was a somnolent quiet about the square in mid-morning. Only half the artists had set up their wares so far, and none of the sidewalk performers were out. Kyle and Jessica strolled past the long row of portraitists and other artists selling their paintings, and sidestepped a horse-drawn wagon with a load of tourists as they crossed the street to the Café Du Monde. The café consisted of an indoor restaurant as well as a roofed open-air area, both nearly full. Kyle squeezed past a few small round tables and claimed one that was empty. A sign on the wall proclaimed the cost of a plate of beignets and coffee, with or without milk. A waiter hurried up to them and laid down two small menus, then scurried off. The hand-held menus closely resembled the sign on the wall.

"This is all they serve?" Jessica asked in amazement.

Kyle chuckled. "It's all they need to serve. Believe me, you'll want to come back every day."

"Okay, I'll take an order of beignets and café au lait."

The scampering waiter, a small, dry, middle-aged man, whisked by and took their order. Jessica was amazed to see him return only minutes later with a tray of beignets and steaming cups of coffee. Kyle paid him, and Jessica watched the man bustle off.

"I thought everyone moved at a slow pace down here," Jessica commented.

"Not at this place. They serve an amazing number of customers. Take a bite."

Jessica glanced down at their meal. Six small square doughnuts covered with powdered sugar sat on a white plate before them. The coffee in the plain white cups was pale with milk. "The coffee looks awfully weak," she commented doubtfully.

Kyle grinned. "Taste it."

Obediently she sipped the hot liquid. It was delicious, rich and strong. "Mmm, terrific. It'd knock you over without the milk."

"Creole coffee. It has chicory in it; it's so thick you could cut it with a knife."

Jessica took another sip. "I've never drunk coffee with so much flavor." She tried one of the messy square pastries. Its taste was beyond description. "Oh, Kyle, this is absolutely sinful, it tastes so good." She polished it off and indelicately licked the remaining powdered sugar from her fingers. "You're right. I'll have to come back here again."

"Told you. When we finish, why don't we walk around the Quarter? I'll show you all the sights. Pirate's Alley, the Dueling Garden behind the church, the Beauregard house, everything."

"Okay. Sounds great. Hey!" She paused in the process of picking up her third doughnut. "I thought you were so big on healthy foods. What are you doing gobbling up all this sugar and caffeine?"

"What good's a rule if you can't break it?" he countered, grinning.

When they finished they strolled past the long buildings of the French Market shops until they reached the actual open-air market with its rows of fresh vegetables and fruits. Kyle bought a couple of peaches, which they ate as they walked on. Juice ran down Jessica's arm, and Kyle wiped it off with his handkerchief, then kissed the fragile inside of her wrist. He led her past the Ursuline convent and various other buildings of historical interest, including a house, now a hotel, fronted by a wrought-iron fence in the shape of cornstalks.

Kyle showed her the typically Creole architecture of the area and pointed out its various features, adding bits of history. He seemed to know everything. Some of the houses remained homes or had been turned into apartments, but most now housed business establishments. They walked past toy shops, dress stores, souvenir shops, perfumeries, candy stores, bookstores, jewelry shops and art galleries, many of them crammed into minuscule spaces. Kyle stopped now and then and introduced Jessica to an owner or manager. Invariably the shopowners were pleased to see Kyle and welcomed Jessica, adding that they admired her mother.

Jessica was taken aback. She had never thought of her mother as being someone people admired for her skill or personality, especially not people as business-oriented as merchants. She was also surprised by the friendship and respect with which they spoke to Kyle. In one antique store the manager even consulted Kyle on the best way to deal with a clerk who had become surly and stubborn. Jessica struggled not to let her amazement show. She couldn't understand why someone as unambitious and little given to work as Kyle was would know so many business people and be well liked by them.

But then, look at how he had charmed her, usually the most practical and levelheaded of people. Of course, it was a romantic relationship rather than friendship or business dealings. If it weren't for her physical attraction to Kyle, she probably wouldn't be friends with him. Or would she? It was hard to say. His blond good looks, the endearing smile, the mouth-watering molding of shoul-

ders and chest and arms and hips, were an essential part
of him. His looks were influenced by his personality and
vice versa. She couldn't imagine what he would be like
without them; certainly he wouldn't be the same.

Still, pretending that she could erase Kyle's sex
appeal, would she enjoy being with him? She thought of
his laugh. He was funny and fun. She remembered the
way she had giggled and joked with him yesterday
evening as they sat on the bed, eating. She hadn't
laughed that much in years. He told enjoyable stories
about himself and others. He was a stockpile of all sorts
of strange and trivial knowledge. And though he was
rough at times in his manner or speech, there was an
essential kindness to him. It was obvious in his eyes, in
the way he moved to help someone. Now that she
thought about it, Jessica realized that she *would* be his
friend even if they were not lovers. So why shouldn't
other people? Obviously business sense or ambition
didn't make a good friend; the qualities that did were
abundant in Kyle.

Jessica looked up and smiled, and Kyle staggered
back, as if stricken by the brilliance of her smile.
"Wow! What brought that on?"

"Nothing. I just smiled."

"But what a smile! Maybe we ought to turn around
right here and go back to your apartment."

"Nonsense," Jessica said stoutly. "You promised to
take me to that perfume shop."

He sighed dramatically. "All right. I'll suffer in
silence. Here, let's cross the street."

They strolled across the asphalt to the cobbled sidewalk on the other side, and Kyle led her into a narrow
storefront. A black-haired woman with dark eyes and a

pale olive complexion was seated on a high stool behind the counter, her head bent over the book in her lap. She seemed lost to the world, not even glancing up at the delicate tinkling of the bell on the door. Kyle cleared his throat ostentatiously, and she jumped.

"Oh, my goodness, I'm so sorry." She looked up, her gaze sweeping past Jessica to Kyle, and she burst into a grin. "Kyle Morrow! It's been ages since I saw you. You must be working too hard."

He laughed. "You know better than that. Annette, I want you to meet Jessica Todd. She's Viv Howard's daughter, and she's staying in Viv's apartment while Viv's in San Francisco. Jessica, this is Annette Folse, the proprietor of this establishment."

"My, you make me sound important. Hello, Jessica, it's nice to meet you. How is Viveca? I haven't seen her in weeks, either. I must have been out of circulation."

"As far as I know, she's fine. I haven't talked to her since she flew to California."

"She's notorious for not keeping in touch. It doesn't matter, though, because everyone likes her so much we go out of our way to keep in touch."

Kyle leaned his elbow on one of the glass counters. "Annette's one of those rare beings, a native New Orleanian."

"Oh, really?" Jessica's interest was piqued. "Are you a Creole?"

"Actually, 'Creole' applies only to those of French and Spanish origin who were here before the U.S. bought Louisiana. But I am of Creole descent on my mother's side. My father's family was German, but over the years the name Foltz turned into the French-sounding Folse.

"Don't let her fool you," Kyle interrupted. "Nobody could be more Louisiana blueblood than Annette. She inherited this shop from her grandmother, Madame Lavoisier, whose great-grandfather was one of the original settlers."

"That's true. And his bride was a 'casket' girl."

"A what?"

Annette carefully explained the name given to the girls of France who had been sent to the New World as brides to the settlers and who had carried their possessions in boxes, or "caskets." "Well, enough history. What can I do for you today?"

"I was intrigued by the sound of your shop. I've never been in a store that sold only perfume. Kyle tells me you make it yourself."

"Most of it. Let me show you our scents." She waved a hand toward the display case of bottles, sprays and jars, some tiny and delicate, others sturdy, some antique, and some boldly contemporary, but all undeniably graceful. She laid out several samples for Jessica to try, and even offered to concoct a special scent of her own for Jessica.

"What? Oh, no, that's very kind of you, but I couldn't let you go to so much trouble."

"Don't be silly. I do it all the time. It's one of our trademarks. It makes your perfume extra special."

"Why don't you mix one, Annette?" Kyle stuck in. "I'd like to get it for her. And put it in this bottle, the blue one with the teardrop stopper."

Annette chuckled. "You're wasted on those apartment buildings, Kyle. You have a real eye for beauty."

"I know. I found Jessica, didn't I?"

Jessica blushed at his bantering, too shy and amazed at his tender, almost loving tone to protest his buying her such an expensive gift. Annette studied the scents Jessica had liked best, then said, "Okay, I've got an idea of what you like. You want to come back in an hour or so and see what I've come up with? If you don't like it, I'll give it another try."

They agreed and left the shop. It was long past noon, so they made their way to a small restaurant, crammed full of people, that made the po-boy sandwiches which New Orleanians loved. Jessica agreed that the sandwich was excellent, but it was so large she couldn't eat even half of it. "You're not trying to gain weight," Kyle admonished her, wagging a stern forefinger at her.

"You make me sound like skin and bones," Jessica exclaimed, making a pout. "I don't look that bad, do I?"

"Are you trying to squeeze a compliment out of me?" Kyle leaned over and kissed her forehead. "You're utterly beautiful." He grinned. "But we can't have you going into a decline. Got to keep your strength up."

"For what?"

He wiggled his eyebrows in a manner she presumed was meant to be leering. Jessica burst into giggles.

"You're awfully deflating to the male ego, I hope you realize."

"I'm sorry." She couldn't stifle her giggles, and Kyle grinned.

"You do look beautiful when you laugh like that." Kyle placed his hands on either side of her face. "I like you this way much better. No more gaunt, frowning career woman in a designer three-piece suit, okay?"

"Okay."

He kissed her lightly on the lips. "Now, let's go see what delightfully sexy concoction Annette's come up with."

The shop was empty when they walked in, but Annette immediately stuck her head out of a door at the rear. "Hi! I'm just finishing. Can you wait a minute?"

"Sure."

She disappeared into the back and emerged a few minutes later with a small blue glass vial in her hand. She pulled out the delicate stopper and applied a touch to Jessica's inner wrist. "How's that?"

Jessica sniffed. "Mmm, lovely."

Kyle raised her wrist so that he could smell it and smiled. "I agree. We'll take it."

"Great. Let me wrap it up so it won't break or spill."

She vanished into the back again, and Jessica turned to Kyle. "You really shouldn't buy this for me."

"Why not?"

"I imagine it's terribly expensive."

"It probably is. Annette doesn't do anything cheap."

Jessica frowned. Kyle was as bad about money as Viv. But she couldn't deny that it filled her with a warm glow to know that he wished to buy something special for her, despite the cost. "Well, thank you. It's—I'll treasure it."

"I hope you do." He smiled down at her, his eyes glowing, and his expression warmed Jessica down to her toes. She moved forward and wrapped her arms around his chest, hugging him. His arms quickly encircled her, and they stood locked together in a moment of unspoiled happiness and affection.

Then Annette emerged from the back room, and Jessica quickly stepped out of his arms. Annette smiled. "Don't mind me."

She handed Jessica the lightweight white box emblazoned with the store's name. Kyle paid the bill, and they started toward the door.

"Come back and see me again while you're here, Jessica," Annette called after her. "Just to talk. I enjoyed meeting you."

"Sure. I'd love to." Jessica turned back to wave and smile. Annette was friendly, and Jessica had had fun talking to her. It wasn't often that she got to visit with other women her own age who were also businesswomen. But now she had plenty of time. Perhaps she would come back.

As they stepped out the front door Kyle looped an arm around Jessica's shoulders and bent his head to nibble at her neck. "You smell delicious. I think I'd like to see you in nothing but your new perfume."

Jessica giggled and tried half-heartedly to wriggle away from him. "Right here on the street?"

"My apartment's not far from here. Would you like to see it?"

"Why do I get the feeling that a tour of your apartment isn't exactly what you have in mind?"

He grinned. "I'll show you around first. But the tour will probably end in the bedroom."

"Probably?" Jessica queried with a flirtatious upward glance.

"Definitely." He kissed her briefly but thoroughly on the mouth, then turned her in the direction of his apartment.

His apartment house was only four blocks away, a narrow three-story building of a faded color somewhere between gray and blue, built flush with the sidewalk. On the upper two floors wrought iron balconies jutted out to overhang the street. Kyle took out his keys and opened the outer door. They stepped into a narrow entryway, and Kyle led Jessica up the polished wooden stairs to the third floor. There was only one apartment door at each landing, and Jessica realized that each apartment must take up an entire floor. It made sense, with such a narrow building.

Kyle stopped in front of the door on the third floor and inserted another key. "Where does that go?" Jessica asked, indicating a narrow metal staircase leading up.

"Onto the roof. You want to see it? I turned it into a sun porch."

"Sure."

They went up the stairs and out the metal door onto the roof. Jessica gasped with delight. Wooden decking had been laid down in paths over the roof and supported several chairs and umbrella-topped tables. Plants, flowers and small trees in decorative wooden tubs were scattered about attractively, giving the place the air of a garden. At the far end steps led up to a wood-encased hot tub. "It's beautiful!"

"I'm glad you like it. I was pleased when I finished it. There isn't a garden here like there is at Viv's apartment, and this seemed a good alternative."

"You did the work yourself?"

"Most of it. Except the Jacuzzi, of course."

"You did an excellent job."

"Why, thank you. We'll come out here some night and sit in the hot tub, have a little wine, and look out at nighttime New Orleans."

He kissed her, and Jessica followed him back down the metal stairway a little breathlessly. Kyle opened the plain, unassuming door to his apartment and stepped back for Jessica to enter. The apartment was one enormous room, large and bright and airy. Only a small kitchen and an equally tiny bathroom were separated from the single main room. A row of uncurtained French doors across the front wall, opening onto the iron balcony, flooded the room with light and made it appear even larger than it was. Farther down the room two bubble skylights added light to the rear of the apartment.

The old cypress plank floor was waxed and polished until it gleamed. There was little furniture, and like Viveca's apartment, it was rather light and contemporary. The ceiling was high, and two old-fashioned fans hung down from it. Kyle had taken advantage of the light and the height of the ceiling to put in a couple of tall palms, which added a cooling touch to the sunny room. About three-fourths of the way down the room two folding screens, one intricately carved wood and the other Japanese lacquered, served to partition off the bedroom area. It was a casual place, but there was an understated beauty about it, an air of elegance and charm . . . and money.

Jessica's immediate response to his apartment was an indrawn breath of admiration. Then her mind began to click rapidly. French Quarter apartments were not inexpensive. Jessica knew what Viveca paid for hers, and Viv's was smaller than this one. Each floor here was a single apartment; his was lovely and modernized; there were a sundeck and hot tub on the top floor. It all added up to an apartment that would cost a pretty penny. Certainly more than what the handyman of a building would earn. Perhaps Kyle got his home as part of his pay, but surely he wouldn't be given one of the nicest apartments. And the furniture in this room, while casual, was obviously quality.

Suspicions which had begun to tickle at the back of Jessica's mind when they were on the rooftop now burst into full flower. She turned to Kyle, eyes wide and indignant. "You aren't poor, are you?"

He laughed. "That makes you mad?"

"It makes me mad that you deceived me!"

"I didn't deceive you. I never told you I was poor."

"You told me you took care of these apartments, Viveca's, and a third building."

"I do."

"Why?"

"Because I own them."

"You own three apartment houses in the French Quarter?"

"Two apartment houses and a condominium complex. This house is actually condominiums, too."

Jessica had some idea of the worth of old, renovated buildings in the Quarter; property values in this small area were sky-high. Owning three such buildings would put one into a rather high tax bracket. "Then you're rich."

Kyle shrugged. "I'm not hurting." His face turned blank, almost hard. "Does that make me more acceptable to you? Now do you feel better about sleeping with me?"

"No! How dare you imply that I'm so—so—"

"Mercenary?" Kyle supplied softly.

Jessica paled. "Yes, mercenary. Is that what you think of me?"

"I think that you're very impressed by status and wealth," he replied calmly. "You revere success, and money is the indicator of success, right?"

"Why didn't you tell me? Why did you let me believe you were a bum?"

"Because I'm the same person, with money or without. I wanted you to make love with me because you wanted me, not because I made some money before I 'dropped out.' "

"You were afraid I would sleep with you because you were wealthy? That I might refuse because you didn't have money? That I was some gold digger who was after your cash?" Jessica's voice rose ominously.

"No, damn it. I wasn't afraid you were trying to get your hands in my pockets. But I didn't want you to think I was something different than I am. I didn't want it to color your perception of me."

"Why? It's not exactly something to be ashamed of."

"I do the work I told you I did. Nothing else. When I left California I liquidated everything I owned and reinvested it in property here. I don't spend my time playing the stock market or trying to multiply my assets. I do physical labor, things that need to be done around the apartments, and I collect and bank the rent. That's it. I'm no financial whiz in hiding; I have no ambitions to do any more than what I'm doing. I really am the bum you thought I was. But I was afraid that if you knew I had money you would assume I was something different, that you'd say, 'Well, he's rather eccentric, but that's okay because he's rich.' I didn't think you'd refuse to accept me because of my money, but I was afraid it might give you false hopes about me."

"False hopes! False hopes of what! Marriage? Financial gain? What?"

He made a disgusted sound. "Jessica, I know you're not on the make for a sugar daddy. But I didn't want you to think that I was really a part of your world, that deep down I was running after money or property. I didn't want you to dream that someday I'd change, revert to that world. That we—"

"Don't worry! I never for a moment was so deluded as to think there could be anything permanent between us," Jessica snapped and whirled around, heading for the front door.

Kyle darted after her, grabbing her wrist as she reached for the doorknob. "Jessica, don't leave like this! Give me a chance to explain."

Her eyes shot sparks. "Why should I?"

"Because I love you," he answered simply.

Chapter 8

JESSICA STARED AT HIM, OPEN-MOUTHED. HER STOM-ach had fallen as if she were in a skyrocketing elevator. Her knees sagged, and Kyle had to grab her upper arms tightly to hold her up. "Come on, baby, don't pass out on me now." He half led, half dragged her to a wide leather chair and eased her into it. He stepped back, studying her with concern. "Shall I get you a glass of water?"

"I'm not about to faint! You hit me with one surprise too many this morning. You conceal the fact that you have money because you think I'm so materialistic it will color the way I feel about you. You've known me only a few days, spent one night with me. I hardly know anything about you—what you used to do that made a lot of money or how you lived or why you quit. And yet you tell me you love me? Just like that?"

"Does it take more time than that? Should I have waited to fall in love with you?"

"You must have been a lawyer, the way you twist everything around."

"No. A doctor, actually."

"A doctor," Jessica repeated numbly. "I—Kyle, would you please just tell me about it!"

"What do you want to know?"

"Everything! Why you wanted to be a doctor, why you quit, what your life was like. You're so secretive!"

"I'm not." She shot him a scathing look, and he sighed. "Oh, all right. It's not that exciting a story. We didn't have much money when I was a kid, but my mother came from an old, genteel family. The kind that once had money and a name, but was down to just the name. All my life there was a financial struggle between my parents. Dad claimed mother was extravagant and snobbish; she blamed Dad for not providing adequately for her children. He was conservative, prudent, very aware of the value of a dollar. Mother was very aware of all the niceties that money could buy and that she felt we deserved." Kyle shrugged and moved away, shoving his hands in his pockets. "I grew up determined to make money, to be a success in both their eyes. I wanted to be wealthy, to have fine things, to be able to buy something without worrying about the cost—or feeling ashamed because I worried."

"And that's why you became a doctor?"

"Basically, yes. It offered prestige and money and admiration. Everything I wanted. It was something I knew I could achieve. I was smart, and if I worked hard enough I could get a scholarship to college and admittance to med school. I studied hard. I had part-time jobs through college and med school. I made a good intern program and then tried like hell to get into a good residency program. After that I went into practice and worked as hard as ever making money. I saw more patients than any sane man; I worked all hours. When I wasn't at the office, I was at home planning my investments. You think we aren't alike? If anything, I was worse than you. Nothing existed for me but my career. I was all push and drive, running myself ragged and driving everyone around me crazy.''

''What happened?''

He faced her, his face drawn in harsh, bitter lines. ''After about three years of practice, I'd had enough. I realized I was killing myself. Nor was I being fair to my patients. So I decided to get out.''

''Just like that?''

''Just like that.''

''You were able to leave medicine without a qualm? Without wishing you could go back?''

''Yeah. I told you; I chose it for the money. Don't think I had any great humanitarian need to make sick people well.''

''I don't see how you could have worked so hard to get through medical school and your internship and everything unless you had some real love for what you were doing.''

''I was an achiever. I was very motivated.''

Jessica grimaced. She didn't believe him, but obviously he wasn't about to tell her the truth. ''What happened to make you give it up?''

''I told you. I wised up.''

''Kyle, something must have happened. You don't just suddenly decide to throw away everything you've worked half your life to achieve.''

''Some people do. I found out that what I'd worked

for didn't mean anything. My wife and I didn't love each other; we merely lived in the same house and shared a name. I realized I'd married her primarily because she looked and acted like my image of a doctor's wife. I wanted her because she was a society girl. She wanted me because I could provide her with money and status and the sort of life she'd grown up with. We had mutual expectations and a modicum of desire for each other. It caused me no pain to leave her. There was nothing for me in our house; I'd spent practically every waking minute at my office or the hospital. My car didn't mean anything—none of my material possessions did. They were symbols of status, not anything personal.''

''And medicine meant nothing to you either?''

''Not any longer. I was burned out, disillusioned with my life and myself and my peers. I was a mental and physical wreck. So I left.''

Jessica sighed and pushed back her hair with both hands. Her head was spinning from the onslaught of surprises. Kyle was wealthy, not poor, yet still the ambitionless, lazy soul she had thought he was. He'd deceived her about the state of his pocketbook because he thought she was so money-oriented it would influence her feelings for him, yet he said he loved her. He had had the drive and ability to work his way through med school and become a successful physician, yet he'd thrown it away. No matter what he said, something must have been the catalyst for his abrupt decision to leave. But what had it been, and why wouldn't he talk about it? Jessica couldn't reconcile the image of a man who'd endured the punishing schedule of an intern and mastered complex medical books with this man she knew, who was happy to spend his days strolling around the French Quarter or painting walls or digging in the dirt.

She rose and walked away from him to stare blankly at the lovely Japanese screen in front of her. "I don't know what to make of you."

"You aren't the first."

A smile escaped her. "I'm sure that's true." Jessica turned toward him. "It hurts that you didn't tell me about yourself."

He glanced down at the floor. "I'm sorry. I never meant to hurt you. Maybe I was wrong not to tell you I owned the apartments, but at the time it seemed easier, safer. Once I'd let it slide by, it was an awfully awkward thing to bring up in conversation. 'Oh, say, by the way, I used to be a doctor and I own this place.' Besides, most of the time I was with you, my former occupation was the farthest thing from my mind. All I could think about was you and making love with you."

"You make it difficult to stay mad at you."

"I try."

"Are you sure you weren't really a con artist?"

A smile started across his mouth. "Maybe I was, at that. I just called it something else."

He came to stand before her, towering over her. It hurt her neck to look up at him. He tangled the fingers of one hand in her hair, his eyes questioning. And behind the question lurked the remnants of his hot desire, the urging to take her to his bed. He brought his hand down, his thumb and then his fingers tracing the line of her jaw. His thumb brushed across her lips. "Forgiven?"

Jessica sighed. "I suppose so."

"Good. 'Cause I've been aching all day to show you my bedroom."

Jessica couldn't stop the teasing, sensuous smile that spread across her mouth. "Oh, really? And what's so special about your bedroom?"

"The fact that you'll be in it."

His hand slid down her arm to clasp her hand, leaving tiny goosebumps of sensitivity behind it. Jessica went with him, still a little unnerved and dismayed by what he had told her, but also aware of a growing warmth low in her abdomen, a sweet anticipation. She thought of what had happened between them last night and knew she would be a liar if she denied that she wanted him again. She was thirsty for him. She wanted to know Kyle in a hundred different ways, to feel him, to be a part of him. She had never had this kind of hunger for a man before, a desire that went far beyond mere physical passion to a need to experience his essence.

The bedroom was as plain as the rest of the apartment, the single exception being a massive, dark, ornately carved armoire that stood against one wall. The room was bathed in the muted light of an opaque skylight. Jessica walked over in awe to the huge wardrobe. "Kyle, this is beautiful," she breathed, reaching out to run a gentle hand over the finely detailed carving of the corners.

"The house didn't have closets originally, and I saw no reason to put one in after I'd seen this." He joined her. With his forefinger he traced a light pattern on the back of her hand. "Jessica . . ."

She turned. "What?"

"I meant what I said a while ago. I love you."

"How can you possibly know that?"

"It's not something I had to think about. I knew it in my gut the first time I saw you. I wanted you so badly it scared the hell out of me."

"There's a difference between wanting and loving."

"Not this kind of wanting. It's bone deep. Deeper than that. It goes clear down to my soul." He wrapped his arms around her loosely and nuzzled her hair. "Last night when I heard your little cry when you hit it, I thought I would burst into a million pieces. I felt like the most victorious male animal in the world, and yet as gooey soft as caramel, grateful for the gift I'd been given."

"Oh, Kyle . . ." Jessica rubbed her cheek against him. His words stirred the banked fire within her. Was this love? she wondered. This hot yearning that sprang up in her at the mere thought of him? Surely not. It was passion, a tremendous, overwhelming passion, true . . . but still just that. Not love. Love took time and understanding and compatibility. Didn't it? When she felt his breath stir her hair and his hands caressing her back like this, she wasn't sure of anything, least of all her own feelings.

She turned her face, seeking his lips, and Kyle moved to meet her. His mouth brushed hers once and then again, as if seeking its home, before settling avidly on her lips. His tongue traced the tender inner flesh of her lips, then slipped fervently into her mouth. Their tongues met and twined in a sensuous mating, and Jessica felt the sudden heat that flashed through Kyle at their touch. His arms tightened around her, squeezing her against him. One hand slid up to spread in her hair, to follow the convolutions of her ear, to skim her throat and cheek.

Slowly, reluctantly, the kiss ended, and Kyle moved back. His breath was ragged, his eyes glittering. "I want to undress you."

Jessica nodded, not trusting herself to speak. With nerve-racking slowness Kyle took off her clothes, rolling up her T-shirt and sliding it up off her arms and head, pushing the shorts down over her hips and legs, then

pulling off the scraps of her underwear. Each movement
was a caress, and his eyes drank in her body as he
revealed it bit by bit. When he had finished Jessica
answered him in kind, almost languidly removing his
shorts and shirt. When she was through she scraped her
fingernails lightly down his chest, and Kyle drew in his
breath sharply. He reached for her, but she blocked his
arms and stepped closer.

He waited, unmoving, for what she would do. Her
tongue flickered out and circled one flat masculine
nipple. It tightened and elongated under her touch, and
she pressed her tongue against it hard as her lips moved
over it, clamping down with moist heat. She moved to
the other nipple, and air hissed out sharply between his
teeth. The sound stabbed Jessica with a white heat. Her
hands skimmed down his ribs and over the sharp, jutting
hip bones onto the hair-roughened flesh of his thighs.
Kyle turned up her face and kissed her as if he would
consume her. His need swelled against the softness of
her belly, and Jessica pressed up against it, offering
herself to him. He groaned.

His hands roamed her back and buttocks, pushing her
into him at every point. "I love the way you feel," he
murmured against her temple. His lips slid down across
her cheek and onto her tender throat. "Like satin. Silk.
Touch me, Jessie. Take me in your hands. Ahhh, yes,
like that. Oh, my sweet. My love."

The intensity of his pleasure at her touch amazed her.
She was not skilled at lovemaking; yet Kyle quivered
and groaned at her caresses. She experimented with her
hands, striving to bring him more pleasure, caressing his
satiny hardness in every way she could think of, until
Kyle began to tremble from the force of his unspent
passion.

"I want you." His voice was low, with a faint underlying tremor. He walked her back until she was against the armoire, its smooth wood cool against her skin. Muscles bulging, he lifted her to fit himself into her. Jessica was too surprised at first to respond, but then she wrapped her legs tightly around his waist and clung to him. His hands dug into her buttocks, supporting her weight. He lowered his mouth to her breasts, taking one delicate pink nipple in his mouth and laving it. He nibbled with his lips, then sucked fiercely. Invisible cords ran from the depths of her womanhood into her nipples, and they vibrated now at the touch of his mouth. It felt as if he were finding and bringing to the surface all her long-hidden femininity. Jessica trembled and dug her fingernails into his shoulders, her head twisting from side to side in wild delight.

He began to work on the other breast, his maleness quiescent but hard and full within her, heightening the intense pleasure in her breasts. Kyle's mouth left her breast and he raised his head to gaze into her face. His eyes were dark and cloudy with desire, his mouth slack and full. Every line of his face spoke of his deep yearning for her and how close he was to losing command of himself. His eyes were heavy-lidded; he seemed almost drugged. He began to move his hips, bracing her against the heavy wardrobe cabinet and thrusting up into her. His eyes drifted closed; his nostrils narrowed. Jessica watched him, feeling her own pleasure spiral within her, and the sight of his desire touched her with a strange combination of tenderness and passion.

Jessica cupped the back of his neck with her hands, teetering on the brink of fulfillment. Her hands slid up and her fingers clenched in his hair. She cried out, pulling his hair, but Kyle didn't notice the pain, lost in his own cataclysm of desire.

They clung to each other, weak and sweat-dampened, trembling with spent passion. Slowly his hold relaxed, and Jessica slid down to stand on the floor. Kyle turned and leaned against the armoire doors beside her, eyes closed. His breath was rapid and uneven as he wiped a strand of hair off his forehead. He opened his eyes to cast Jessica a sidelong look. A smile hovered on his lips. "Oh, baby. I can't describe what you do to me."

"You don't have to. I feel it."

He took her wrist and pulled her with him to the bed, where they stretched out, exhausted and blissful. He curled an arm around her shoulders and smoothed back her hair. "I wish I could take time and stop it, freeze this moment, bottle it—somehow store it so I could take it out and savor it whenever I wanted."

"Oh, Kyle. I wish I could, too." It would be so wonderful, she thought, tears burning at the back of her eyes, if she could have this moment to experience again when she was gone, cold and lonely and aching for Kyle's presence. But, no, leaving was something she wouldn't think about. She refused to spoil this precious time with thoughts of the future.

Jessica managed to avoid all thoughts of the future during the next few days—and all thoughts of the past, as well. She refused to think about what Kyle used to do or what had made him give up medicine. She wouldn't consider the disparities between them, the conflict of philosophies or lifestyles. Nor would she allow herself to dwell on what a short time she would be able to spend with Kyle, or how she would feel when she returned to

Atlanta. For once in her life she was determined not to examine the consequences. This time was hers, and she planned to enjoy it. Nothing was going to spoil it, including her own worrying.

She and Kyle spent most of their time together, laughing, talking, often making love, but even more often simply enjoying each other's presence. Jessica accompanied him on the jobs he did at his buildings, sitting on the sidewalk beside him as he dug weeds in the garden, handing him his tools as he lay stretched out beneath a kitchen sink working on the plumbing, even helping him repair a low brick wall. The rest of the time they spent simply having fun.

Kyle insisted on taking her out in his sailboat on Lake Pontchartrain, though Jessica balked when he mentioned it.

"Why?" he countered. "Are you scared of the water? Do you get sick?"

"Yes, a little, to both your questions," she answered.

"You'll be fine. Can you swim?"

"In a swimming pool I can, but I've never done it in a lake."

"Same difference."

"A swimming pool is not hundreds of feet deep."

"You can drown in a foot of water."

"I know. I know. But I'd have to really try to do that. Drowning in deep water's easy."

"Don't be silly. You'll wear a life jacket."

"But I've never been on a sailboat. Don't you have to run around and tie ropes and lift sails and stuff like that? I wouldn't have the least idea what to do. I'll probably tip us over."

"No, you won't. I'll do most of the work, and I

promise I'll explain to you whatever I ask you to do. You'll like it. I promise. We'll take Dramamine in case you get sick.''

"Kyle, I'm not sure . . ."

He leaned back and studied her. "You're afraid of doing something you don't know, aren't you? Something you aren't competent at, don't have control over. Is that it?"

Jessica shrugged. "Partly. I hate to have you see me foul up."

"You won't be the first person I've seen do it. I've done it myself quite a few times."

"Yeah, but . . ."

"But what?"

"That's different."

"How is it different?"

Jessica glared at him, exasperated. "Because it wasn't *me*!"

He laughed. "That's refreshingly honest. Come on, Jess, I won't laugh at you or think you're any less of a person if you can't do everything right the first time you set foot on a sailboat. It would be crazy to expect you to know what to do. Would you expect me to be able to march into your office and do your job?"

"Of course not. You don't know anything about it."

He glanced at her significantly. "You wouldn't get mad at me? You wouldn't think I was an idiot? Lose all respect for me?"

"No! You're twisting everything around, as usual. The difference is that I'm a woman. Men are excused for not knowing things; women are considered incompetent fools."

"Talk about chauvinism," he muttered. "Where do you come up with these ideas? Let me put it as plainly as

I can. I couldn't care less whether you know a bow knot from a square knot or anything else about sailing. I just want you to be with me because I enjoy your company. Okay? And I want to show you my boat and my lake. Will you come?''

Jessica smiled sheepishly. "How can I refuse?''

"You can't.''

They went sailing, and much to her surprise, Jessica had a marvelous time. She had been in New Orleans over a week now, and the time of concentrated rest and good eating habits had invigorated her. She felt better than she could remember feeling in months, maybe years. The lake was enormous and blue, dotted with other brightly colored sailing craft. Once she got over her initial nervousness Jessica settled down and enjoyed the soothing bobbing of the boat and the warmth of the sun. Kyle handled the sailing, now and then throwing her a careful, precise instruction which she was easily able to follow.

When they returned to the marina Jessica asked eagerly, "When can we sail again?''

"Did you enjoy it?'' Kyle smiled.

"I loved it.''

"I'm glad. Sailing's a favorite pasttime of mine.''

"You know, that's one of the nicest things about you.''

He glanced at her, puzzled. "What? Sailing?''

"No, silly. Not saying 'I told you so.' You could, you know; you told me I'd like it if I went. And most people would remind me about it.'' Guiltily Jessica recalled a few occasions when she had done the same thing herself.

Kyle shrugged. "What's the purpose in it?''

"One-upsmanship,'' Jessica answered promptly. "Reminding me that you were right, and I was wrong.''

"I don't care whether I was right about your sailing. What I care about is whether you had a good time."

"But don't you see? That's what's so unusual." Jessica smiled to herself. "Besides, I always have a good time when I'm with you."

"I'm glad."

Jessica drew in a deep breath of satisfaction, and the sudden rush of air into her lungs made her cough. She looked away, knowing the expression of grim disapproval that would appear on Kyle's face. He hated her smoking. Jessica coughed again, but tried to suppress it, which only made it worse, of course.

When they reached Kyle's car, Jessica pushed in the cigarette lighter, an automatic action with her whenever she got into a car, and fumbled in her purse for her package of cigarettes. When she brought out a cigarette and picked up the car lighter, Kyle suddenly grabbed the cigarette from her fingers and broke it. Jessica gasped, staring in disbelief as he stuffed the mangled cigarette into the ashtray.

"Just what do you think you're doing?" she demanded.

"Trying to keep you from killing yourself," he replied grimly.

"And just who appointed you my watchdog?"

"Me. Somebody has to take you in hand. You're obviously not going to save yourself."

Jessica glared at him. "I don't need to be 'taken in hand,' thank you. I've managed to take care of myself for quite a few years without your help."

"You haven't exactly done a sterling job of it. When you showed up at Viv's apartment you were a pretty good example of what not to do with your health."

"I was run-down. But now I'm fine."

He grunted. "Yeah. Except for sounding like you need to enter a TB ward."

"Listen, what I do with my life is my business. I don't need you interfering and domineering all over the place."

For a moment they stared at each other in a grim contest of wills. Then Kyle sighed and started the engine. "Okay, I'm sorry. You're right. I have no business telling you what to do. If you want to go to hell in a handbasket, it's your right. But I'll tell you, it hurts like hell to have to stand by and watch you kill yourself."

Jessica's chin jutted out a little farther and she retrieved the pack of cigarettes from her purse to pull out a defiant smoke. The package was empty! Disgustedly she crumpled it into a tight ball. "Now we'll have to stop at a store."

"Can't last thirty miles without a smoke, huh?"

"Just shut up and drive. All right?"

Kyle put the car in gear and pulled out of the parking lot. There was a combination gas station, grocery and bait shop not far from the marina, and Kyle drove up to it. Killing the engine, he turned toward her expectantly.

Jessica hesitated. Suddenly she was repelled by her panic at finding herself without cigarettes. It was awful, really, to be so driven, so—out of control.

Jessica leaned her head against the window and sighed. "Never mind. I'll get some at home. Let's go on."

He shrugged and started the car. Jessica stared pensively out the side window as they crossed the long causeway to the city. Kyle glanced at her curiously a few times, but decided not to disturb her obvious contemplation. When he pulled his old beaten-up Jeep into his parking space, Jessica turned to him. There was a strange look on her face, partly excited, partly scared. Kyle's heart jumped a little, infected by her emotions.

"I've decided to quit."

"What?"

"I said, I've decided to—"

"Yes, I heard what you said. What do you mean? Quit what?"

Jessica grimaced. "Smoking, of course."

He looked at her silently. "Why?"

"What do you mean, why? I thought you'd be pleased."

"If it's really what you want to do, of course I am. But I don't want you deciding to quit for my sake and then hating me because I forced you into it."

"You're really twisted."

"No, I've just known a lot of smokers. I mean it, Jess. I don't want to be the reason for your quitting."

Jessica frowned, searching her reasons. "You're not. Honestly. I don't know exactly why it just struck me. Maybe because I feel better. Or because I know you're right, and I was being stupidly defiant. Anyway, all of a sudden I hated the way I felt when I realized I didn't have a cigarette. You're right about me. I like to be in control. I didn't like knowing that the habit was ruling me, not the other way around. So I decided to stop."

There was a long pause while Kyle studied her face. Then he burst into a grin and leaned across to kiss her. "Congratulations."

"Will you help me?"

"Absolutely. Believe me, you won't get a smoke past this guard." He jumped out of the car and went around to open her door. "Okay. First thing—we need to dump out all your cigarettes."

Jessica swallowed. "Dump my cigarettes?" she squeaked out. "But I have practically a whole carton in your apartment."

"So? You aren't going to smoke them, are you?"

"No."

"Then why keep them?"

"I—I guess you're right."

They walked to his apartment, Kyle's hand under her elbow hurrying her along. Once there, Jessica moved on increasingly dragging feet into the kitchen and picked up the carton atop the counter. She went to the trash can and poured the packages into it. As she watched the cellophane-wrapped packs tumble into the scraps of food and paper, panic stabbed through her briefly, but she straightened her shoulders and tossed the empty carton in on top of them.

"Here's a pack I found lying on the coffee table." Kyle held out a half-empty pack.

With trembling fingers Jessica took it. That meant there were no more cigarettes in the entire apartment. She dropped it into the trash.

"Now, how about your matches and lighters?"

"Oh, but . . . do I have to throw them away, too?"

Kyle shrugged. "It doesn't matter to me. But you won't need them, will you?"

"No . . ." She opened her purse and dug through it, finding three partially used books of matches and a disposable lighter. They followed the rest of the stuff into the trash.

"Now. We need to go over to your apartment to do the same thing," Kyle said as he picked up the plastic trash bag and twisted it to tie it.

"Now? But why? I could do it tomorrow when I go over there."

"You can if you want to. But it'll be easier tonight."

"I guess you're right."

Kyle carried the trash out and dumped it in the outside can, and they walked to Jessica's apartment. There she found every lighter, matchbook and cigarette pack in her suitcases and drawers and atop all the various surfaces. With a sinking heart she watched them tumble into the trash can, which Kyle again emptied into the larger one outside.

Flushed with success and hope, Jessica managed to get through the evening without once running to dig in the large dumpster outside to retrieve her cigarette packages . . . though she thought of doing it more than once. When they went to bed she wished fleetingly for a final cigarette of the day. Why hadn't she thought to wait to stop until after she'd taken a last smoke? But she gritted her teeth and got into bed, and it didn't take as long as she thought it would for her to go to sleep.

The next morning when she awoke and made her way to the kitchen for her first cup of coffee, she looked around automatically for a package of cigarettes. Then she recalled that she had dumped all her smoking paraphernalia into the wastebasket the night before, and she felt as if she had been punched in the stomach.

Good heavens! What kind of insanity had come over her last night? Jessica started for the bedroom to get dressed. There was a café three doors down the street which had a cigarette machine. She stopped, gnawing irresolutely on her lip. What would Kyle think of her? What would he say when she broke her resolution after only one night?

She waffled, and the moment was lost. Kyle strolled into the kitchen, bursting with good cheer, and kissed her. "Hello, sweetheart. Want something to eat? How about pancakes? I'll make them."

Jessica couldn't bring herself to leave in search of cigarettes right in front of him, so she leaned rather grumpily against the counter, sipping her coffee and watching him bustle around the kitchen. Somehow she got through the rest of the morning, occupying herself with eating, showering and dressing. Nervously she wandered around the apartment, picking up and straightening. She rummaged through all the kitchen cabinets and found a half-empty can of peanuts, which she ate as she worked. A later search turned up a package of gum. Eagerly she unwrapped a piece and began to chew it. Two hours later the package was empty and her jaw was sore. Jessica headed for the kitchen again.

"It's a good thing you need to gain weight," commented Kyle, who had been watching her nervous movements all morning. "Tell you what. Why don't we walk through the Quarter?"

"All right." Jessica seized on the opportunity to do something. She couldn't let this thing get the best of her. She had sworn off smoking, and she would do it—if it didn't kill her first.

The day continued to be full of horrors. Although walking and looking into shop windows helped calm her nerves and gave her something to do, it seemed as if everyone she saw was smoking. Her mouth watered for the taste of a cigarette. She stopped several times on their walk to buy a bag of popcorn, a candy bar, a roll of mints, a can of toffee peanuts. She had to have something in her hands; she had to have something to put in her mouth. When she went into a hotel lobby to buy a bag of hard candies from the little hotel drugstore she became thoroughly disgusted with herself. She couldn't go through life eating like this or she'd not only gain back the weight she was supposed to but keep on until she was a blimp! What good would it do her to stop smoking if, in the course of doing it, she gained thirty pounds?

Sensing her frustration, Kyle linked his hand in hers and murmured, "Let's go home."

She knew it wouldn't help, but Jessica sighed and agreed. When they reached his apartment Jessica walked straight into the bedroom and dumped out the contents of her purse on the bed. She pawed through the mess, hoping a stray cigarette had slipped out of its package and would show up now. There were lots of tobacco crumbs, but no cigarette. Jessica groaned and flung everything back into her purse. Think about that, she told herself. There'd be no more getting tobacco crumbs beneath her fingernails when she searched her purse if she stopped smoking. And no more trying to get the smell of smoke out of her clothes. And—and—surely there were other benefits.

Jessica grabbed her purse and hurled it onto the chair, letting out a shriek of frustration. Kyle was in the bedroom in an instant, and she whirled on him. "I can't do it!"

"What?"

"I'm sorry, but it's utterly impossible. I don't have the willpower or the desire or whatever it takes. I'm a nervous wreck. I keep eating, and I've chewed so much gum I feel like my teeth are about to fall out. I can't do it! I'm going out to buy some cigarettes."

"Wait." Kyle reached out and stopped her. "I have something I want to try first."

"What?"

A lazy smile grew on his face. "Something that should occupy you for a while. And it's guaranteed to calm your nerves."

"What?" she repeated suspiciously.

He drew closer, his eyes fixed on hers. Jessica felt a telltale pulse begin to throb in her throat. Kyle's lips touched hers lightly, then grazed her cheek and nuzzled through her hair to her sensitive earlobe. His breath rasped in her ear, and she shivered. With his tongue he traced the delicate folds of her ear before his lips closed on the lobe and began to suck gently.

"This is a remedy for smoking?" Jessica asked unevenly.

"Dr. Morrow's Patented Smoking Cure. It's yours for free."

His mouth traveled downward, traversing the tender column of Jessica's throat. A smile touched her lips. "I think this is definitely better than acupuncture."

Kyle chuckled and swung her up into his arms.

Chapter 9

FOR THE NEXT WEEK KYLE WAS WITH HER ALMOST constantly. Sometimes Jessica felt as if he were her jailer. One day when he offered to go with her to the drugstore she shouted at him that she didn't need a keeper. But Jessica knew that she did. Kyle was the main thing that kept her from sneaking a cigarette. She was embarrassed to smoke in front of him after making her big announcement that she was quitting. And when she showed signs of restlessness and nervousness— when she started prowling the room, or glancing around a restaurant for the location of the cigarette machine—he would take her mind off smoking. Sometimes he took her to bed and made love to her as he had that first day. Once he'd even started an argument just to give her an opportunity to blow off steam.

But usually he simply tried to keep her entertained. They took daily walks through the Quarter. They took a paddleboat ride along the Mississippi River, and another day they went on a boat trip that wound its way through the murky, moss-hung bayous. Kyle drove out with her along the old River Road, pointing out the antebellum houses which they passed. "These used to be sugarcane plantations," he explained. "Some of them were pretty fancy. There's even one, up near Baton Rouge, where the owner had indoor plumbing."

"Indoor plumbing! When was it built?"

"Before the Civil War. What he did was put a huge cistern on the roof and pipe the water down into the house."

"Good grief."

"This road follows the Mississippi all the way to Baton Rouge. Of course, back then most people went by way of the river instead of the road. In fact, most of the houses face the river because that's the direction people usually approached from."

"Are we going to stop at any of the houses? Are they open for visitors?"

"Oh, yes. You can't really see many from the road. They're set back close to the river. We're going to see a good example of steamboat Gothic."

"What in the world is 'steamboat Gothic'?"

"It's the term they used to describe a certain type of architecture. The houses had a lot of ornate carving and fretwork along the roofs and columns that resembled the 'wedding cake' look of steamboats. Some of them were very colorful."

The first house they went to, called San Francisco, was a classic steamboat Gothic, trimmed in a multitude of gingerbread and ironwork. It was a cream-colored building trimmed in bright blue, and beside it stood a little round silo, also bright blue. Kyle explained that the matching outbuilding was a cistern for catching and holding rainwater.

When they headed up the drive to the next plantation on their schedule, Jessica let out a long sigh. "Now *this* is a plantation house."

Named Houmas House, it was the epitome of most people's idea of a southern plantation house. Two-storied, with three dormer windows on the sloping roof, it was a white Greek Revival building with evenly spaced, enormous round columns. The grounds around the house were dotted with ancient, gigantic oak trees, all draped in Spanish moss.

Kyle smiled at Jessica's comment. "Well, architecturally it's very typical of Louisiana houses. It's much simpler inside than it looks. There are the verandahs upstairs and down running around three sides of the house, and inside there's a long central hall on each floor and a breezeway running across the back. Nearly all the windows are French and open onto the verandahs, with louvered shutters. It's built for ventilation and keeping out the heat."

"Are those big cisterns out in back?"

Kyle smiled. "No, those are called 'garconnières.' Bachelor quarters. When the boys of the family became teenagers they were often put out there to live until they got married and established homes of their own. It gave them a sense of independence, I suppose."

"As well as keeping them from bothering the rest of the family," Jessica added with amusement. "I know a few parents who'd like to do that today."

They strolled through the house, exploring leisurely. With all the doors and windows open, shaded by the huge trees, the house was amazingly cool even without air conditioning. Jessica wandered onto the upper floor verandah and leaned against one of the massive columns, drinking in the lovely picture before her.

"I feel like I've been transported back in time."

"Expecting to see Rhett Butler soon?"

Jessica chuckled. "No. He resides back where I came from. Atlanta."

"Oh, that's true." Kyle sat down on the railing. "Nervous?"

"No. Why should I be nervous?"

"Not smoking."

"Oh." Jessica paused to consider the thought. "Isn't that weird? I had almost forgotten. Wow! That must be some kind of milestone, actually forgetting for a couple of hours that I was kicking the habit."

"It's a good sign."

Jessica smiled, then turned serious. "You've helped me more than I can tell you. I don't know what I'd have done without you."

Kyle smiled faintly. "Good. I hope you don't try to find out."

Kyle made sure she was entertained in the evenings, as well. Almost every night he took her to one New Orleans nightspot or another, going to Preservation Hall to hear classic jazz without any trimmings, or to a razzle-dazzle revue atop a downtown hotel, or to the celebrated Pat O'Brien's. Often they simply went to a quiet bar in the lobby of one of the old Quarter hotels, where they drank Ramos gin fizzes and listened to a soft piano. Jessica tried to remember the last time she had gone out like this, purely for fun rather than for business purposes. She thought it was a year ago, when Alan had landed their first really big client. But even that had had something to do with business. Everything about her life in Atlanta had something to do with business.

But not here. Not in New Orleans. Not with Kyle. And for the moment that was all she would allow to exist. Later, she told herself. She'd straighten it all out later, when she felt better, when she was rested. Right now all she wanted was this strange, newfound happiness.

One morning Kyle had to leave her alone while he went to do a job at one of the apartment buildings which he assured her was too long, dirty and tedious for her to accompany him. He hesitated, eyeing her uncertainly, until finally Jessica had to laugh, unsure whether she should be amused or angry.

"I can manage one morning by myself, I think," she told him. "You can go ahead. If I start wanting a cigarette, I promise that I'll go for a walk."

"Well, if you're sure . . ."

"I'm sure."

After he left she sat down to read, but soon she found that she was nervous after all, and a little frightened at facing a morning without cigarettes all on her own. She jumped up and grabbed her purse and left her apartment. On their daily walks through the Quarter, she and Kyle often stopped to visit with Annette Folse, who owned the perfumerie, and Jessica decided to go to her shop now. She walked the short distance to the shop and stepped inside, feeling a little awkward and foolish. There was a customer in the store, whom Annette was busy helping, but she looked up at Jessica's entrance and flashed a welcoming smile.

"Jessica! How nice to see you. Be with you in a moment."

"Don't hurry." Jessica dawdled near the door, examining a display of tiny vials, bottles and jars. The white-haired woman at the counter spent a few more moments vacillating and finally left, saying that she wanted to think about it a little more.

When she had gone, Annette let out a groan. "Oh, that woman! This is the third time she's come in in the past two days, and she still can't make up her mind. You'd think she was buying a diamond necklace instead of a little bottle of perfume. Well! Forget her. How are you doing? Still on the wagon?"

"Yes." Jessica held up her crossed fingers.

"Where's Kyle?"

"Working. I began feeling antsy sitting there by myself, so I thought I'd come visit. I hope you don't mind."

"Heavens, no. I'm glad. I like Kyle, but it's hard to have a really cozy chat with a man around. You know what I mean? Would you like some coffee? A Coke?"

"Coffee would be nice, thank you."

It was easy to talk to Annette. In fact, it was sometimes hard for Jessica to get a word in. Annette could carry on almost an entire conversation by herself. "What do you think of that storefront next door?" she asked Jessica now, as she went to the small back room to pour a couple of cups of coffee.

"I hadn't really noticed it. Why?"

"Because it's up for rent in two months. The lady who's been leasing it told me this morning that she was giving up the business. I'd love to have it, but I don't know exactly what I'd put in it."

"Expand your store?" Jessica suggested.

Annette raised one shoulder. "No. I don't have enough business to warrant it. I've thought of putting in an antique store. I love antiques, but I'm afraid I don't know enough about them to really run a store. Do you like antiques?"

"I've never really thought about it," Jessica admitted.

"Why don't I take you over to the stores on Magazine Street one day?" Annette offered eagerly. "I love going there. That's where most of the best antique places are. The ones in the Quarter are a lot smaller and more touristy. But I could happily spend *days* on Magazine Street. Anyway, I don't think I'd be able to make a go of antiques."

"How about a dress store? Or jewelry? Either of those would go with perfume."

"Yeah, that'd be nice. I don't know anything about jewelry, either, but I imagine I could do the clothes." Annette's eyes brightened as her mind whirred with ideas. Then she sighed. "No, it's not possible. I can't run two stores. I have enough trouble with one."

"You could hire extra help. It wouldn't be hard for someone else to sell the clothes, anyway."

Annette cocked her head on one side. "It's a very interesting idea. You know, I'm really tempted. Of course, getting the capital would be a problem. And it's kind of scary starting a new venture. I mean, I've known this place since I was a kid; it was no problem taking it over. But something entirely new . . ."

"I know what you mean. I was scared silly when Alan and I left our jobs to start our own firm. But it's exciting, too."

Annette smiled at her. "I really enjoy talking to you. Why don't you and I go out shopping sometime? Do you like to shop?"

"You mean for clothes?"

"Sure. Anything."

"Frankly, I've never done much of it. I don't have the time."

"I love it. I don't have enough time for it, either, but I usually manage to squeeze it in somehow. On Mondays my sister-in-law subs for me in the store. Why don't we go out next Monday? I'll show you all the boutiques, and we can have lunch. It'll be just like being in college again—except now we have enough money to buy something."

Jessica laughed. "Okay. I'd love it."

The following Monday she went out with Annette, who showed her all the fashionable places to shop in New Orleans. Jessica found she loved shopping. Always before, clothes buying had been a necessary but boring and time-consuming chore which she had accomplished with as much speed and efficiency as she could. Now, however, she was eager to look good for Kyle, and for that she needed an entirely different type of outfit from any she had. All her clothes were either dressy but plain and businesslike office clothes, or the outfits she wore at home, which she chose for their comfort, not their looks.

She yearned for more feminine dresses, things that were soft and pretty and emphasized her best features. She wanted outfits that were sexy, that would make Kyle get that certain look on his face and suggest that they stay home instead of going out. So she tromped happily from store to store, trying on dresses and spending her money recklessly.

It was also fun being with Annette. The other woman was witty and sophisticated and could appear elegantly polished, but when she was alone with Jessica, she displayed a thoroughly practical, down-to-earth, warm side, as well. In recent years Jessica had had little time to develop any friendships, especially with other career women like herself, who were as rushed as she was. She found that she had missed having a woman to talk to about her problems and hopes and the ordinary details of daily life. By the end of the day she was happy to accept Annette's invitation to spend the next Monday looking at antiques on Magazine Street.

The next morning Jessica and Kyle woke late. They puttered around, dressing, eating breakfast and reading the newspaper. "I had an idea," Kyle mentioned, putting aside the sports section. "Since we didn't see each other much yesterday, I thought we might take an excursion today."

"Sounds great. Where shall we go?"

"I was thinking of a cemetery."

Jessica's jaw dropped. "Cemetery?" she repeated weakly.

"Yeah. The old St. Louis one, over on Basin St."

"Why would we go to a cemetery?"

"The ones in New Orleans are fascinating. Wait'll you see. Didn't Viveca ever show you one?"

"No. I told you, I didn't visit her very often—and I certainly didn't stay long enough for us to get so desperate as to visit cemeteries."

He chuckled. "Just wait."

When they reached the gates of the ancient cemetery on the edge of the French Quarter, Jessica understood why he had wanted to show it to her. Rather than the grassy area dotted with low tombstones that she thought of when she heard the word cemetery, this was a jumbled collection of tombs standing above the ground like little houses. Many were taller than she was, and a few were imposing monuments. Scuffed paths meandered through the jumbled cemetery, and Jessica started along one, fascinated in an eerie way.

"They call it the City of the Dead sometimes."

"That's exactly what I was thinking it looked like," Jessica replied in a hushed tone. "Why is it built like this?"

"Because New Orleans is right on top of water. The city sits in a bowl, like this." He cupped his hands together. "It's actually below sea level. You can't dig six feet down. At first they'd fill in the land, making the cemetery higher than the land around it, but after a while they began putting the bodies in tombs instead. The wealthier families have family tombs, like this." He pointed to a large vault with a smaller one on each side, all encircled by a black wrought iron fence. The plaster had crumbled away from two of the tombs, revealing red brick beneath.

"What are those huge ones? Particularly famous families?"

"No. Those are the 'society' tombs. You know, the French Society. That's the biggest one. The Italian Mutual Benevolent Society. That's the marble circular one over there."

"I see." She stopped and stared at the high brick wall that ran around the cemetery. "Are those vaults in the wall?"

"Yeah. They're the less expensive ones. The French called them *fours* because they looked like bakers' ovens. That's the French word for oven."

"How gruesome. But they do look like that." They strolled along a meandering path. There were no trees or shrubs. Old, sagging slabs jutted out into the path, and sometimes a vault would cut off the walkway altogether.

"Here's the most famous one." Kyle led her to a family vault covered with chalked x's.

"What in the world?" Jessica looked at the inscription. It was written in French, and she could understand nothing except that it seemed to be the vault of a family named Paris.

"This vault is the Widow Paris's. That's Marie Laveau."

"Who?"

"The Voodoo Queen. Haven't you heard of her?" Jessica shook her head. "She was a famous practitioner of voodoo among the blacks here. People visit her grave and mark x's on it for good luck."

"You're kidding. Did she die a long time ago?"

"The 1880s."

"Good heavens. And they still come to her grave?"

He shrugged. "She was supposed to have powerful magic. She conducted voodoo rituals in the yard of her house. She'd dance with a snake. Everybody would drink rum and dance."

"Sounds like a wild party to me."

"Yeah, but they were also quite serious about it. She was greatly feared." They strolled away from the tomb toward one of the large monuments. "I can't believe you've visited New Orleans before and know as little about it as you do."

Jessica shrugged. "Oh, Viv may have told me some of this stuff, but I probably didn't listen. You know me. I've never paid much attention to things like that— folklore and history and—"

"And the world around you," he finished ironically. "But you seem interested in it now."

"Sure. It's fascinating. There's something so unusual and peaceful, and yet spooky, about this place. But when I used to come to New Orleans I didn't have the time to do things like this. I'd be here for a weekend or for a conference, something like that."

"You must be the only person in the world who came

to New Orleans for a conference and actually went to the meetings.''

Jessica laughed. "You think I'm an old stick-in-the-mud, don't you?''

"No,'' he replied softly. "Just someone who likes to see the world with blinkers on.''

"I don't know which description is more unflattering.''

Kyle stopped her and turned her to face him, putting his hands on her shoulders. "I don't mean to say anything to hurt you. I love you; you know that.''

Jessica quivered inside as she had the other time when Kyle had told her he loved her. She didn't understand how he could love her, yet it made her whole world sunny to hear him say it. Why did she enjoy the idea of his loving her . . . unless she felt the same way?

No, surely not. Why not? What else could it be? Half the reason she was stopping smoking—the most painful thing she'd ever done in her life—was to please him. Whenever Kyle entered the room, she lit up like a sparkler. His kisses and caresses aroused her in a way she'd never felt before, and his lovemaking was a shattering, beautiful explosion of joy. Whenever she let herself think of returning to Atlanta, which wasn't often, pain ripped through her heart. How could she call it anything but love? It didn't matter that she'd known him only two weeks; her heart had known him a lifetime.

She loved Kyle, and he loved her. Yet it was a terrible, terrible mess, and nothing could ever come of it. The futility, the pain of it, wrenched her.

"Don't cry." Kyle tilted up her chin so that he could look into her face. "Oh, baby, I'm sorry for what I said.''

She shook her head. "No. It's not that.''

"Then what?"

"Nothing."

"That's no answer."

"It's quitting smoking," she told him, seizing the first explanation that came into her mind. "It makes me nervous and weepy."

"Then you're sure you weren't hurt by what I said?"

"No, of course not."

"Jessica, you enjoy being in New Orleans, don't you?"

"Yes, I love it. How can you ask that?" She focused her luminous, tear-filled eyes on his face. "I'm very happy."

"Are you this happy in Atlanta?"

"What?" She paused, struggling to remember how she felt in Atlanta. "I—I've never thought of my life there in terms of happiness. I . . . yes, I suppose I was happy. In a different way. At least, until I got so tired and all."

"You didn't have to think about it to answer that you're happy here. Did you know you've been in New Orleans over two weeks? When you came, you said you were going to stay only a couple of weeks."

"Oh. Well, I—the doctor told me to take off a month, but at first I didn't want to. I guess I've decided to stay the whole month."

"I'm glad." He bent and kissed the top of her head. "I think you've changed, Jessica. There are things inside you that shine out now, and they didn't show before."

"I suppose I have. You changed me."

He smiled. "I'd like to take the credit. Maybe I've been a catalyst, but it's you who's done the changing. You're freer, happier, even lovelier." He smoothed back her hair from her face, his eyes warm and soft with love, telling her a thousand things more precious than words could express. "I love you, Jessica."

She went up on tiptoe to kiss him, her arms sliding around his neck. "And I love you."

Jessica called Alan that evening at his home. His wife Lynn answered the phone, and when she heard Jessica's voice, she exclaimed delightedly, "Jessica! How are you? We've been wondering about you."

"I'm feeling much better, thank you. I'm even trying to stop smoking."

"My goodness. You're really going all out, aren't you? Maybe when you come back you'll be able to persuade Alan to do the same."

"Is Alan there?"

"Yeah. You're lucky to have caught him, though. He just flew in from Florida today, and tomorrow he's going to Savannah."

"Oh, dear." Jessica experienced a twinge of guilt. "Sounds like he's pretty busy."

"Isn't he always?" Lynn replied dryly. "Let me get him on the phone."

There was a moment of silence, then Alan's hearty voice came on the line. "Jessica, how are you?"

"Fine, just fine. How about you?"

"We're chugging along. Listen, I hired a fantastic assistant. You're going to love her. She's the hardest worker we've ever employed. She's sharp, too; it didn't take her any time to catch on to practically everything."

"Good. Then you've been able to handle the workload?"

"Sure, no problem. Don't you worry about it."

"Great. Because I've decided to stay the full month."

"I figured you must have. I was surprised you didn't

call before, though. Everybody was expecting you to phone in every day to check up on things."

"Frankly, I've hardly given the business a thought," Jessica admitted. She felt another surge of guilt. She really shouldn't leave Alan in this situation any longer; she was well enough to return to work. And she knew the workload was too much for him, even with an able assistant.

"Good. That's what the doctor ordered, huh?"

"Yeah. I'll call you in a couple of weeks and let you know exactly when I'm returning, okay?" Jessica firmly suppressed her guilt. She was determined that she was going to have the next two weeks with Kyle, no matter what. She was going to seize all the happiness she could before it had to end. Surely two weeks with the man she loved wasn't too much to ask.

"Okay, talk to you then."

They said their good-byes and hung up. Neither of them liked to linger on the telephone. They had had to spend too much of their working lives talking on the telephone to want to do any extra on their own time. That was why Lynn nearly always answered the phone at Alan's house.

The following two weeks went by far too quickly for Jessica. No matter how often or how long she was with Kyle, it never seemed to be enough, because looming in the back of her mind was the knowledge that soon it would all be over. Soon she would have to leave New Orleans and return to the real world. At times she dreamed that Kyle would decide to go back to medicine, that he would tell her that he would move to Atlanta when she did and set up a practice there. Because he loved her he might realize that her world wasn't so bad, after all. Maybe he'd see that he could fit in. But Jessica tried not to let herself hope.

The two weeks passed, but Jessica made no move about going home. She determinedly ignored the calendar and let herself drift into staying another day, then another, until soon it had been five weeks since she arrived in New Orleans. Perhaps, somehow, if she did nothing, everything would work out. She couldn't bring herself to be the one to smash their lovely, private little world into smithereens.

Not smoking had grown easier daily until finally it began to seem as if she were free of the habit. She no longer thought of smoking every waking moment of the day, and she could now see another person smoking without longing to light up a cigarette herself. She walked past cigarette machines and the cigarette counters in stores without giving them a second glance. Best of all, there was no longer the awful physical need for nicotine. She could laugh now without coughing, and wake up in the morning without feeling that her chest had acquired a two-pound weight during the night.

She turned to Kyle one afternoon, her eyes gleaming. "You know what? I think I've kicked it!"

Kyle grinned. "Congratulations! I was beginning to hope that myself. When did you realize it?"

"Just now."

"We'll have to celebrate, then. How about going out for dinner tonight? I wanted to do something special tonight, anyway."

"Why?"

"Because it's a special night."

"You mean because I've quit smoking?"

"Well, that, too. But there's something else."

"What?"

"I can't tell you. You'll find out tonight."

"Meanie. Now I'll spend all the rest of the day wondering what it is."

"Don't worry about that. Just dress up extra special and we'll make it a night to remember."

Chapter 10

JESSICA LINKED HER ARM THROUGH KYLE'S, A SMILE breaking sunnily across her face. Tonight she was walking on air. She wore a vivid turquoise dress of shiny silk jacquard which she had impulsively bought the day before in a boutique on St. Charles Avenue. The high neck of the dress covered her throat up to her chin, falling in soft folds; the long sleeves had a small puff at the shoulders. But it was the bright, almost spangled appearance of the material that gave the dress its flair; that and the bias draping on one side at the thigh, which lent a touch of femininity to the severe lines of the dress and pulled it to a clinging tightness above the knees.

Jessica felt as feminine and vivid as her dress. She had arranged her hair atop her head in a tangle of curls with a few seductive wisps trailing down her neck and around her face. It wasn't a style she was used to wearing, but she found she liked the way it looked. With Kyle she could look pretty. She didn't have to worry about whether she appeared frilly and empty-headed, or no-nonsense and even threatening.

Kyle glanced down and caught her smile. He grinned back, his eyes studying her lovingly. "You look beautiful tonight."

"Thank you. I feel . . . just super."

"Good. So do I. Tonight's a perfect night for a very special dinner."

"When are you going to tell me why it's special?"

"Later."

Jessica made a playful grimace. "That's cruel."

"I'll tell you this much: We're going to a restaurant to suit the occasion."

Jessica had worn this dress because Kyle had told her to wear something fancy. But it had surprised her when he arrived at her apartment as dressed-up as she was. He wore a fitted cream-colored silk suit with a muted tie and shirt, tastefully expensive. Jessica had stared and thought that the restaurant they were going to must be elegant indeed to warrant Kyle's attire.

When they entered the restaurant Jessica's guess was confirmed. It was tucked away in a narrow blue building in the French Quarter, thoroughly unprepossessing on the outside. The inside, however, was plush. An antique pink-and-green patterned Persian rug lay over the gleaming hardwood floor. Crystal lights adorned the ceiling, and the walls were paneled halfway up, then covered with muted, textured wallpaper above the paneling. Ornate plaster moldings ran along the tops of the walls and spread out on the ceiling around the large chandelier. Antique tables and chairs dotted the room, and in one corner stood a short, highly carved mahogany bar. A tuxedo-clad maitre d' glided up to them and asked in hushed tones whether they had a reservation. When Kyle gave his name, the man said, "Ah, yes, the garden table."

He turned and led them through the dining room and into a narrow paneled hallway. They emerged onto a bricked patio lushly decorated with greenery. A central fountain flowed in a slow, soothing trickle. On two sides of the enclosed garden were the ancient brick walls of other buildings, draped with ivy. Glass doors fenced in the patio on the other sides so that many tables in the restaurant had a view of the garden. There were only a few tables actually placed on the patio, and each was sheltered by small trees and other plants, conveying a sense of privacy.

"Oh, Kyle, this is beautiful," Jessica whispered as the man seated them and left with a courtly bow.

He smiled. "You don't have to whisper. It's not sacred."

"It's so lovely it seems like everything should be hushed."

"I thought you'd like it. They have an upstairs dining room, too, with tables on the balcony overlooking the street. It's quaint, but noisier and not so private."

"I prefer this. You can't even hear those people at the next table." Jessica glanced through the fronds of a palm to the table in question. A family sat there, two children and their parents, all dressed to the teeth and chatting happily to each other, but Jessica and Kyle could hear nothing of their conversation but a low murmur. This was definitely a private place to dine. Jessica slipped her hand into Kyle's rough palm, and he closed his hand around hers. They gazed at each other, content simply to be close to each other. Jessica couldn't remember when she'd been happier.

The meal was as leisurely and delightful as the atmosphere of the garden. Kyle continued to refuse to discuss the occasion for the ''special'' evening, but Jessica went along with him laughingly, willing to enjoy the dinner without racing to find the reason. About halfway through the meal, a woman's high-pitched voice sliced through the air. ''Jimmy!''

Jessica and Kyle swung around, startled, toward the table nearest them, where the family group sat. Jessica stared uncomprehendingly. The family seemed to have suddenly gone wild. The father was slapping the little boy on the back. The mother's face was contorted with fear, and the daughter sat stiff and staring. The boy's arms flailed wildly and his face blazed with panic, but no sound came from his throat. Before Jessica could even realize what was happening, Kyle lunged from his chair and vaulted across the low brick planter separating their table from the section of the patio where the other table sat.

He reached the boy in an instant and pushed the parents aside. The father stumbled backward, gaping. ''What—''

Kyle didn't bother to even look at the man. He hauled the child out of his chair, and without a wasted motion, braced his foot on the chair seat and tossed the sturdy youngster face down along his thigh. The boy lay at a strong downward slant.

Kyle struck the child hard on his back, and at the same time bellowed, ''Get me a knife—sharp and small. Fast! And a straw!''

Waiters, quick to sense a crisis, were already gathering, and fortunately one was quick-witted enough to race for the kitchen as soon as Kyle shouted. The child jerked and thrashed about, and his mother continued her high-pitched screeching. The father reached out to pull the boy away. "Hey, wait a minute! What the hell do you think you're doing?"

"Damn it, I'm a doctor!" Kyle snapped. "He's choking."

Jessica stood frozen, her fingers gripping the edge of the table, and stared at Kyle and the boy. She knew that Kyle was battling death. There was no time for ambulances, paramedics or hospitals. In a matter of minutes without oxygen the child would be dead. She couldn't move, couldn't think, hardly breathed. But her entire soul and heart rushed out to Kyle, willing him all her strength.

The waiter reappeared on the run from the kitchen, a paring knife in one hand and a straw in another. Kyle moved quickly but with an almost inhuman calm. He laid the boy down on the bricks, dipped the knife into the father's glass of brandy and sloshed more on the boy's throat. "Hold him down," he ordered, steel in his voice. "Keep him perfectly still. It'll hurt."

Obeying the authority in Kyle's voice, the father went down on his knees and placed his hands on the boy's widespread arms. The waiter grabbed his legs, and Kyle straddled him, one hand thrusting the child's chin up and holding it still. The other hand held the knife. The straw went unorthodoxly between his teeth. He lowered the knife and made a shallow, precise cut. The boy's body bucked, his agony made all the worse by the fact that no sound came from his open mouth. Kyle set down the knife and inserted the straw in the slit in the child's throat. Air whistled in and out of the straw.

Kyle sat back on his heels, his rigid body slumping. Jessica realized that the child had been saved. At last her legs moved. She went around the planter to where Kyle sat. "Call an ambulance," Kyle ordered, his voice weary. "He needs to go to a hospital and get the piece of food removed from his throat. The tracheotomy needs attention so that it won't get infected."

The mother, crying now, knelt beside her child, smoothing back his hair from his forehead. Tears were streaming from the youngster's eyes, too, but the awful panic had left his features. The waiter released the boy's legs and ran for a telephone. Kyle moved off the boy and sat on the bricked flooring, resting his forehead on his knees. Jessica squatted beside him and slid her arm around his shoulders. There was blood on his fingers and a spot of it on one of his cuffs. His forehead and upper lip were damp, his hands cold.

Kyle glanced up and offered her a faint smile. "Not exactly a restful evening out, is it?"

Jessica shook her head, smiling, tears standing in her eyes. She was filled to bursting with pride and love. "You saved his life," she whispered.

He tilted back his head and released a long breath. "Yeah. Thank God they got me that knife in time."

By now the maitre d' and waiters had gathered to ring the drama, blocking it from the view of the other patrons, and soon another employee arrived with a folding screen from another part of the restaurant, which they set up to block the view from most of the rest of the diners. Kyle stood up and took Jessica's hand, starting back to their table.

The father ran after them. "Wait! Just a minute." Kyle turned, and the man reached out to pump his hand. "Thank you. Thank you. My God, when I think what would have happened if you hadn't been here . . . And I tried to stop you!"

"It's all right. I was here, and the boy's okay. It was

perfectly understandable that you protested what I did. But I didn't have time to explain.''

"My name's Jim Sommers. If I can ever . . . ever do anything for you . . .''

"It's quite all right, Mr. Sommers. Go on back to your wife and kids.''

The man babbled his thanks a few more times, and Mrs. Sommers came up to weep over Kyle a bit. Finally the maitre d' extricated them from the uncomfortable situation and led them back to their table. "We are so grateful for your quick action, Dr. Morrow,'' he told him quietly as he held out Jessica's chair for her to sit down. "The management can't thank you enough. Is there anything we can do for you?''

"No. I just need to clean up a bit.'' He lifted his arm with the blood-stained cuff.

"Yes, of course. Come with me, please.''

He led Kyle off toward the bathroom, while Jessica sat down at their table. In a few minutes two paramedics arrived and loaded the boy onto a stretcher. "Cut sure looks professional,'' one of the attendants remarked. "Looks like a surgeon did it.''

Was that what Kyle had been? A surgeon? Jessica realized that she had never asked him what his specialty had been. Her chest felt suddenly, strangely heavy. She wondered if she really knew Kyle at all.

Kyle returned and flopped down in his seat. Sighing, he brushed the hair back from his forehead. "Do you want to stay?'' He gestured toward their half-finished meal.

Jessica shook her head. "No. I couldn't eat, not now.''

"Me either. Let's go.''

He signaled to their waiter, and when the man arrived,

he asked for their bill. The waiter shook his head emphatically. "Oh, no, sir, there's no charge. Mr. Walters, the maitre d', specifically told me that your dinner tonight was to be compliments of the house. A token of our appreciation for what you did."

"Oh. Well, thank you. And Mr. Walters, of course."

After much nodding and bowing the waiter let them leave, and they slipped through the hallway to the street outside. Kyle took Jessica's hand and swung their intertwined hands gently between them as they walked. Jessica glanced at him. His face was closed and distant. He seemed very far away from her. She wondered what feelings and memories the emergency had stirred up in him. "Kyle . . ." she began softly. "What kind of doctor were you?"

His gaze flickered toward her, and he smiled. "The best."

Jessica grimaced. As always, he was using humor to escape talking about something he didn't like. "You know what I mean. What was your specialty?"

"Surgery."

"Why did you quit?"

He shrugged. "I didn't want to do it any longer. Too much pressure."

"You aren't telling me the whole story, and I know it."

"Does it really matter?"

"Yes! It matters to me. I can't understand how you could leave such a profession just to . . . to loaf around. Don't you miss it? Don't you ever regret it?"

"No. It's simply part of the past."

"I can't believe that. I mean, if we were talking about a stockbroker or an insurance salesman or someone like that, I could understand it. But you were doing something useful. Something important and productive! When I think of what you did for that boy—he would have died if you hadn't been there!''

''Probably,'' Kyle agreed. ''It's fortunate I was. But stop trying to lay a guilt trip on me. Emergencies like that are rare. Usually the absence of one doctor in this world doesn't make a bit of difference. There are plenty to take my place. People aren't dying because I left; they simply go to another physician.''

''I'm not trying to make you feel guilty!'' Jessica snapped. ''I'm trying to understand how, with all you had going for you, you could have dropped out.''

''How do you know what I had going for me?'' he retorted gruffly.

''I can imagine what it must feel like, doing something so important and necessary. I mean, my accomplishments thrill me, but they're nothing compared to what it must be like to save lives every day.''

''Oh, I had a God complex, all right.'' Kyle's voice was light and bitter. ''For a long time I thought I could do no wrong. I got a wonderful rush of power every time I stepped into the operating theater. I was Super Surgeon. Patients loved me; they thanked me all the time for saving their lives or the lives of people close to them. Nurses scurried to do my bidding. Other doctors listened to my advice. I was on top of the hill, and there was no such thing as taking a fall.''

''What happened?''

His smile was brief and twisted. ''I fell, of course.''

''What do you mean?''

''I killed a boy.''

For a moment Jessica was too stunned to do anything but stumble along after him, her mouth hanging open in shock. Kyle didn't look at her, just kept on walking until they reached his building. He opened the front door and climbed the steps, Jessica following closely behind him.

After they entered his apartment, Jessica planted her fists on her hips and demanded, "What are you talking about? What do you mean, you killed a boy?"

"Just what I said." Kyle's tanned face was drawn and weary, his usually warm brown eyes blank. "I performed an appendectomy on a child, a routine thing, something I did all the time. But his heart stopped while he was on the table, and I couldn't revive him. He died."

Jessica frowned, her heart contracting in pity and love. "Oh, Kyle, I'm so sorry." She moved forward and put her hands on his arms. "I know how it must have hurt you. But surely that wasn't your fault. I've read about cases like that before. Any time a person goes under anesthetic, there's a chance of his heart failing, isn't there?"

Kyle shrugged. "It's not common, but neither is it inconceivable. There's always a risk a patient may have an undetected heart defect. It's happened before. You know: The operation was a success, but the patient died."

"It's not your fault! You didn't do anything wrong! Things like that happen. It's fate. No one could have foreseen—"

"But I didn't need to operate!" Kyle ground out. "I could have left his appendix alone. It wasn't an emergency. I should have waited to see what developed instead of jumping in and cutting him. But my schedule was full for the next two or three days. I knew I'd have to cancel one of the other operations if his appendix got worse and I had to operate. So I moved him up to Tuesday, even though he didn't require the surgery yet. For the sake of my schedule!''

Kyle swung around and began to pace the room, words pouring out of him like long-trapped water through a broken dam. His nostrils were pinched, his lips white and taut. ''You know why I didn't want to mess up my schedule? Because it would mean less money for me. I talk about you chasing money—hell, I played with people's lives in order to get it! So what if the kid didn't need the surgery that day? I had an open slot on my schedule, an hour that wasn't making money. If I had to reschedule him later, I would be pushing aside a money-making operation. If I operated on him immediately, I'd be making more money. He might never have needed that appendectomy! I could have waited and seen whether he did, but I was too interested in making a buck.''

Kyle stopped at a window and leaned against it, staring out, his arms crossed above his head and resting on the glass. He gazed at the street below, not seeing it, as if he were watching a movie in his mind. ''For three years I chased the almighty dollar. When I wasn't operating I was investing my money, talking to my financial adviser about tax breaks and investments. I overworked myself; I scheduled too many operations; I worried too much about what I should do with my money. I had to invest it; I sure as hell didn't have time to enjoy it. I got a Mercedes; it was a status symbol. And a gorgeous house—another status symbol. I was never in either one enough to enjoy them. My wife chose all the furnishings and pictures for our house. I didn't have the time or interest; none of it meant anything to me except as proof that I had made it.'' He swung around to face Jessica, his features etched with scorn and self-hatred. ''You think you're ambitious? You're an amateur compared to me. I was eaten up with ambition. And I killed a child for it!''

Jessica gazed at him, her eyes swimming with sympathetic tears. She felt his anguish inside herself, his self-blame and searing pain. ''Oh, Kyle. Darling, I'm so sorry.'' She slid her arms around him, wanting to comfort him. He clung to her, his arms digging painfully into her ribs, pressing her so tightly to his chest that she could hardly breathe. Jessica closed her eyes, her mind racing to think of something to say, the right words to ease the pain of years. Don't hurt, she thought fiercely. I don't want you ever to hurt. She wanted to share his burden, to take his tragedy upon herself, to ease his load, yet she knew it was impossible.

''Ah, Jessie, Jessie,'' he breathed against her hair. ''I feel better just holding you. I love you.'' He kissed her hair. ''I need you so much it scares me.''

Gradually his hold loosened. He dropped his arms and moved away. Flopping down on the couch, he linked his hands behind his head and stared up at the ceiling. ''Well, that's it. After that boy died, I took a good, hard look at my life. I saw what my greed and ambition had gotten me: an empty house; possessions I didn't need or use or care for; a lot of money that didn't do a damn thing for me; a wife I didn't love and who didn't love me. There wasn't any happiness or love or joy in my life. I'd forgotten how to live—if I ever knew how. And I'd sacrificed a child on the altar of whatever I worshipped, though I wasn't even sure what that was. It was a pretty miserable picture.''

He was silent for a moment. Jessica prompted, ''So you gave up your practice?''

''Yeah. I realized what idiocy it all was. I sold the house, the car, everything, and gave away what I couldn't sell. Of course, Beth wasn't having any of that. She told me I was crazy and filed for divorce. I came to New Orleans to rest and sort out my life. I'd been here once before when I was in college; it was the only vacation I'd ever taken. When I got here I fell in love with the city and stayed. I bought these old houses in the Quarter and fixed them up, rented them as apartments. The life suited me. The peace and quiet, the atmosphere, the people. It's endlessly fascinating, slow-paced, accepting. It was exactly what I needed.''

"And is it still?" Jessica asked softly.

Kyle glanced at her in surprise. "Why, yes, of course. This is where I belong."

Jessica placed her hands together carefully, searching for exactly the right words. "Kyle," she began slowly, "you mustn't continue to blame yourself for that boy's death. It doesn't do anyone any good. Perhaps you acted selfishly in doing the operation early, but if you'd waited for the appendix to get worse, he would still have reacted the same way when you *did* operate on him. Suppose you had waited two days until it became an emergency? His heart wouldn't have gotten any stronger; it would still have failed.''

"His appendix might not have gotten worse. I might not have had to operate."

"It's also very possible that it would have."

"Oh, yeah, it was a gamble. But I was gambling with someone else's life!''

"Kyle, please . . . even if you made a mistake, you aren't the first person to do so. Not even the first doctor. You're only human. You can't expect to know everything, to be perfectly right every time. The consequences can be tragic when a doctor makes an error, but the fact remains that doctors will make errors, just as all of us will. You have to forgive yourself. You can't keep on punishing yourself.''

"Punishing myself? What do you mean? I'm not punishing myself. You asked me why I left medicine, and I told you. I don't sit around and dwell on it.''

"What do you call giving up your career? Cutting yourself off from the thing you worked so long and hard to achieve? It's penance.''

His brows rushed together. "Didn't you hear anything I said? I had no love for medicine, no great calling to help my fellow man. My career was nothing but self-aggrandizement. Ambition. Selfish ambition and greed. Can't you understand? I didn't love my career. I have no desire to return to it. When that boy died I realized what a shallow sham my life was. I'll never go back.''

Sadness settled on Jessica, seeping through her skin and down to the center of her bones. She hurt for Kyle, whose tragic mistake haunted him. And she hurt for herself, for she faced the shattering of the tender, almost unformed dreams she had harbored for their future. Despite their differences, she had hoped that somehow things would work out between her and Kyle. Down deep she had dreamed that Kyle would decide to resume his practice of medicine and move to Atlanta with her.

But now she saw that he would never leave New Orleans. He loved the city. And something far stronger than a mere decision to change his lifestyle had prompted Kyle to leave medicine and pursue his present life. A child's death had tainted medicine for him forever. He was dedicated to living a life that was totally opposite to the one he'd lived before; he'd never change, never go back. He'd never fit in with Jessica and her life.

Tears glittered in her eyes, and Jessica turned her head aside so that Kyle wouldn't see them. She wanted to burst into tears, but that wasn't her way. Instead she walked away from Kyle, pressing her lips together to hold back the sorrow.

It was over now. She had to face it. The idyllic time she had spent with Kyle was a dream, a moment stolen out of time. It couldn't last forever. She had delayed as long as she could—longer, really. Now she must give it up. She had to return to Atlanta. That was her life, everything she had worked for since she was an adult. She couldn't give up everything now that the firm was really on the brink of success.

Even if she were willing to throw her own life aside and move to New Orleans to be with Kyle, a future between them would be impossible. She'd get another job here; she'd work and strive as she always had. It was her nature. It was what she wanted. She wouldn't fit into Kyle's indolent life. It had been fun for a while, but eventually she'd get itchy to do something. Their passion had had an opportunity to ripen because she had been told to rest and relax for a month. Once she started working again, once she returned to her old self, the lovely relationship between them would crumble.

Kyle would resent her activity, her absences; he'd want her to slow down, to do things with him as they had this month. He'd want to go sailing on the lake when she was rushing to meet a deadline. He would irritate her. When her alarm rang early in the morning and she rushed to dress and reach the office on time, she'd resent his lying in bed snoozing. Soon she would begin to prod him to do something, to return to medicine, to be productive.

It was obvious that they could never have a life together. She'd known it from the start. She had simply let herself drift along dreaming for a few weeks, hoping that the situation would somehow resolve itself. But after what Kyle had just told her, she knew her dreams were futile. Kyle wouldn't change. And she wouldn't either. It was time to admit it. She would have to say good-bye to him and return to Atlanta.

Tears spilled over and coursed down her cheeks. Kyle came up behind her softly and rested his hands on her shoulders. "Here, what's this? Why are you crying?"

Jessica shook her head, forcing a smile, and brushed away the tears. "It's just a sad story. I'm sorry that it happened to you."

Kyle turned her around, and his hands cupped her face. For a long moment he studied her, taking in every detail: the smooth skin, now lightly golden from the sun; the lips, softened with emotion; the green eyes, sparkling with tears. "How lovely you are," he breathed. "This wasn't the way I meant the evening to go at all. I was going to—"

Jessica raised her hand to his lips, stopping his words. "Don't. It doesn't matter now. Make love to me, Kyle. Please, make love to me."

Chapter 11

JESSICA AWAKENED, PRODDED TO CONSCIOUSNESS BY A
confusing, troubled dream. Beside her Kyle lay sprawled
across the bed in sleep, the sheets twisted around his
legs, one arm flung off the mattress and dangling. It
looked as though he'd had as restless a night as she had.
Wearily Jessica sat up and combed her fingers through
her hair. A dull ache settled in her chest. Their lovemaking last night had been slow and soft and sweet, with an
element of sadness twisting through it; it was as if Kyle,
too, had sensed that it would be their last time together.
The beauty of it made it all the harder to leave this
morning.

But there was no sense in putting it off. Jessica flung
back the sheet and slid out of bed, moving quietly so as
not to awaken Kyle. She gathered up her clothes, then
slipped into the bathroom to shower and dress. By the
time she was finished and her hair wound into a wet knot

atop her head, Kyle was awake. He opened the door to the bathroom just as she reached for the knob to leave. Seeing her, he smiled sleepily, rubbing a hand through his rumpled hair and yawning. "Hello, sweetheart." One long arm snaked out to wrap around her shoulders and pull her close. He planted a kiss on the top of her head. "Mmm, you smell good."

Jessica slipped out of his arms, suddenly finding his embrace unbearable. She had to get this over with. It wouldn't get any easier if she put it off. Even though her heart and body longed to stay, even though she ached to linger in Kyle's strong arms and put off her leave-taking, she knew she must not. With every moment she remained, the agony of leaving would simply get worse. She didn't want to go; yet she knew that sooner or later she would have to. There was no other choice for them. The longer she kept silent about it, the longer she would have to struggle with this horrible indecision, the hurt, the dread of pain, the frantic wishing that somehow it could come out all right.

A clean cut. *Do it now.* Even though it would hurt, it would at least be over. Jessica walked out of the bathroom, leaving the door open. Behind her Kyle began to lather his cheeks and chin. Jessica laced her fingers together and studied them. Heart pounding, her stomach like ice, she turned to look back at Kyle. He was humming as he shaved, thrusting out his chin to shave his throat. "Kyle?" she began, her voice tremulous.

"Hmm?" He turned his eyes toward her briefly and continued with his shaving.

"I need to talk to you."

"Okay. Shoot."

"I—it's been over a month since I came here. To New Orleans, I mean. And, well, my time's up."

His hand stopped in mid-stroke. He lowered the razor and turned to face her. "What do you mean?"

"I took four weeks off from the firm, and that's gone now. I've already stayed longer than I told them I would. In a few more days I'll have been here six weeks. I—I have to go back to Atlanta."

"No!" he bit out sharply, his brows meeting in a dark frown. "Jessie, you can't."

Jessica drew herself up. "I can. I must. It's time—I'm healthy again. I've even stopped smoking. I have a job, and I have to go back to it."

"You don't have to do anything," he countered roughly. "If you go, it'll be your own choice."

"All right, then. I choose to go back to Atlanta."

His eyes flared with a dark light, and he swung back to the mirror. With movements that were too swift, too precise, he continued to shave. The muscles of his body were tight with strain. Jessica waited, surprised at his seeming acquiescence. Then, abruptly, he swished the lather from his razor and flung it down on the counter. Whirling, he took three long, aggressive strides toward her. Instinctively Jessica backed up, her heart pounding at the hard, bright glare in his eyes.

"Why!" he barked. "Why have you suddenly decided to go back to Atlanta? How can you just walk away?"

"It isn't easy!" Jessica flared. "I don't want to leave you."

"Then why are you doing it?"

"I have to. I can't stay here forever. I have a life, too, you know. Something outside of this little dream world we've inhabited the past few weeks."

"A life? Is that what you call it? It sounds to me as though all you have there is a job. An all-consuming career. You've had more of a real life here than you ever had in Atlanta.''

"It's *not* real.'' Jessica crossed her arms across her chest and walked away from him. "It's been a fantasy, that's all. I can't live like this. What would I do? It's all right for a few weeks, but—''

"All right? Is that what you think of the time we've spent together? Merely all right?''

"No, of course not. Quit twisting my words. Our time together has been glorious, beautiful. It's the most wonderful thing I've ever experienced.''

"Then why are you running back to Atlanta?''

"It wouldn't last! Why are you making this so difficult? Don't you see? It can never work between us. This has been wonderful, but it was a dream. It was an idyllic period, a moment of time taken out of reality. There were no pressures, no obligations, no other people. It wasn't real!''

"Reality is only hard and serious?'' Kyle challenged her, hands clenched on his hips. "Only drudgery and pain are real? Why can't this be real? Why can't we go on as we have? Jessica!'' He moved forward and clamped his hands on her shoulders, forcing her to look into his intent, determined eyes. "I love you. I want to marry you. That was the big occasion last night, the reason for the fancy dinner and dressing up—before everything got all fouled up. I was going to ask you to marry me. I still want it. Even though this isn't a particularly romantic setting, I'm asking you now. Marry me. Stay with me.''

Jessica's throat tightened chokingly. She couldn't have had her choice presented more clearly: work or love; emotion or reason; her mother's life, aimless and controlled by feelings, or her own, firmly directed and controlled solely by herself. She had never imagined that it could hurt so much to choose the life she had always wanted, that love could threaten to pull her so far off course. "Kyle, I—I—it's not that simple."

"It *is* that simple. You're the one who's making something difficult out of it."

"This is one brief month. But what's back there in Atlanta is twenty-eight years. It's my life!"

"This one month is what your life could be. Freedom, love, fun . . . God, Jessica, why do you want to go back to that trap?"

"Trap? My career is not a trap!" Jessica flared, jerking out of his grasp. "It's what I want to do. It's what I've worked for all my life."

"It's a cage you've built for yourself, a negative reaction to your mother's lifestyle. It's nothing of what you feel or want, merely fear of being like Viv."

"How dare you!" Jessica quivered with anger, hardly able to speak she was so enraged. "I'm not the one who's trapped myself. It's you! You're the one who ran away in fear because you'd made a mistake. You misjudged something, and it was costly. And it scared you so badly you took cover in New Orleans. You threw away your whole life, everything you'd worked for, because you were so afraid you might make another mistake. Don't try to tell me that you have no love of medicine; no one works that hard for all those years if they have no feeling for it. There are lots of other, faster ways you could have made money."

She whirled away, her rage feeding itself, and stalked across the room. She turned back, her eyes narrowed. "Oh, no, it wasn't that you decided to give up chasing success for a peaceful lifestyle. You cut yourself off from your profession, from something that was very dear to you. You forced yourself into a mold that was the opposite of what you had been because you didn't have the guts to stick with it after you'd failed once. You let one mistake, one failure, ruin you. You're the one who's living in a trap of his own making, not me!''

Kyle's mouth whitened and turned grim; his nostrils flared, then pinched. He stepped back. ''I see.'' His hand half rose, then fell back down in a defeated gesture. ''Well, I guess there's nothing left to say, is there?''

Jessica's heart froze. Why had she said that? Why? Kyle had infuriated her with his assumption of superiority, and she had lashed back instinctively. But why had she had to say something that would hurt Kyle so much? She believed what she'd said; Kyle *had* made a trap for himself. But she needn't have been so harsh, so cruel. She wished she could take back her hastily uttered words. But she had said them, and they'd be with them forever. There was nothing she could do or say to put it right. It was over between them; she'd known it had to end. And now her angry words had killed whatever chance there might have been for them to part with any amiability or friendship. Kyle was hurt and furious with her now. Jessica swallowed and looked away. ''Yes. Well, good-bye, Kyle.''

''Good-bye, Jessica.''

She walked blindly out of the bedroom and through the living area of Kyle's apartment, grabbing her purse from the coffee table. She shoved back the heavy bolt and stepped out into the hall, pulling the door to behind her. Almost running, she went down the stairs and out the main door into the heat of the French Quarter street.

It didn't take Jessica long to leave New Orleans after she had made her decision. As soon as she reached

Viveca's apartment she pulled out her suitcases and began to pack, pausing only to call for an airplane reservation and to let Alan know she was returning. With the ruins of her love affair crumbled around her, she had no desire to stay any longer than absolutely necessary. She was an expert in packing, and she soon cleaned the place of all her possessions and stuffed them into her bags. She hesitated for a moment over the delicate bottle of perfume Kyle had bought her in Annette's shop, and tears threatened to pour from her eyes again. But sternly she blinked away the tears and wrapped a steely control around her emotions. She slipped the bottle into the suitcase and carefully surrounded it with soft clothing so it wouldn't break in flight. When she had finished packing she phoned for a cab and carried her suitcases to the gate of the courtyard. Then she returned to lock up the apartment and dropped the key into her bag. When she got back to Atlanta she would mail the key to Viveca in San Francisco.

Jessica caught an evening flight to Atlanta and arrived before ten o'clock. The airport was very familiar; yet after her absence it seemed curiously foreign as well, like something out of a far distant past. Shrugging off the uneasy feeling, Jessica collected her luggage and caught a taxi to her apartment. When the cab pulled into the parking lot she saw her small, foreign-made compact in its assigned slot. There were the same trees, same hedge, same pothole in the middle of the lot; it was all just as it had been when she left. But again, she knew the almost queasy sensation that it was far removed from reality and the present.

She carted the bags into her apartment and hastened to turn on the air conditioning to cool the hot, stale rooms. After opening her bags on the bed she began to efficiently unpack as she always did after her trips. After a few minutes she rebelled. She simply couldn't do this right now! Almost desperately Jessica cast around for something else to do. She needed to get out, to do something. The heat was stifling, and the walls of the apartment were suffocatingly close. Had Viveca's apartment been that much bigger than this one? No, it was simply that Viv's place had had more windows, which gave it an airy, sunny appearance.

Jessica had never noticed before how dark and cramped her own apartment was. She ought to move; she could afford it. Why hadn't she done so? Surely it wouldn't take that much time to find an apartment. She'd start looking in the newspaper ads that weekend.

Jessica thought of the empty cupboards and refrigerator in the kitchen. That was a good excuse to get out. She'd go shopping. She whisked her purse off the dining table and hurried out. It was good to be outside again, she thought as she clattered down the metal and concrete steps to her car. The sun was hot on her skin, but at least it wasn't muggy like it was in New Orleans. Atlanta had a much nicer climate. It was good to be home, really. She glanced around the apartment complex and sighed. Then why did everything look so dreary, so boring, so . . . so ordinary?

She went to the supermarket where she had usually shopped when she was home—when she remembered to shop, that was. It was a huge, modern building with the latest in shopping carts, check-out counters and computerized cash registers. Even this late in the evening, it was busy. A woman in high heels and a slightly bedraggled gray suit clicked quickly past Jessica, her chin thrust forward purposefully. Jessica watched her hurry down the aisle and remembered all the times she herself had dropped by after staying late at the office, speeding with her cart through the aisles to grab a frozen dinner, or milk and cereal for her breakfast the next morning. She couldn't recall ever purchasing an entire week's worth of groceries at one time, or buying from an organized list. She doubted that she had ever gone to any check-out counter except the express lane, where she fretted and fumed over customers in front of her who wrote out checks and clerks who rang the groceries up too slowly.

Jessica dawdled along the aisles, perusing the packages of meat spread out in the refrigerated meat section. Every cut was set on a white foam tray and covered tightly with plastic wrap, a white price and weight tag stuck on the top. Jessica thought of the chin-high old butcher's counter at the little grocery in the Quarter where she had gone. There had been a window running the length of it and inside chickens, fish, shrimp, beef and pork had been laid out. When she ordered what she wanted, the apron-clad butcher behind the counter whisked it out, cut it up and wrapped it in white butcher paper, sealing it with a strip of red tape and scribbling the price on the front in pencil. Not as sanitary as this, she supposed, but Jessica couldn't stop a little twinge of nostalgia.

She smiled, thinking of the expeditions she and Kyle had made to the grocery, arguing playfully over what they would buy, gossiping with the butcher and the middle-aged lady at the front cash register. Jessica's eyes misted with tears as she remembered Kyle curling his arm around her shoulders and leaning his head down to hers to whisper something highly indelicate in her ear.

She would laugh and blush a little, happy and excited by his presence and the trace of wickedness in his voice. Oh, Kyle!

Suddenly his absence was a sharp pain slicing through her. She trembled and tightly gripped the handle of the cart, stiffening her arms to keep from bending over with the pain. Kyle was gone. Gone from her forever. She would never see him again, never touch his skin, never taste the warm delight of his lips. Her life shimmered before her, a long, empty vista, an aching loneliness that would never be filled or even soothed. My God, what had she done?

Jessica stood dead-still, staring at the rows of blood-red steaks. What did her job matter? What did any of it matter without Kyle? Atlanta, New Orleans—Tucumcari, New Mexico. She didn't care where she lived, as long as it was with Kyle.

She abandoned her partially stocked cart and whirled around, striding rapidly to the automatic doors. Kyle. Kyle. She had to get back to him. Jessica jerked the keys from her purse and slid behind the wheel of her car, fumbling for the ignition. Tears blurred her eyes. She couldn't find the ignition, and in her haste she dropped the keys to the floor. As if that were the last straw, she began to cry. Noisy, painful sobs wracked her chest. She crossed her hands on top of the steering wheel and rested her forehead upon them. And there, in the parking lot of the local supermarket, she wept broken-heartedly for the loss of her love.

When the sobs finally stopped Jessica wiped her tears away, using up all the tissues in her purse. She bent over and retrieved the keys and fitted them into the ignition. She drove home with great care, her fingers trembling on the wheel, the world vague through her teary, swollen eyes. Mechanically she pulled into her parking slot at home, got out and climbed the stairs to her apartment. This time when she entered she hardly noticed the dark, cramped interior. She dropped her keys and purse on the floor inside the door and walked through the living room into her bedroom, where she flopped down on the bed. Jessica flung an arm across her eyes, sighed and waited. She wasn't sure what she waited for—the end of pain, sleep, a return of control over her emotions. But she knew she lay in a listless limbo.

She couldn't give up everything she'd worked for. The pain would pass; that was what everyone said. Eventually you got over loss, any loss. If she waited and concentrated on her work, gradually the hurt would ease and then disappear entirely. In future years Kyle Morrow would be nothing but a bittersweet memory that would bring a faint smile to her lips. It was unthinkable that she should change her mind and run back to him. She always stuck by her decisions. This, like most of her decisions, was based on logic and firm reason. It hadn't been clouded by emotion or tiredness or weakness, as her thoughts were now. Having charted the best course, the only thing to do was to stick with it. That was the way she was, the way she lived. It was how she had achieved so much at a comparatively young age. She was goal-oriented, and once her goal was established, she steamed unswervingly toward it. Obstacles held her up sometimes, but nothing stopped her completely.

Just because she felt weak at the moment, just because she was grief-stricken for the love she had turned her back on, there was no reason to give in to her emotions. No reason to break the habits and principles of a lifetime.

For twenty-eight years she had striven to get where she was, and she couldn't—wouldn't—allow her treacherous heart to betray her into throwing it all away.

It was the sort of pep talk Jessica had always given herself when she was down or defeated or frustrated. From long-ingrained habit, she swallowed the lump of sorrow in her throat and squeezed back the tears. She tightened all over, as though struggling physically with her problem. She wouldn't give in. She wouldn't! Jessica Todd never gave up! Jessica sat up and rather wearily rose from the bed. She compressed the painful, swollen feeling in her chest and tucked it away deep inside herself. Later, when it was easier, she'd get back to it. But right now the important thing was to reestablish her routine, to act normally. To just live day to day until finally the pain went away. Jessica opened her suitcases again and began to methodically take out each item and store it away in its place.

The alarm went off the next morning at six-thirty, jangling Jessica's nerves. She slapped the snooze button and rolled over, curling into a ball. Just a few more minutes . . . When the alarm went off again in ten minutes she jerked up and turned it off, barely restraining her desire to hurl it against the far wall. What a shrill, obnoxious noise it made! Not a very good way to start off a day. Jessica staggered to the bathroom, yawning and promising herself to buy a clock radio that came on with soothing music instead of a loud clang.

She was all thumbs this morning: dropping the shampoo in the shower; burning her thumb twice on her curling iron; ripping a run in a brand-new pair of pantyhose. She seemed to have forgotten how to dress quickly, and she was almost twenty minutes late leaving her apartment.

The extra minutes made a lot of difference in the amount of traffic she had to face. It was almost eight o'clock by the time she got onto the expressway, and traffic had slowed to a crawl. Jessica glanced at her watch and grimaced, a knot of irritation forming in her chest. There was nothing to do but sit in the car and creep forward as best she could. Jessica wished she had something to do with her hands, and for the first time in days she wished she had a cigarette. It wasn't the last time she wished it that day.

When she reached the office, almost forty-five minutes later than her normal arrival time, she was greeted by gratifying cries of welcome from the receptionist and the secretary, and Alan gave her a quick squeeze. Then he pulled her toward a woman she had never seen before. "This is our new assistant, Mary Brindley. Mary, this is Jessica Todd, the one you've heard us all talk about so much."

"It's so nice to meet you," Jessica said automatically, stepping forward to shake the woman's hand. Mary was short and plump, and there were permanent worry lines printed between her eyes. She wore half glasses, now pushed up on top of her head, and as she chatted with Jessica and the others, she rolled a pen up and down between her palms. Her hair was light brown with streaks of gray in the front, and Jessica judged her to be in her late thirties. She had a serious, efficient air, and Jessica suspected that there wasn't a speck of humor anywhere in her.

"Come on in my office," Alan suggested. "Mary and I will fill you in on what's happened while you've been gone."

"Sure." Jessica followed the other two into Alan's office.

Alan pushed around a few files and located a yellow legal pad while the receptionist bustled in with cups of coffee for them all. Jessica took hers with a grateful smile. The way this day had begun, she was going to need something to perk her up. She took a sip and sighed with satisfaction. She'd forgotten how much better it tasted than the decaffeinated stuff Kyle had had her drinking lately.

Kyle. Her heart twisted painfully. Don't think about him, she reminded herself. Just think about business. "Ah, here we go," Alan announced triumphantly and handed Jessica a sheet of paper. "These are your classes that I took over. Mary's been in charge of your paperwork and correspondence. She's done it admirably, I might add. I don't know what I would have done without her the past few weeks."

Jessica glanced over the paper Alan had handed her. He hadn't even asked her if she had enjoyed her vacation. He consulted a chart. "Let's see, I've got you scheduled for Harper and McMann in Augusta tomorrow. Billie's made your reservation. Thank goodness you called yesterday and said you were returning. I can make a sales call here that I thought I would have to cancel." He glanced over at her and grinned. "It's Bankston, Bauer, Lipscomb, etc."

He had named one of the biggest law firms in Atlanta. She and Alan had been trying to get a foot in the door with them for months. If Alan sold them a program, it would be a real feather in his cap.

Jessica summoned up a smile. Alan obviously expected a response from her. "Well, good. That's . . . great. Just great."

Alan looked deflated by her lukewarm reaction, but he made no comment, just turned back to his chart. "You'll be in Augusta for two days. The next day, I've booked a couple of appointments with firms there. Jarrell Manufacturing and Country Cousins, Inc. Billie'll bring you the files so you can bone up on them. They're both good prospects. Cousins contacted me because they needed help, and their banker recommended us. You taught a course at the bank, and they were very impressed. I guess you'll need to write them a thank-you."

"Sure." Jessica glanced around. She hadn't thought to grab a pad for jotting down notes before she came in Alan's office. "Can I borrow a sheet of paper?"

Alan looked a little surprised, but handed her one. He smiled. "You've been gone too long, Jessica," he joked. "I don't think I've ever seen you without a notepad and pen on you somewhere."

"You forget a lot in a month," Jessica admitted, scribbling down the names of the companies in Augusta and a reminder about the thank-you letter.

"While you were gone I scheduled a few courses for you next month. You already had several on your chart. It won't fill your month, of course."

"I imagine I'll need the extra time for the sales appointments we had to cancel."

"Yeah. And there's an individual counseling commitment you'd signed up for with a firm in Charleston that you'll need to take care of. I postponed it; I didn't have the time to squeeze them in."

"Oh, yeah." What was that firm's name? "A manufacturer of clothing, wasn't it? Children's clothing?"

"I think so. SweetSuits, or something like that."

"Right. I'll get in touch with them."

"That's all I have for you at the moment. Mary can fill

you in on the correspondence. She's been handling the letters, cancelling your appointments and setting up new ones, all that. She also wrote up a couple of tentative plans for companies from your notes. What else, Mary?"

"There are a few new prospects that have inquired about our services," Mary replied. "I wrote thanking them and offering to set up an appointment as soon as you returned. The usual sort of stuff. I used your file letters, of course, but I imagine you'll want to check them over."

"Fine. Thank you for taking over so admirably."

"Oh, I enjoyed it. I've been swamped with work since I set foot in the door, and that's the way I like it!"

"You ought to fit in well, then," Jessica responded. She wasn't sure that *she* did anymore, though. She was overwhelmed by the amount of work Alan and Mary had tossed in her lap during the last few minutes.

"Let me show you what I've done," Mary offered. "The files are in your office."

Jessica tossed Alan a quick good-bye and followed Mary out the door. For the second time she wondered at Alan's lack of curiosity about her trip and New Orleans. Had things always been this impersonal and businesslike between them? She had thought of Alan as her closest friend, yet she couldn't remember many times when they had spoken about extracurricular interests. It had always been the "office," the "firm," the "business."

Mary scurried down the hall, not pausing to glance back at Jessica. When Jessica reached the doorway of her office, she found Mary standing inside by Jessica's desk. There was a tall stack of files on the desk beside her, and she held a file in her hand, which she extended to Jessica. "Here's the correspondence from while you were gone. These that I've clipped together were the ones I didn't feel competent to handle and that Alan didn't take care of. The rest I answered, and I have my replies clipped to them, as you can see. I thought it would be easier keeping them together instead of having to go through all the individual files. But I made a separate file for each new prospect, and I put copies of the letters in the pre-existing files. Here are the individual folders in this stack if you want to refer to them. Now, let's see. What else? Oh, yes.'' She pulled open a drawer and dug out a thick sheaf of notes. ''Telephone messages.''

Jessica spent the next hour watching Mary retrieve the work she'd done over the past few weeks and set it on Jessica's desk. Every item involved a precise, detailed explanation. Jessica jotted down notes and struggled to keep her attention on what Mary said. Would the woman never stop? She wondered what Kyle was doing right now. Was he just waking up, stretching in his rumpled bed, muscles rippling beneath his tawny skin? She imagined him yawning and rubbing his bristly jaw as he always did.

No. He had probably gotten up early and gone to work in one of the gardens before the heat became too sweltering. He might be squatting in the brick courtyard of Viv's apartment house, digging weeds out of the tiny flower bed. He would be shirtless and in cut-off shorts, and there would be a dizzying expanse of bronzed flesh exposed to the eye of any watcher. Jessica remembered the sheen of his sweat-dampened skin as he worked, the flash of bright gold the sun brought out in his hair, the darkening patches where his hair was soaked with perspiration.

A fierce pain stabbed Jessica, and it was all she could

do to keep the tears from starting. She didn't want to hear about all these businesses and their problems. She didn't care what Mary had said or written to them. She wanted Kyle. Everything in this office was dull in comparison to his wit and passion.

Jessica squeezed her eyes shut and forced the vision of Kyle from her mind. Listen, she admonished herself sternly, forget about him. Forget about New Orleans. Pay attention to what you're doing! Sternly she fixed her attention on the other woman's words. She listened patiently while Mary finished bringing her up to date on everything she'd done in Jessica's absence, but it was a relief when the new assistant finally left Jessica's office. She wasn't used to not being on top of everything that was going on in their business, Jessica thought. That was why it made her uncomfortable to have Mary and Alan explain things to her. Once she got back to work, things would return to normal.

That was an assurance she repeated to herself several times during the day with appropriate variations for the circumstances. But the mantle of normality never settled over her. First Jessica applied herself to the files piled on her desk. As she reviewed the correspondence she found that Mary had done a more than adequate job of taking care of it. Taking up the few letters that had not been answered, Jessica reviewed the account files and dictated answers for Billie to type.

After she had worked for an hour and still hadn't managed to plow through the correspondence, Jessica became aware of a restless urge. She pushed it away once or twice, struggling to concentrate on her work, but finally she sighed and leaned back in her chair. What was the matter with her? She was oddly bored and she wanted to do something—get up and go somewhere, walk around, anything. She needed to get out of this office.

The thought surprised her. Jessica glanced around. She had never noticed before how small and cramped her office was. Their offices lay on the inside hall of the building and consequently had no windows to give the illusion of space. The rent was cheaper on the inner side, and she and Alan had agreed that they had no need for windows. They were often out of the office, and when they were there, they didn't waste time looking outside. But now Jessica wished she could gaze out at a view instead of staring at four pale beige walls.

There was too much junk in the room, too. Too much furniture, too many files and books and materials stacked haphazardly around. Nothing hung on the walls; she'd never had time to shop for pictures. All in all, Jessica thought, it was a bland, dull, suffocating place. She would have to do something about it. Perhaps they had outgrown their space. She'd discuss it with Alan later.

She returned to her work, but the itchy feeling remained. Finally she realized that she was simply tired of sitting. She wanted to walk around and get some exercise. Jessica smiled faintly. She had never thought the day would come when she would actually miss exercise. But during the past few weeks she'd become accustomed to walking every day. It was the most feasible way of getting around in the Quarter. And she and Kyle had taken time for a lot of physical activities—sailing, tennis, gardening. Her muscles had grown used to it, and now the morning of inactivity bothered her. She'd have to make do with a walk at lunch.

A little before twelve, Billie stuck her head in the door. "I'm going for lunch. You want me to bring you back a sandwich?"

Jessica looked up and smiled. "No, I'm going out for lunch. I need the exercise."

Billie looked surprised, but she made no comment, merely waved and was gone. Jessica propped her chin on her hand and gazed after the woman. Obviously she'd startled her secretary with her answer. Jessica knew she had often eaten her lunch in the office because she didn't want to waste the time going out, but had it been such a regular habit? Thinking back on it, Jessica realized that it had; she'd eaten lunch at her desk practically every day when she wasn't on the road. She shook her head. Amazing. It was a wonder she hadn't gone nuts stuck in this cubicle all day long. Well, today she was going to start a new habit. She had to get out, at least for an hour.

Jessica stood up, swung her purse over her shoulder and left the office. She bought her lunch at a nearby deli, which was packed with its usual noon crowd. Several people were eating their lunch standing up at the long wooden counter which ran around the wall. Jessica decided that she preferred to eat her meal in more peace and quiet than that, so she carried the brown bag containing her lunch across the street and down several blocks to an office building that boasted a quaint little courtyard. It, too, was crowded with workers eating their lunches from bags, but at least there was room to sit on a low brick wall, and she could listen to the soothing rush of the fountain in the center of the patio.

Her mind wandered as she ate the thick sandwich, going to New Orleans and Kyle. Immediately her spirits plummetted. Why couldn't she get her mind off Kyle? Why did everything and everyone somehow remind her of him? Would she never escape him? In disgust Jessica rolled up her half-eaten sandwich in its tissue wrappings and threw it into a nearby trash barrel. Dusting the crumbs from her fingers, she made her way through the building and onto the sidewalk. She walked briskly through the crowd, trying to ignore the frequent jostling. A dress caught her eye in a store window and she stopped to look at it. She drifted on and was lured through the door of a department store by an array of bright, soft silk scarves.

Thirty minutes later she left the store with two scarves and a set of earrings she hadn't been able to resist buying. It was almost one-thirty when she walked back into the firm's outer office. Billie sat behind the receptionist's desk, relieving the other worker during her lunch break. When she saw Jessica, her eyes widened. "Where have you been? I was beginning to get worried about you."

"Me? Why? I told you I was going out to lunch."

"I know. But you were gone over an hour, and I—well, it isn't like you."

Jessica shrugged. "I stopped to do some shopping. Look what I bought." She pulled out her purchases to display them. Billie was appropriately admiring, but Jessica sensed an uneasiness in her manner, as if she didn't know quite what to make of Jessica. Jessica grinned. "Have I changed that much?"

"I'm sorry. I didn't mean to—well, yes, you *have* changed. It's not just that you aren't tired-looking and terribly thin anymore. You seem more . . . I don't know, relaxed, I guess. Slower-moving. Used to be nobody could ever keep up with you. You didn't go out for lunch; you never went shopping, especially for things like accessories."

"The doctor did tell me to slow down." Jessica gave a half-laugh. "Or maybe New Orleans got in my blood."

Billie looked at Jessica consideringly, started to

speak, hesitated, then went on in a rush, "You look kinda sad, too."

Jessica glanced at her, startled. "Do I? I didn't realize . . ." She trailed off and absently stuffed her purchases back into the sack. She forced a smile. "It's difficult readjusting after a long time away."

"Yeah, I guess so." Billie's faintly frowning face didn't look convinced.

Jessica picked up her sack and headed back to her office. The afternoon turned out to be even longer and grimmer than the morning. She finished the correspondence, but then she had to bone up on the prospective clients Alan had scheduled for her in Augusta. After that she had to run through the course to refresh herself. She'd been away a long time. By the time she was adequately prepared for the several days in Augusta, it was long past quitting time, and the other three women had left. As she strolled down the hall she spotted Alan seated at his desk. She called out a good-bye to him, and he glanced up.

"Oh, Jessica. Wait a minute. Come in." Wearily Jessica turned into his office. She didn't want to talk now. The day had been dreadfully tiring, and she had to pack and get ready for her flight out tomorrow. Alan went on, "We need to have a financial meeting now that you're back."

"Oh, Alan, no. Now?" Their monthly meetings about the state of the firm's finances were always squeezed in haphazardly, for the meetings received lowest priority in the firm's busy schedule. "Couldn't it wait?"

"I'll be gone Friday when you get back. Then I'm out the first two days of next week, and you're away the rest. We haven't discussed our financial state in almost two months."

Jessica sighed and set her purse down. "All right. Shoot."

"We need to make some decisions. We're starting to show a healthy profit these days." Alan pulled out another notepad from his desk and began to rattle off figures. Jessica was amazed. Were they really making that much money? What was she going to do with it? She'd always been prudent enough over the years to make small investments in money market certificates and other financial paper that was easily liquidated. But this! Her accountant was already after her to buy a house for the tax benefits and to get into other tax-free investments. It looked like she was going to be forced to look into such things now, even if she didn't have the time or energy.

Alan droned on about incorporation, Keogh plans, pension plans, taxes and investments. Jessica twitched impatiently. "What does our accountant say we ought to do?"

Alan grimaced. "You know him. Carl leaves it up to us. He says it depends on what our goals are. He's full of pluses and minuses, as usual. We can save a lot of taxes with these plans, but then we're stuck with them, and if we expand, get new employees, they'll have to be covered, too. . . ."

Jessica rubbed a hand across her forehead and tried to shut out his voice. "What do you think is best?" she asked. "I'll go along with your decision. Really, I'm not up to thinking about this now."

Alan frowned. "Are you okay? You look healthy, but you've been acting funny all day. You don't seem like yourself."

"I'm beginning to wonder if I am," Jessica commented wryly.

"What does that mean?"

"I don't know. Look, Alan, let's delay this discussion. Please? I'm not back in the swing of things yet. Give me a few days to adjust. I've been away a long time. In another week I'm sure I'll be going full blast. I promise."

"Sure. Okay. I didn't mean to press you."

Jessica smiled and left the office, aware of Alan's puzzled gaze on her back. She rode downstairs in the elevator, leaning back against the wall, her eyes closed. Surely what she had said to Alan was the truth. It was just going to take her some time to start pumping again. In a week she wouldn't feel so overwhelmed, so uninterested, so restless. A few days on the job and she'd be back to her old self. She had to be! Jessica sighed and opened her eyes as the elevator jerked to a stop. If only she could believe that.

Chapter 12

KYLE WAS BEGINNING TO THINK HE WOULD GO OUT OF his mind. Jessica had been gone only a week, but it seemed as if he'd gone through months of misery. At first he had raged against her, angry and bitter. He told himself that she was selfish and immature. Any woman who would give her love only if he changed his life for her wasn't worth having. His mind understood the concept, but there was no convincing his heart.

For two days after she left he fumed, pacing the apartment until he went almost stir-crazy, unwilling to admit that he wouldn't leave the apartment because he hoped she would phone and confess that everything she had said had been a mistake. The phone rang only once, and he jumped on it as if it were a lifesaver, but it turned out to be only a tenant at one of the apartments. It had taken all his willpower not to hang up on the poor old woman.

Gradually the anger seeped out, leaving behind only pain and the realization that Jessica would not come back. She'd chosen her career over his love. Jessica was a determined woman; she wouldn't be weakly calling up in a few days to tell him that she'd changed her mind. That was a fantasy. There was no hope. He wasn't going to return to medicine and the rat race he'd once lived. She would not leave the firm she loved. So there they were: impasse. It was over.

The only thing to do was to face it and get on with his life. But after a week without her, Kyle began to wonder whether his life was worth getting on with. He missed her. Jessica's absence was a constant stabbing pain. There wasn't a thing in his apartment that didn't remind him of her. He tried working at the other buildings, but it didn't help. He envisioned her sitting beside him in the gardens, laughing, or crouching down beside him to hand him his tools as he worked on a sink, or a door that had come off its hinges, or a brick that had been pried loose from the patio pathway. There was no surcease anywhere. Her memory invaded the entire French Quarter; he couldn't even walk down the street without remembering how she had looked as they walked along the same street, or what she had said, or the way she had tilted her head, laughing up at him. Even sailing on his boat was no longer a comfort; Jessica lingered there, too.

He remembered how he had felt when his wife, Beth, left him. The mild regret for their failed marriage that he'd felt then was laughable compared to this. The only thing that even approached it in terms of pain was the agony of the soul he'd suffered when that boy had died under his knife. But even then he'd been able to leave it behind, to separate himself from it to some extent by giving up his past life and moving far away. There was nothing he could give up now, no move he could make that would take any of this pain away. Jessica was going to be with him forever.

Not a day went by that Kyle didn't start to pick up the phone and call her to beg her to come back. Sometimes his pride stopped him. At other times he realized how hopeless it was; even if he begged, Jessica wouldn't return. Twice he was unable to keep from dialing the number of her apartment in Atlanta, but there had been no answer. Then jealousy had gnawed at his vitals—not jealousy of another man, but of her precious job, which had taken her away from him and was no doubt the reason she was not at home.

There was nothing he could do but accept it, he told himself now. He had to learn to live without her, no matter how impossible that seemed. For the only way he could get Jessica back would be to give up everything he believed in, to go to Atlanta and practice medicine again. Kyle closed his eyes against the thought. He couldn't commit himself to such self-destruction, even for Jessica. How could she have asked it of him?

But then, she hadn't understood what it meant to him. He hadn't been able to get through to her how useless that life had been, how thoroughly he'd hated it. She refused to believe that he hadn't really loved medicine. She insisted that he was merely hiding from what he loved because he was afraid of making another mistake as disastrous as the one he'd made with the appendectomy.

Again Kyle felt a flash of rage, just as he had when she'd suggested that idea to him. It was ridiculous. Preposterous! But now, as soon as he rejected her opinion, doubt started to creep in. Was he really so sure she was wrong? He remembered the eagerness he had felt in medical school, the desire to learn, to know, to help. He recalled the awe and joy he'd experienced in the obstetrics section of his internship when he had delivered a child and felt the red, wrinkled little scrap of flesh suck in its first breath in his hands. Or the time in the emergency room when he'd forced a heart to beat again and stolen his first patient from Death's hands. Those times had had nothing to do with money or success. There had been nothing there but the love of what he had learned to do, the joy of contributing to life.

Kyle shook his head sharply. No! Those times had been few and far between. The rest of the time there had been only ambition, only struggling and weariness and no time for any decent life of his own. But did it have to be that way? He began to chew at his lower lip. Couldn't there be some sort of compromise? Some way of getting the good things out of medicine without taking on the parts he'd despised? Maybe he could try it again in a small way and find out whether there was still any love of medicine left in him.

There was a free clinic on a street just off of Elysian Fields. He'd passed it once or twice. What if he volunteered to help out there once or twice a week? After all, he was licensed to practice in Louisiana. The state had reciprocity, so it had been easy to obtain the license when he moved to New Orleans. He hadn't really wanted to bother to get his license, but one of his medical friends back home had insisted that he do it, and he'd finally agreed just to get him off his back.

No doubt the clinic would jump at a physician's offer to donate his time. He'd find out whether there was anything left for him in the field, or if he had been right in telling Jessica that he would never return to medicine. At least it would give him something to do, something to

take his mind off Jessica and his pain. And if he found he
didn't hate it, maybe, just maybe, he could start practicing again. Perhaps he could work out some sort of
compromise with Jessica then, or . . . Oh, hell, if he
could stomach practicing again, he'd give up New
Orleans and move to Atlanta if it meant getting Jessica
back.

As the days passed Jessica discovered that she didn't
settle into her old routine as she had hoped she would.
Nor did she attack her job with the same relentless
enthusiasm she'd once had. In fact she was bored, tired,
harried and miserable. She wondered how she had
managed to do it before.

After years of teaching the same class she found her
course presentations stale and uninteresting. Before her
vacation Jessica had greeted the classes with weary
gratitude, for teaching the familiar material had been
easier than selling or consulting. But now, unencum-
bered by tiredness, the course was no longer a welcome
rest but a dull chore. Selling their services wasn't
boring, but it exhausted her mentally and emotionally.
She had to stay constantly on her toes with prospective
clients, prepared to reassure, explain, or seize an opening. It was much harder than before to smile and be
diplomatic when a client was rude or sexually interested
in her or just plain dull. The falseness bothered her, and
the pressure was exhausting.

She couldn't keep up with her work. Jessica felt as if
she were constantly running. She hated hurrying through
airports and juggling flight schedules, appointments,
hotel reservations, dinner meetings, cocktail meetings,
and rental car check-outs and check-ins. She hated the
long meals of rich foods, the rounds of drinks, the

pleasant-faced, meaningless chatter with clients. She hated staying up late and snatching every spare moment on planes and in departure lounges to catch up on her work. With all the traveling there was never enough time for her office work unless she kept at it eighteen hours a day.

By the end of the first week Jessica's nerves were shot. She knew she should have spent Saturday and Sunday in the office, working on her files and correspondence, but she had neither the energy nor the desire. Amazingly enough, she simply didn't care. What did it matter if she landed one less account? What did it matter if she didn't squeeze enough time out of her week for another day of lecturing?

She spent the weekend in her apartment, giving it the most thorough cleaning it had received in years. She disposed of piles of junk that had accumulated because she had never taken the time to sort through it. She dug through her closets and the boxes under her bed and the stacks of books and magazines shoved into every available space. Most of the latter, she realized, had remained unread, though she had set them aside to read "when she had the time." There were mounds of paperbacks with perfectly intact spines, and magazines that were two years old and yellowing without having been opened once!

What a pack rat she had become! Jessica shook her head, thinking of how light her family had traveled. They hadn't had many possessions because of lack of money, and what they owned was often discarded because it was too much trouble to pack every time they moved. Jessica sat back on her heels, a thoughtful frown marring her forehead. Was that why she hadn't thrown this stuff away? Had she been trying to make up for what she hadn't had as a child? Or, as Kyle had suggested, was it a case of trying to prove she wasn't like her mother?

Jessica sighed and glanced down at the greeting cards in her hand. Birthday cards from the staff at the office where she'd first worked. A Christmas card from a college chum. A scribbled letter from a man she had once dated. She looked back into the box. Knickknacks. Mementos. Reminders of people she'd known, places she'd been. None of it seemed important any longer. It wasn't worth keeping. Jessica dumped the cards into the trash.

The housework helped her to work out some of her frustrations, but it did nothing to ease the ache in her heart or clear her mind of Kyle. Jessica had hoped physical labor might do the trick, since her more cerebral work all week hadn't managed it. She had known when she left Kyle that it would hurt, that there would be times when she cried, nights when she yearned for him. But she had never imagined it would be so awful!

Kyle had been on her mind constantly since she returned to Atlanta. She had thought that if she concentrated on her work she wouldn't think about him and in time she would forget him. The job she loved so much, her all-consuming career, would fill the empty spot inside her. Jessica couldn't believe that she had been so wrong, so foolishly naive. It wasn't just an empty spot; her insides were a huge, aching void. Work didn't banish Kyle; rather, he banished the concentration she needed to work. When she read a letter, his face intruded. When she looked through a file, her thoughts drifted to memories of their laughter and lovemaking, of soft, sensual nights in New Orleans. While she stood in line to board a plane, while she ate, while she talked with clients, while she brushed her hair in the morning—Kyle was always there.

She missed his laugh, his voice. She missed the warm bulk of his body in her bed when she woke up. During the night she often rolled over and woke up to realize that she was reaching for him. When she saw something that struck her as funny she would start to turn to him to see if he thought it was funny, too. She had known him only six weeks, yet they had been so close during that time, both physically and emotionally, that he had become a necessary part of her life. Jessica was lonely and hurt . . . and she was hungry for his touch.

That was another thing she hadn't expected. She'd gotten along perfectly well without sex before she met Kyle, and she had presumed she would after she left him. But then, sex with Kyle hadn't been like anything she had ever known; she should have realized being without it wouldn't be the same, either. She missed the rapturous heights, the exploding waves of fulfillment, the pleasure that was so fierce it was almost a torment. Kyle had known her, mind and body. His every touch, his every look, had gone straight to her core.

Without him, her body betrayed every firm declaration that she would get over him. She woke at night from dreaming of Kyle and found that her skin was scorching hot and there was an unsatisfied pulsing between her legs. Recalling their lovemaking turned her throat dry and set her blood to throbbing. She wanted him, and the lust swelled and burned and begged inside her.

It seemed absurd that in only six short weeks Kyle could have come to mean so much to her. Nothing, even her career, seemed more important. Jessica was amazed and scared. She didn't know what to do. For the first time she had no control over her mind and emotions. She wasn't directing her life, but being pushed hither and yon by some outside force—no, by her own treacherous feelings.

Jessica wasn't used to admitting defeat. Nor to changing her mind. She couldn't go back to New Orleans and ask Kyle to take her back. That would be crawling, she thought disdainfully, and she had never crawled in her life. Then she would think traitorously: Wouldn't crawling be better than this pain and emptiness?

She reminded herself that Kyle probably wouldn't even take her back. She had been cruelly blunt with him at the end. Disappointed, and in pain herself, she had lashed out at him. There had been some truth in what she said, but she had been harsh and abrupt and far too biting. She had wounded Kyle to the quick; she had seen it in his eyes and the bitter twist of his mouth. He had dismissed her after that; he'd plainly said it was over between them. How could she go back? He had looked at her as if he despised her.

Besides, she had been right. They weren't alike. She'd get bored with his life; he would feel pushed by her. The fact that it was unbelievably painful being away from Kyle didn't mean that she had not taken the correct course. Just because her job hadn't soothed her hurts, it didn't mean she should abandon everything she'd worked for and run back to Kyle. There was no future for them. No hope of a future. It would be tough, but she wouldn't give up. She'd grit her teeth and bear it. She'd get through the pain somehow.

But the second week wasn't any better than the first. Jessica wished she had someone to talk to about it, but she had no real personal friends. She had lots of business acquaintances, both men and women, but none of them were the kind of close friend with whom she could let down her hair; there was no one she could allow to see her as she really was. Except Kyle.

She jerked away from that thought. There was Annette, of course. During Jessica's time in New Orleans they had developed a friendship. While they hadn't discussed anything very intimate, the relationship had been warm and personal. She wouldn't be surprised if Jessica called her and talked about her problems, and Jessica felt sure she would be happy to give advice. However, Annette was also a friend of Kyle's, and she loved New Orleans. Jessica doubted that she could give her an impartial judgment. In fact, Annette might be furious with Jessica for hurting Kyle.

She couldn't imagine discussing her problem with her brothers—or any man, for that matter. That left only Viveca. Jessica smiled faintly at the thought. She'd never gone to her mother for help or advice. Viv was lovable, but flighty and vague. She simply wasn't the problem-solving kind of mother.

But Jessica's thoughts kept returning to Viveca. San Francisco was a lovely city, a nice place to visit when one's spirits needed a boost. And Viv was an amusing companion; she could lift anyone out of the dumps. Maybe it wouldn't be a bad idea to fly up to see her over the weekend. Granted, it was a long way to go just for a weekend. But Jessica knew she needed a special shot-in-the-arm right now; it might be worth it.

She thought about the idea off and on all week as the struggle with her work grew worse. Thursday was the final straw. She had been working with the plant manager of a textile mill on an individual consulting basis. They had toured the plant in the morning, and she had spent the afternoon dragging the plant's problems out of him. He was at best slow and a little hostile; at worst he was downright obstructive. It was something Jessica had dealt with many times before; the manager interpreted his company's hiring her as an insult and a threat. The company must think that he wasn't doing his job right, or there wouldn't be any need to call in an outside management consultant. Jessica knew ways to placate and cajole him, to reassure him even as she wrestled more information out of him.

But it was draining and taxed her nerves. She would have liked to grab his shoulders and shake him hard, shouting, "Can't you see I'm trying to help you?" Of course she didn't, but the tension built up inside of her. Then, after a whole day of pulling information from him and putting up with his caustic comments, he gave her a leer and suggested they go out for drinks.

Jessica exploded. "I've been trying to help you, and you've done everything you could to make it difficult for me! Now you think I'm interested in going out with you? You must be crazy!"

He shrugged. "Hey, that was work. I'm talking about relaxation. It must get pretty boring, spending your evening in a strange town, nothing to do but sit in your hotel room." He smiled suggestively. "You look like somebody who likes to have fun."

"Well, an evening with you would hardly qualify," Jessica replied bluntly, carried away by her fury. "For your information it will be a distinct pleasure to eat by myself and spend the evening alone. I've had more than enough of your company today. I don't know why you guys think that just because a woman is away from home for the night she's eager to jump into bed with anybody who asks her. But I want to make it perfectly clear to you that that is not the case."

"Okay! Okay, lady." He raised his hands in mock self-defense. "Sorry I asked."

Jessica left the office fuming. As she stormed through the main lobby she spotted a refreshment area off to the right. She swerved and marched to the cigarette machine. She fumbled for change in her purse, then fed the money into the slot and pulled the handle. A package of cigarettes popped out, and Jessica grabbed it. Her fingers trembled slightly as she ripped off the red strip of cellophane and the paper on one side of the seal. She tapped out a cigarette and, after picking up a book of matches from a table, lighted it.

She took a long drag, closing her eyes in bliss as the smoke swept into her lungs. She stuck the package in her purse and left the building, cigarette in hand. It didn't taste the same. There was a raw, acrid quality to it, a bitter aftertaste. The smoke seared her lungs and throat. Still, Jessica continued to smoke as she got into her rental car and drove back to the hotel. When she finished the first one, she lighted another. By the time she arrived at the hotel, her head hurt. Jessica stepped out of her car and looked down at the half-finished cigarette between her fingers.

What in the world was she doing? First she had exploded at a customer, something she'd never done before, and now here she was puffing away like a fiend. After all the misery she'd gone through getting unhooked! Jessica stubbed out the cigarette and crumpled the package, putting all her anger into crushing it. She tossed it into a nearby trash can and strode through the lobby to her room. There she picked up the phone and dialed her mother's number in San Francisco.

Viveca's voice answered with its usual little inquiring

uptilt, as if she were a little unsure even about saying hello. Jessica smiled. "Mom? This is Jessica."

"Why, hi, honey! How are you? Are you still in New Orleans?"

"No, I got back a couple of weeks ago. Didn't you get the key? I mailed it to you."

"Oh, that's right. It came while I was in the middle of the bird picture. I was surprised it had already been four weeks."

"Well, actually, it had been more like six."

Viveca laughed merrily, as she always did at her own foibles. "Oh, dear. Really? I've been so involved in my painting since I came up here that I lost all sense of time. It's been going so well; I've gotten into this new technique that's absolutely marvelous. I don't know why I never tried it before."

"Well, good," Jessica cut off her mother's flow of words before she could get really rolling on the subject. When she got started on her art, she could go for hours. "You can tell me about it this weekend."

"This weekend?"

"Yeah. I thought I might come see you if you didn't have anything planned."

"Why, Jessica!" Viveca's voice rose in delight. "That would be super! When are you coming?"

"Tomorrow. I'll call and change my reservation to a flight to San Francisco instead of Atlanta."

"You mean you aren't in Atlanta? I can't ever keep up with you. You must be my daughter, after all," Viveca quipped. "When will you get in? I'll be there to get you."

"Oh, no, that's too much trouble. I'll catch a cab. Just give me your address."

"Don't be silly. I'll pick you up at the airport."

Jessica opened her mouth to protest, then shut it firmly. Why not let Viveca meet her? There wasn't any reason to be so blamed self-sufficient. It would be fun getting off an airplane and having someone there to greet her. "Okay. As soon as I make the reservation I'll call you back and let you know the time and the airline."

"Good! Oh, Jessica, I'm so glad you're coming. It'll be such fun."

"That's what I'm counting on."

Viveca was at the airport to meet Jessica, her face glowing. A surge of love rose up in Jessica, and she hurried into Viveca's outstretched arms. One thing you could say about Viv, Jessica thought: She was always there with emotional support. Maybe that was more important than supplying a child with a normal routine and a stable environment. Jessica had learned early in life that she could take care of herself physically and mentally, but she had discovered of late that her feelings were not so hardy.

"It's so good to see you," Viveca declared, smiling, as she linked her arm through Jessica's and started down the long airport hallway. "You look much better than the last time I saw you."

Jessica chuckled. "Thank you—although that's not saying much, considering how I looked when I left the hospital."

"New Orleans must have agreed with you."

"Oh, it did. It did." Jessica sighed. "In fact, it agreed with me a little too much."

"Oh?" Viveca turned her face to Jessica curiously. "What do you mean?"

Much to her surprise, Jessica poured out the story of

her relationship with Kyle Morrow. She couldn't remember ever before confiding a problem to her mother. Viveca had enough trouble struggling through life herself without trying to solve anyone else's problems. Jessica hadn't intended to tell Viv about Kyle; she'd meant to spend a nice, pleasant weekend with her mother, having fun and not worrying about her problems. Yet here she was, telling her everything as they walked through the airport with people streaming around them.

When Jessica finally wound down, Viveca shook her head sadly. "I never thought about your meeting Kyle, let alone falling in love with him. I should have known, I guess. There's a quality about him that's always reminded me a little of you. He straightens things out when they're in a mess, like you do."

Jessica grinned wryly. "Well, I'm afraid this is one mess I haven't the slightest idea how to straighten out."

Viv wrinkled her forehead and pushed back her unruly hair with one hand. "It seems pretty simple to me."

"Things always seem simple to you, Mother. That's how you wind up in trouble."

Viv arched an eyebrow expressively. "And who's in trouble now?"

"All right. All right. What seems so simple to you?"

"First of all, you're in love with Kyle. He loves you, too, and wants to marry you."

"He did," Jessica interrupted. "After our fight, I'm not so sure."

Viveca waved that objection away. "Don't be silly. You both said things you didn't mean because you were angry and hurt. Kyle's taking you back is not the problem."

"I'm not sure I want him to 'take me back.'"

"You just told me you loved him. You miss him desperately. You're miserable without him. How could you not want to get back together with him?"

"We're so different. I don't know how we could make a go of it. What if we can't stand each other after a couple of months? What if it doesn't work out?"

Viveca gave an indelicate snort. "You think you're ever going to find a man that you'll be assured you'll love for the rest of your lives? There isn't any promise of happiness when you fall in love. So what if you're different? That makes life more exciting. You want to marry somebody who's exactly like you? How dull. You'd always know what he's thinking, what he's going to say, what he'll do. It would bore you to tears."

"I suppose so."

"Look. You lived with the guy for over a month, and you were happy. Right?"

"Yeah. Although we weren't actually living together all that time."

"Close enough. You love him, and you were happy together. That sounds like a good basis for assuming you'd be happy if you were married. Goodness, honey, these things aren't written in blood. Sometimes you have to take a chance!"

"I know. But this is such a commitment. I'd have to leave Atlanta and give up my half of the firm. I'd have to throw away everything I've worked for."

"Nonsense. You wouldn't lose everything. You'd still have the skills, knowledge and experience you've gained during that time. You'd have money; surely Alan would buy out your half, wouldn't he?"

"I imagine we could work out something."

"So you would be taking something valuable with you."

"I never thought of it like that."

"Of course not. You're too close to it. You're bored with your job. So why are you leery of leaving it? You could find another job as interesting in New Orleans. Or you could start your own business. Maybe you should go into another field. Heavens, it's not as if New Orleans were a small town where the opportunities are limited. With your ability and experience you could write your own ticket with any number of companies. You could pick and choose, take what's really appealing to you. Surely your ties to Atlanta aren't that strong."

"No. I imagine any large city would offer me enough opportunity. And I do like New Orleans."

"See? I told you it was simple."

"But I know Kyle will never change. He wouldn't even consider going back to medicine."

"Is it so important that he be a practicing doctor?"

"No, of course not. It's just—well, he's throwing it away, and that goes against everything I believe."

"Tell me something. Would you love Kyle more if he were different? Is your love conditional on his changing and being what you think he ought to be?"

"No! I can't imagine loving him any more than I already do."

"Then why should your marrying him be conditional on his changing?" Viveca inquired gently.

Jessica turned a stunned face toward her mother. "I—I'm not sure. Maybe I hate for all the change to be on my side. I give up my job; I move to where he is. It's always the woman who moves and gives up and gives in."

"That's not true. I didn't. I never let a man keep me from drawing. Once I left your father I charted my own course."

Jessica smiled. "I never thought about it. I guess you were a really liberated woman."

"I certainly was, at least for my day and age. But the point I'm trying to make is that you don't *have* to give those things up. If your job and staying in Atlanta mean more to you than Kyle, then stay. If you don't want Kyle unless he changes to suit you, then don't marry him. But, for pity's sake, don't sit around missing him and being unhappy just to satisfy some picture you've created of what your perfect life would be. Life never turns out to be what you want or expect. You have to do the best you can with what you're given, because you won't get perfection."

Jessica was silent and thoughtful as they walked into the baggage claim area. Her mother's words had amazed her with their perception and practical wisdom. Suddenly it seemed ridiculous to be slaving away at her job, trying to bury her love for Kyle under a pile of hard work. She loved him and wanted to be with him. Why was she holding back?

"Oh, there's Ben." Viveca waved across the vast room at a young man dressed in a three-piece suit. "He thought we ought to be alone to greet each other. He's cautious about such things."

Jessica eyed the man making his way through the crowd toward them. She could see the resemblance to the teenage boy she had known years ago when Viv and Ben's mother, Debby, had been friends together here in San Francisco. Dark-haired and gray-eyed, he was handsome in a rather conservative way, but he didn't seem like the artist type Viv usually favored. "Viv, are you having an affair with Debby's son?"

Viveca glanced away from her daughter's sharp gaze. "Not exactly."

"Not exactly? How can you 'not exactly' have an affair?"

"Well, he'd like to, and we've moved in that direction a few times. But I'm not sure. I mean, he *is* Debby's son, and that makes me feel a little awkward."

"I should think so."

"Don't be so censorious, Jessica."

"I'm sorry. Truly, I didn't mean to be. It's just that I hate to see you do something foolish."

Viveca shrugged. "It's happened before. Being foolish is something I'm willing to risk." She cast a meaningful glance at Jessica. "I happen to think love's worth it. But his being Debby's son isn't the worst part. The fact is, he's a banker."

Viveca delivered the statement in much the same tone another person might say, "He's a drug dealer." Jessica whooped with laughter and gave her mother a hug. "Oh, Mom, you're a classic. Nobody else would be concerned about his character because he's a banker."

"Right now he's loving and considerate, but I'm afraid if we get really close, he would start criticizing and trying to change me. You know, telling me I'm silly and emotional and I ought to get my life in order."

"You mean like I do?" Jessica asked a trifle shamefacedly.

"Frankly, yes. Only, men can be so much worse."

Jessica grinned. "Well, someone once told me—you have to take a chance."

Viveca grimaced. "There's nothing worse than a child feeding your own advice back to you."

Ben reached them and extended his hand to Jessica. "Hello, Jessica, nice to see you again."

Jessica returned his greeting, studying him as he turned to Viveca and smiled. His expression changed when he looked at her mother, his face softening and glowing with affection. He loves her, Jessica thought. What does it matter that he's Debby's son and younger than Viv? Or even that he's too normal for her? With the love that shone in his eyes for Viveca, he couldn't be bad for her. "You know, Mom . . ." Jessica turned to her mother and winked. "He might be just the thing for you."

Viveca laughed. "I hope you're right."

Chapter 13

OVER THE WEEKEND JESSICA BEGAN TO LOOK AT HER mother in a new light. She had always dismissed Viveca as an inept, emotionally stormy, thoroughly unstable person. She was charming, lovable and pretty, true, but not the sort you could rely on. She was the kind who had given women the undeserved reputation for being undependable and overly emotional. But after talking with her mother that afternoon, Jessica looked back on Viveca's life and saw that she had a great many other qualities which her daughter had ignored.

Viveca had been strong and devoted to her career. She had succeeded in raising three children largely without the help of any man and without giving up any of herself or her career, either. That was quite an accomplishment, particularly given the mores of the age in which she had done it. It was even more astonishing when you considered that she had been only sixteen years old when she had borne Jessica. Rather than give Jessica up, she had married a seventeen-year-old boy and endured all the woes of a teenage marriage. She had been frightened, lonely, uncertain and caught in a trap. No doubt that was the first and most lasting impression of Viveca that Jessica had received. She had continued to hold it throughout her life, despite the fact that her mother had grown and matured over the years.

Jessica hadn't perceived Viveca's struggle to maintain her own identity and support her children. She had seen only the constant moving, the bizarre lifestyle, the differences from other families. Yet if anyone had given her a role model of an independent, career-oriented woman, surely it was her mother. Strange . . . why hadn't she realized that before?

She watched Viveca with her friends and with Ben, who adored her. Jessica and Viveca walked together, laughed, talked, went sight-seeing, and Jessica had a better time with her mother than she had had in years. She enjoyed Viveca. So what if she wasn't like herself? So what if she was unpredictable and vague? It was part of her charm. Yes, she had faults; she could improve. But she was human. Only children expected perfection from a parent, and Jessica wasn't a child anymore. She realized that she loved her mother just as she was. She wouldn't have changed her if she could.

Jessica thought of the childhood she had hated and knew that she wouldn't have changed it, either. In many ways it had been rough. But it had also been unique, exciting and enriching. She had seen more places by the time she was ten than many people did in a lifetime. She had met all kinds of people from different backgrounds. She had been forced to assume responsibility young, to grow up quickly because her mother was immature and struggling, but Jessica's maturity and experience were an asset to her as an adult. If she had been raised differently, she doubted that she would have become organized and efficient. She wouldn't have learned how to carry on intelligent conversations with adults or how to be at ease in practically any situation. Viveca had shaped her personality, often as a model of what not to do, but also, though Jessica hadn't realized it at the time, as a model of what a woman could achieve.

More of her came from Viveca than she had ever guessed. Jessica knew she had suppressed her awareness of it for years because she hadn't wanted to be like her mother. Kyle had been right when he said that much of what Jessica did was not Jessica, but simply anti-Viveca. Judging her mother to be wrong, she had forced herself to be the exact opposite. She had craved success and security as if they would make her life perfect. But was that what Jessica really wanted? Or just what she was determined to have because it wasn't like Viveca?

She hadn't really created her own life, merely a reaction to her mother's. She was as much shaped by Viveca as if she had followed exactly in her footsteps. She had rejected anything that resembled Viveca and accepted what seemed the opposite. She had chased success, order and stability, giving them more importance than her own happiness and freedom.

She loved Kyle, yet she had rejected him, not because she loved her career so much—she had found that she didn't—but because she had feared being like her mother. She had been afraid to let her emotions guide her because that was the way Viveca would have acted. She was afraid to give up her un-Vivecalike life. What a silly basis on which to decide her future! The weeks she had spent with Kyle had been the happiest she'd ever known.

He had freed her from her self-imposed straightjacket, and she had enjoyed herself without care for the consequences or what someone else might think.

Perhaps the very freedom of what he offered had scared her. Maybe that was why she had run from Kyle. Or maybe it was just out of habit, a clinging to what she had always known. But when she had returned to her life after that brief taste of freedom it had seemed dull, stifling and tiring. She hadn't liked it, and for the first time she hadn't been running the treadmill so hard that she didn't notice her unhappiness. Two months ago it had taken getting ill and breaking down to make her leave her trap. But now—now she knew, and she could walk away freely.

It wouldn't be easy. She wouldn't kid herself about that. It was hard to break away from the habits and preconceptions of a lifetime. Nor was it safe and sure. Kyle was different from her; he had his own problems. Nothing could guarantee that their love would last a lifetime. She wasn't even sure he would take her back! But she had to try. As Viveca had said, love was worth the risk.

As soon as she returned to Atlanta Sunday evening, Jessica called Alan. She knew he was flying out of town early Monday morning, and she was determined to get this over with as soon as possible. Without any preliminaries she announced, "Alan, I've decided to quit the firm."

There was a long silence at his end of the line; then he sighed. "I can't say I'm completely surprised. You've been different since you got back from New Orleans. Well, all right. I sure hate to lose you, kid. Are you certain this is what you want?"

"Positive."

"I know you well enough not to argue, then. I should be able to buy you out. Would that be agreeable to you?"

"Perfectly."

"Okay. Then let's think about the terms while I'm gone. As soon as I come back we'll discuss it."

"Sure."

Monday Jessica dived into her work with an enthusiasm she hadn't had since she returned. She had to get all her accounts straightened up and out of the way; she couldn't leave Alan with a mess on his hands. She would have to finish the two consulting jobs she'd started, and she would need to inform her clients that she was leaving the business and assure them that they would get the best of service from Alan. It would be better if Alan could take over her sales appointments, since the companies would have to deal with him in the future, anyway. But she ought to teach the courses she had planned, at least for the next couple of weeks. After all, Alan would have a lot on his hands trying to hire new help or find a partner or whatever he decided to do.

Jessica's thoughts jumped forward to what she would do, and she felt the quickening excitement of a challenge. A new field. Viveca was right; that sounded intriguing. The thought of owning her own business appealed to her. Annette had mentioned that the small shop next to hers was coming up for rent soon. They had even daydreamed about the kind of business to put in there. She'd have to think about it. There was no hurry.

The only matter that was pressing was seeing Kyle. As soon as she made her decision, Jessica had started to phone him, but she had stopped even as she reached for the receiver. No. This wasn't the sort of thing she could say over the phone. She wanted to be face-to-face with Kyle when she told him that she wanted to move to New

Orleans and marry him. She considered jumping immediately onto a plane to New Orleans, but her training wouldn't let her leave Alan in the lurch. She couldn't break her scheduled appointments without notice. No, she decided. She would have to wait until this weekend to fly to New Orleans and tell Kyle of her decision.

Her stomach fluttered nervously at the thought, remembering his anger and scorn at their last meeting. Then she raised her chin. He loved her. No matter what he said, he couldn't have simply switched off his love. He might be angry at first, but eventually she'd bring him around. Jessica knew she was too determined a woman to be held off forever. She was used to succeeding.

Jessica quit work early Friday afternoon in order to make the five o'clock flight to New Orleans. She wanted to squeeze every last minute out of this weekend. The flight wasn't long, but today it seemed interminable. When the plane landed at the New Orleans airport she was surprised to find that they had arrived on schedule. Anxiety, which had been slowly rising in her stomach all afternoon, flooded her. What if Kyle wasn't at home? What if he'd decided to go somewhere for the weekend? What if he refused to listen to her? What if—what if he didn't want her anymore?

Jessica hauled down her carry-on bag from the overhead rack and made her way along the aisle and out the door of the airplane. When she emerged from the exit tunnel into the airport she walked briskly toward the lobby, struggling to ignore her wayward doubts and fears. Once outside, she hailed a taxi and directed him to take her to the French Quarter, giving him Kyle's address.

When the cab pulled up in front of the pale gray

building with its black wrought-iron balconies, her heart began to thud so hard that she could feel it all over her body. Her hands were icy, and her knees were a trifle weak as she paid the driver, gripped her bag and made her way up the three shallow steps and into the hall of the apartment building. Inside, she raced up the flights of stairs to the top floor, her pulse pounding in her ears and her throat dry with anxiety. She stopped outside Kyle's door and swallowed. Suddenly she couldn't bear to find out; she couldn't knock on the door. For a moment she stood frozen, and then, as if to force her to get on with it, the door opened before her.

Jessica jumped, and so did the middle-aged black woman on the other side of the doorframe. The woman gasped, one hand flying to her chest, then she visibly relaxed and smiled. "Why, Jessica! You nearly scared the life out of me!"

It was the woman who came in to clean Kyle's apartment three afternoons a week. "Hello, Sybil. I'm sorry. I was just standing here trying to work up the nerve to knock."

"Am I glad to see you back!" the other woman went on. "Kyle's been looking terrible since you left, and his temper's gotten worse by the day."

A flutter of hope came to life inside Jessica. "You think he's missed me?"

Sybil gave a brief, mirthless laugh. "Missed you? That's an understatement. I've never seen him act like this."

"Is—is he here?"

"No. He's at the clinic. He always works there late on Fridays. Everybody gets scared about the weekend coming up and goes in to make sure they aren't going to die."

"The clinic?"

"Oh, yeah, I forgot. That's happened since you left, too. You want to wait for him here or go over there? It's off Elysian Fields. I'm about to leave. If you want to dump your bag here, I'll drop you off on my way home."

"That would be marvelous," Jessica replied gratefully and set her bag inside the door. "I'd rather not wait."

They walked to Sybil's car, which was parked a few blocks away in Kyle's rented parking space. It took almost as long to reach the car as it did for Sybil to maneuver through the narrow streets of the Quarter and into the dilapidated area around the street named Elysian Fields. Sybil double-parked in front of a grimy, faded narrow building. There was a simple sign on the front door announcing in red letters: CLINIC. Jessica looked back doubtfully at Sybil. Kyle was in there?

Sybil chuckled. "It's clean on the inside, at least. I guess the outside don't matter. You can go on in. He's there. See, his car's parked down the street.

Jessica followed the woman's pointing finger. Sure enough, there was Kyle's rather weatherbeaten Jeep wagon parked against the curb several car lengths in front of them. Sybil must be right. But what was Kyle doing here? Had he bought another building? And what exactly was the "clinic"?

She thanked Sybil for the ride and slid out the passenger door. Taking a firm grip on her purse, she marched up to the door of the clinic, doing her best to ignore the man sprawled across a doorway two doors down and the four men lounging against one of the cars farther on. She opened the door and stepped into a small room. The walls were lined with folding chairs, all empty, and there was a desk against one wall.

"Kyle?" Jessica asked uncertainly, advancing into the room. There was a door beside the desk, and Jessica wondered if she should go on through it. As she hesitated the door opened and a woman came out. She was dressed all in white and carried a handbag slung over her shoulder. She looked very weary, and her face fell when she saw Jessica.

"I'm sorry, ma'am, but the clinic's closed for the day. Can you come back Monday?"

"I—I just came to see Kyle Morrow. Is he here?"

The nurse stuck her thumb backward over her shoulder. "He's finishing up with the last patient."

Patient? Jessica's breath stilled. Patient, clinic, a woman dressed like a nurse . . . It seemed obvious, but could it really be that Kyle had returned to medicine? Had he let go of the fears that had blocked his career? Jessica began to smile. "I'd like to wait for him, if that's all right."

"Sure. Sit down. He'll leave this way." Pleased to have resolved the problem without any effort on her part, the woman smiled at Jessica and walked out the door. Jessica sat down on one of the plastic seats and waited. Finally she heard the rumble of voices in the hall and moments later a short, stocky man emerged. Jessica could see nothing of the person behind him except the lean, long fingers curving around the door edge to hold it open. The short man walked through the small waiting room, and, seeing Jessica, gave her a brief nod. He went out the front door, and behind him the door to the back hall was released and began to ease to.

Jessica jumped to her feet. "Kyle! Wait! No!"

Instantly he grabbed the door again and this time stepped forward into the doorway, astonishment written on his face. "Jessica!"

Jessica nodded, unable to utter a word. She could only gaze at him, drinking in his dear familiarity and examining the differences. He was dressed in tan slacks and the sort of light pullover shirt he usually wore, but atop it was a hip-length white coat, open down the front. A stethoscope was folded and stuffed into one of the front pockets of the jacket. His hair was a little darker—or was that just the poor lighting? Shaggier, too. His face seemed thinner, more careworn, less tan. But the eyes were the same, dark chocolate brown, warm and alive. He stared at her, arm raised to prop back the door.

His first word had been an exclamation of disbelief. Now he whispered, "Jessie," as his face shifted and warmed, dissolving into belief and then joy as he started toward her. "Jessie!"

Jessica ran to him, flinging her arms around his neck and clinging as if she would never let him go. Kyle didn't appear to mind her stranglehold. Rather, his arms encircled her tightly, and he lifted her off the floor, squeezing her against his chest. He kissed her hair and face, raining kisses everywhere he could reach, murmuring her name over and over in delight. "You're back. Oh, Jess, Jess, I love you so."

His mouth fastened on hers in a deep, searching kiss. Jessica shivered at the delicious, familiar taste of him. Her senses were filled with his scent, the touch of his breath on her face, the warmth of his flesh. Her hands went to the nape of his neck, rediscovering the smoothness of hard bone and skin and the prickle of short hair. She spread her fingers upward, separating the strands of his thick wheat-colored hair and letting them slide sensuously through her fingers.

Kyle groaned, and he pressed her hips against his hard form, making her aware of how aroused he was already.

His fingers dug into her soft buttocks, kneading and rubbing. Jessica gave a sigh of satisfaction and responded by wiggling her hips against him. Kyle's intake of breath was swift, and his face was suddenly fiery against hers. He changed the angle of their kiss, digging his lips into hers hungrily, as if he would consume her.

Kyle broke their kiss and leaned back to look at her. His face was slack with desire, lids drooping slightly over the hot passion in his eyes. "I've never seen you before in a business suit," he murmured huskily. "Is this how you look every day?"

Jessica nodded. A faint smile touched his mouth. His fingers crept down her legs and under her skirt. "You look very untouchable," he whispered as his fingers slipped up her thighs and under the elastic of her panties. Jessica moaned at his intimate touch and moved her legs apart. His eyes closed briefly and then reopened, soft and hazy. His fingers explored beneath the flimsy silken undergarment, and when he touched the moisture between her legs, he smiled. "I like doing this to you, seeing that nice, cool, business-as-usual look turn to fire." Suddenly he pulled his hands out from under her skirt and lifted her up and into him, burying his face against her breasts. "Oh, God, Jess, I've missed you so. Don't ever leave again. Please."

"I won't."

He lifted his face to kiss her, his mouth wild and demanding. Both of them were on fire, and they kissed and caressed in a delirium of passion, unable to get enough of each other. Kyle's breath rasped loudly in the still office, with Jessica's softer panting an arousing counterpoint. Finally he broke away from her and strode to the door, snapping its lock closed with an impatient motion. He turned to Jessica. His face was flushed with desire, his body rigid and tensed. "I have to have you," he told her huskily. "I can't wait."

Jessica nodded in agreement and mutely held out her hands to him. He was at her side in an instant, lifting her into his arms and carrying her through the back door. Jessica nestled her head against his shoulder, caught somewhere between supreme contentment that he loved her and a raw, blazing need to feel his passion. The door led into a dim hall, which Kyle traversed rapidly. He sidestepped into a tiny room and kicked the door closed behind him. Carefully he set Jessica down on a high, padded table. It was covered in paper, which rustled beneath her as she moved.

Kyle stripped off his trousers and underwear, and Jessica watched, thrilled by the magnificence of his lean-hipped, intensely masculine body. He jerked off his jacket and tossed it aside and went to work on the buttons of his shirt. Halfway through, he made a low, impatient sound and climbed onto the table, covering her with his body. Jessica melted inside at the familiar, primitive pleasure of his body sinking onto hers.

Kyle kissed her feverishly as his hand fumbled at the buttons of her blouse and skirt. Haphazardly he pulled her clothes from her, leaving her jacket and blouse beneath her and tossing her skirt and underthings onto a nearby chair. But there was no haste in the way he bent to take her breast into his mouth, adoring her with lips and teeth and tongue. His mouth was hot and yearning, and it sent desire stabbing through Jessica's abdomen. Her own passion lay low and heavy within her, swelling and throbbing with sweet life at each caress of his fingers and lips.

Jessica groaned and twisted beneath him, begging

wordlessly for him to fill the aching void within her. Kyle answered by parting her legs and slipping his fingers down to caress the moist, throbbing folds of her femininity. At this delightful new torment, Jessica arched her hips, sobbing, "Kyle, please. Please, love me."

He waited no more then, but with a long groan of pent-up desire, he entered her, filling her welcoming flesh with his hardness. They moved together, locked in a primeval dance of love, conscious of nothing else in the world but each other and the undeniable need within them. At last their world exploded in a shimmering flash, and they clung together, suspended for an instant in a heavenly union. Slowly they drifted down from the bright peak of gratification, collapsing in a warm, tangled heap of limbs and bodies.

It was much, much later that Kyle lifted his weight onto his elbows and looked down at her. Jessica sighed; she thought she could have lived forever quite happily with his heavy body draped across her. She smiled at him, unshed tears sparkling in her eyes. Never in her life had she been this happy, this content. She hadn't even dreamed that such a time and place existed. Kyle's gaze explored her face as his fingers drifted lightly across her brow and cheek and lips.

"I can't quite believe you're here. I'm scared maybe I dreamed it."

"If I could make up a dream like that, I'd probably stay asleep forever," Jessica joked.

He smiled and rolled from her, jumping lithely off the table. "This isn't the most romantic place in the world." He cast a wry glance around the examining room.

"Sorry. I didn't think I could wait long enough to take you home. Hell, I didn't think, period. All I knew was that I had to have you again."

His eyes met hers, devoid of joking. Jessica gazed back, her love shining in her eyes. "I love you."

Kyle leaned over her, bracing his arms on the table on either side of her. "I can't let you go again. Marry me, Jess."

"I will," she answered simply, and he gave her a brief, hard kiss. He turned away, grinning, and began to pick up their scattered clothes. Jessica sat up on her elbows and watched him. She glanced down at the examining table on which she lay. "So this is what doctors do on these things. I always wondered."

He flashed her a mockingly stern look. "Have you no respect for the medical profession?" He tossed her clothes at her and began to pull on his own. Jessica slipped into her underwear, skirt and blouse, but opted to go barefooted, shoes in hand. Content and happy as she was, the tight knot of her hair seemed restricting. Besides, she was sure it was a mess after Kyle's fingers had roamed through it. She pulled the pins from her hair and let it fall in tousled strands upon her shoulders. She sat idly combing it with her fingers, a faint smile playing about her lips as she recalled their torrid lovemaking here on the table a few minutes ago. All sense of time and reason had deserted them.

She glanced up to find Kyle's gaze on her, steady and warm. "You better stop that, girl," he warned softly, "or we may never get out of here."

Jessica cast a thoughtful eye at the narrow table. "Well . . . it might get a little uncomfortable after a while." She turned back to Kyle, suddenly serious. "What *is* this place? That nurse said something about a patient. Are you . . .'' She trailed off, afraid he might interpret her interest as pressure.

But Kyle merely nodded, seemingly undisturbed by the question. ''Yeah. After you left, I thought about what you had said—that I was cutting myself off from medicine because I was afraid of making another mistake. I wondered whether you were right, so I decided to go back to medicine part-time to find out whether I enjoyed it or hated it. Besides, I needed something to do. I was driving myself crazy thinking about you.''

''Oh, Kyle, I'm so sorry.'' Jessica leaned out and took one of his hands in hers. ''I'm sorry I hurt you.''

''It's all right, as long as you came back. That's all I care about.'' The love in his eyes melted her. He broke their gaze and cleared his throat. ''What was I—oh, yeah. I was scared about being out of practice, of not knowing what's happened in the field for the last two or three years. But I knew there was a clinic here, and I figured most of their business would be minor, things I could do pretty easily. So I volunteered to work here in the afternoons. Needless to say, they jumped at the opportunity to get a doctor to donate his time. I've been here for two weeks.''

''Do you enjoy it?''

He paused, considering. ''Yeah, I do. It's different from what I used to do. More general practice. I've seen a little of everything in here: colds, cuts, broken legs, pregnancies, emphysema, you name it. It's been a real education. But I feel useful. Productive, like I'm contributing something. When I was practicing surgery I never felt that way. I saved people, but I saw it as something to my credit, not theirs. You know what I mean? It was all money and praise and esteem. But here medicine is helping people who are sick and poor. It's more satisfying. And I have time for myself. I'm not married to my job."

He studied his hands as he continued in a low voice, "Jess, I've given it a lot of thought. I love New Orleans, but I love you more. I'll move to Atlanta and set up a practice there, if that's what you want."

"Is that what you want to do?"

"What I want is to marry you, and if that's what it takes, then I'll do it," he replied bluntly. "I was planning on going to Atlanta tomorrow to tell you. Frankly, I've reached the begging stage. At first I was determined that I'd wait until you came back to me." A wry grin twisted his mouth. "But pride isn't very good company."

Tears glimmered in Jessica's eyes. "Thank you. It makes me feel very . . . very special and loved for you to be willing to do that for me. But it isn't necessary. You see, I came here to tell you that I'm quitting the firm. I'm moving to New Orleans."

Kyle let out a whoop and pulled Jessica off the table, lifting her high in the air. He whirled around, grinning up at her, his face alight with joy. Slowly he let her slip down his body to the floor and bent his head to kiss her. His mouth was light and loving on hers. "Oh, baby, I love you. You're everything I want in a woman. After you left, I was miserable. I kept hoping and praying you'd come back. Nothing could take my mind off you, not even the clinic. I can't think of anything more perfect than marrying you and living here, continuing my work at the clinic." He pulled back suddenly, frowning. "But will you be happy moving here and giving up your job?"

Jessica smiled up at him and linked her hands behind his head. "When I got back to Atlanta I discovered that I didn't feel the same way about my job. You were right. I was just trying to be different from Viveca all these years, not doing what I truly wanted. I no longer liked my job. The only important thing to me is being with you. I love New Orleans. My time here was the happiest I've ever known. That's what I want for the rest of my life.'' She leaned her head against his chest and snuggled up happily. ''Maybe we used to be worlds apart, but I'm determined we're going to create our very own special world right here. Just us.''

Kyle kissed the top of her head. ''I like the way that sounds.'' He squeezed her lightly and released her. ''Let's get out of here. I want to go home and show you how happy I am you're back.''

''You mean you haven't already?'' Jessica cast a teasing glance up at him.

Kyle grinned. ''Just wait. I haven't even begun.''

READERS' COMMENTS ON
SILHOUETTE INTIMATE MOMENTS:

"About a month ago a friend loaned me my first Silhouette. I was thoroughly surprised as well as totally addicted. Last week I read a Silhouette Intimate Moments and I was even more pleased. They are the best romance series novels I have ever read. They give much more depth to the plot, characters, and the story is fundamentally realistic. They incorporate tasteful sex scenes, which is a must, especially in the 1980's. I only hope you can publish them fast enough."

S.B.*, Lees Summit, MO

"After noticing the attractive covers on the new line of Silhouette Intimate Moments, I decided to read the inside and discovered that this new line was more in the line of books that I like to read. I do want to say I enjoyed the books because they are so realistic and a lot more truthful than so many romance books today."

J.C., Onekama, MI

"I would like to compliment you on your books. I will continue to purchase all of the Silhouette Intimate Moments. They are your best line of books that I have had the pleasure of reading."

S.M., Billings, MT

*names available on request

If you enjoyed this book...

Thrill to 4 more Silhouette Intimate Moments novels (a $9.00 value)— ABSOLUTELY FREE!

If you want more passionate sensual romance, then Silhouette Intimate Moments novels are for you!

In every 256-page book, you'll find romance that's electrifying...involving... and intense. And now, these larger-than-life romances can come into your home every month!

4 FREE books as your introduction.

Act now and we'll send you four thrilling Silhouette Intimate Moments novels. They're our gift to introduce you to our convenient home subscription service. Every month, we'll send you four new Silhouette Intimate Moments books. Look them over for 15 days. If you keep them, pay just $9.00 for all four. Or return them at no charge.

We'll mail your books to you *as soon as they are published.* Plus, with every shipment, you'll receive the Silhouette Books Newsletter absolutely free. *And Silhouette Intimate Moments is delivered free.*

Mail the coupon today and start receiving Silhouette Intimate Moments. Romance novels for women...not girls.

Silhouette Intimate Moments

Silhouette Intimate Moments™
120 Brighton Road, P.O. Box 5084, Clifton, NJ 07015-5084

☐ **YES!** Please send me FREE and without obligation, 4 exciting Silhouette Intimate Moments romance novels. Unless you hear from me after I receive my 4 FREE books, please send 4 new Silhouette Intimate Moments novels to preview each month. I understand that you will bill me $2.25 each for a total of $9.00 — with no additional shipping, handling or other charges. There is no minimum number of books to buy and I may cancel anytime I wish. The first 4 books are mine to keep, even if I never take a single additional book.

☐ Mrs. ☐ Miss ☐ Ms. ☐ Mr.   BMM325

Name	(please print)
Address	Apt. #
City ( )	State Zip
Area Code Telephone Number	

Signature (if under 18, parent or guardian must sign)

This offer limited to one per customer. Terms and prices subject to change. Your enrollment is subject to acceptance by Silhouette Books.

Silhouette Intimate Moments is a service mark and trademark.

IMIM-R-A